Don't Tell Anyone

Don't Tell Anyone
Published by Laurie Boris

Copyright © 2012 Laurie Boris
Cover art: Paul Blumstein
ISBN #13: 978-1481152099

1

As Liza's professor scrawled diagrams of molecules across his whiteboard in an attempt to explain osmosis and the sodium-potassium pump, something began to ring. That bothered her. There was only so much organic chemistry she could fit into her head, and the ringing took up too much space. She nudged her leg against her husband's. "Make it stop."

He grunted.

"Adam..."

He said something that sounded like, "Beer me."

Right, Liza thought, slowly waking. They'd been down the hill at the Miller's Halloween party; apparently it was still in full swing in Adam's head. She wondered if he was still dancing with Cara Miller's breasts.

Ring. Alert now, Liza could identify it as the telephone. She forced open her eyes, crusted with last night's congealed makeup, and peered at the clock through a clump of disheveled auburn hair. Four-thirty.

As she fought her way out of the covers for the cordless handset, which should have been on the nightstand, several thoughts seeped through her muzzy brain. One, it had been warm in bed next to her passed-out husband. Two, she almost had the sodium-potassium pump story down pat. And three, dressing up like a flapper and drinking three glasses of zombie punch at the Miller's Halloween party two days before her organic chemistry midterm had been a very bad idea.

"Where'd he leave that stupid phone?" Startling her orange tabby, Liza followed the sound down the hall to the top of the washing machine. When she picked up, she heard heavy breathing.

You've got to be kidding. I was in the middle of a perfectly efficient REM cycle. It had to be one of her neighbors, who'd come to the party dressed as a flasher and had been a little too deep into his character, the punch, and every woman in the room.

"It isn't funny anymore, Ted."

The breathing became a tiny, wheezing, nasal voice. It creaked out, "I'm Estelle's upstairs neighbor? I just called 911."

Liza froze. Her own voice failed her. She swallowed. "We'll be right there." Still holding the receiver, she bolted toward their bedroom, calling her husband's name.

Nothing.

She shoved his arm. It flopped over like a dead halibut. "Adam."

"Huh?"

"It's your mother."

A groan emanated from the pillows. "What about my mother?"

"A neighbor called. She's on her way to the hospital."

"She's what?"

Oh, for the love of— "Adam. Get dressed."

* * *

There was no time for coffee or hygiene, no time to remove the physical or emotional remnants of the party. Adam and Liza threw on jeans and grabbed car keys and bolted from their yellow ranch house halfway up the hill on Sycamore Street.

Now it seemed surreal to Liza that such a short time ago, they were drinking and dancing in the Miller's living room. That only three hours ago, they'd argued whether Adam perhaps enjoyed a little too enthusiastically the lewd comments Cara Miller had made about the tight leather pants of his punk-rocker costume. That two hours ago, when they'd arrived home, Adam, possibly thinking about Cara's hydraulically raised breasts in her Naughty Nurse outfit, had attempted to make love to Liza but passed out instead.

Just as well, Liza thought. She hadn't wanted that to be the story of how their first child was conceived.

As she drove her baby blue VW bug out of the neighborhood, not trusting Adam behind the wheel, Liza noticed a dribble of cars still parked in front of the Miller's house. Talking Heads' "Psycho Killer" pulsed from the windows. What looked like a human form lay on the side of the Miller's lawn. Another human form swayed rhythmically atop it.

"Unbelievable," Adam said. "Is that Cara?"

More to the point, Liza thought, *is that her husband?*

* * *

In Liza's observation, it had hit Adam somewhere around the New Paltz Thruway entrance that a call to 911 at four-thirty in the morning could mean bad news. He'd sobered up enough to be scared and quiet. He seemed to completely disappear when Liza asked the emergency room guard where they could find Estelle Trager.

The guard made a phone call and pulled a glass screen closed.

Adam's compact body seemed to flinch. "Why's he doing that?" He knocked on the glass. "Hey—"

The guard ignored them. He talked into the phone and nodded. Then slid the partition open. "They'll come get you soon."

"Soon? What the hell is 'soon?' It's my mother."

"They're trying to stabilize her."

Adam's voice climbed an octave. "Stabilize her? What does that mean?"

"Adam…"

"No, damn it. We should be in there." He turned to Liza. "Shouldn't we be in there?"

"Soon," the guard said. "Have a seat."

* * *

Adam and Liza clung together in the tiny, mostly empty waiting room. The buzzing overhead lights drained the remaining color from his boyishly handsome face and turned his greenish-blue eyes a shade of pale mud. The smeared eyeliner and blue tips in his short, sandy brown hair made the horror of the situation worse. It no longer mattered what Cara had said, Liza realized, or where her neighbor might or might not have put her hands. She just wanted to make it better. She wanted to scrub last night off her husband's face and hair and tuck him into bed.

Adam said, "Maybe it's just an allergic reaction."

"Maybe."

"I don't even remember the last time she was sick."

Finally they heard the slide of the glass. "Mr. and Mrs. Trager, you can go back now."

Liza cringed, a reflex sharpened over the past five years, at hearing someone call her "Mrs. Trager." That title belonged to Adam's mother. She was Liza Stanhope. But at the moment it wasn't worth an argument.

* * *

No one showed them which partition shielded Estelle Trager. Liza felt lost and small as she and Adam wandered amid the bustle of hospital personnel and equipment. People ignored them, as if bedraggled Halloween party refugees drifted through every night. On one gurney was a man in jeans, work boots, and a sleeveless T-shirt. He was out cold and, from the odious cloud surrounding him, dead drunk. Atop another lay a mountain of a black woman surrounded by family and a minister who recited scripture.

"Here." Adam tugged at Liza's arm.

All she saw was a rumple of bedclothes, spent equipment, and plastic wrappers on the floor. "But there's no one…" Then she spotted the dyed red shock of Estelle's hair sticking up out of a sheet. "…here."

"Christ," Adam muttered. "Jesus H…."

"Are you the son?"

Adam hadn't moved. Liza normally thought of herself as sanguine, but she had to force her attention from the tube in her mother-in-law's throat, from the sallow hue of her face, and from the rhythmic wheeze of the machine that thrust

Estelle's chest out and in, out and in.

Standing behind them was a ridiculously young woman in a lab coat.

"Yes," Liza said. "He is. Well. The only son in the country at the moment."

The young woman blinked at him and forced a bit of a smile. "Halloween party?"

No, Liza thought, glaring. *My stockbroker husband just likes to dress up as Sid Vicious on the weekends.* "What happened?"

"First I need to ask you some questions about her history. She's not in our database."

Liza waited.

"How long has she been sick?"

Adam shrugged, still staring at his mother. "Didn't know she *was* sick."

"Has she ever had surgery?"

Adam failed to respond. Liza shook her head.

"Taking any prescription medication?"

Again, not a word came from the son who was supposed to supply the answers. "I don't think so," Liza said.

"Allergies?"

"None that I'm aware of." *Why have I made myself the keeper of Estelle Trager's medical history?*

The technician scribbled at her chart. "I'll leave that as 'unknown.' And how long has she had the tumors?"

A knot tightened in Liza's throat. Adam went wooden against her. Finally, he snapped out of his focus and looked at the technician, his brow wrinkled in confusion. "How long has she had *what*?"

* * *

At three-thirty that afternoon, two large men bundled the still-unconscious Estelle Trager onto a different gurney, rolled her into and out of various elevators, eventually arriving in the ICU. Adam stood in the corner of her assigned cubicle, out of the way, still apparently in shock. It hurt Liza too much to see his stunned, smeared face or to watch the things the orderlies were doing to his mother with tubes, IV poles, and monitors. So she twined her arm through his and turned him toward the window. A crack in the drawn curtain revealed a view of the Catskill Mountains. The sky was perfectly blue. Orange and brown leaves drizzled down and piled in the streets. Schoolchildren shuffled through them, swinging book bags, shouting to each other. They didn't know that inside these cinderblock walls, a chest X-ray of a sixty-five-year-old woman revealed bilateral breast tumors so large and distinct the security guard could have made the diagnosis. They didn't know that a respirator pumped oxygen into Estelle Trager's medically controlled lungs. In and out, out and in. Nurses injected things into her IV and gave Liza and Adam soothing looks. *It's not that bad*, they said. *She's almost out of the woods*, they said. *With pneumonia you want to be cautious.*

But in the darkened room, his black-lined eyes hollow, Adam looked like death. Liza didn't imagine she looked so great herself. All they'd had since four-thirty that morning was bad coffee from a sympathetic ER nurse. She ought to get Adam some food.

"You should eat something," she said.

"My mother has breast cancer." His voice cracked. Liza focused on the rise and fall of Estelle's pigeon-like chest. "When was she planning to tell me?"

"Apparently," Liza drew in a breath, "never."

He lifted a lost, greenish-blue gaze to hers. He looked about eight years old, his mouth and jaw slack. "How...how do you...how can you know you have something like that and do nothing?"

"Maybe she didn't know."

Then he narrowed his eyes, suddenly a grown man's. "Please. She knew. She knew damned well. She always knows exactly what she's doing."

2

A couple of days later, Liza sat on her back deck with Cara Miller and Patty DeAngelo, another woman from the neighborhood, who, like Liza, was slim and dark-haired, a perfect visual foil for Cara's blonde pulchritude. Although the sunny November afternoon was unseasonably warm, Liza found little to enjoy about it. Still tired from several trips to the hospital, she hadn't been feeling particuslarly up for company. But hearing through the neighborhood gossip net about what had happened to Adam's mother, the women had simply appeared. They brought food. Discovering that Adam had been unsuccessfully tackling a few home repairs, Cara called her husband, Dan, who brought tools and beer.

As Cara concluded yet another story about one of her patients, Dan Miller, big and burly, came out onto the deck and pulled the sliding glass door most of the way closed. Liza considered that progress, since Dan usually left it wide open, inviting flies she had to chase around her kitchen with a dishtowel after he and Cara went home. Dan had a death grip on a sweaty beer. Apparently, from the puckered track marks in the fabric, he'd used his Giants T-shirt to twist off the cap.

"Ladies." He nodded at Liza and Patty. Then he took a long swallow and raised his eyebrows at his wife. "Cara."

"Asshole," Cara said in the same lilt, smiling at him, her small blue eyes twinkling. "Are you done yet?"

"I wish. Adam and me, we're going up the hill, see if we can borrow a torque wrench." His gaze landed on the patio table and Cara's cigarette lighter. "I thought you quit."

"I did." She slid a coy glance toward the other women. "For a while."

He pointed a callused index finger at his wife. "You better not be smoking around here when Adam's mother comes home."

Cara threw up her hands. "I won't. I swear. I'll go on the

patch again." But she reached for her lighter the second Dan's truck pulled out of the driveway. "Tomorrow," she said with an impish grin. She shook out two cigarettes, one for herself and one for Patty, who shouldn't have been smoking, either.

"So Adam's mother is really going to be staying here?" Patty said.

Liza nodded, her shoulders sagging as she anticipated the fight Estelle would put up about it. "For a while. Until she can manage on her own." *Will she ever be able to manage on her own?* Liza wondered. "Or until…whenever."

"Cripes," Cara said with a mock shudder. She nodded toward Patty. "Hey, remember when Jean's mother-in-law moved in? What was that then, her gall bladder?"

"I think it was the stroke," Patty said. "The first time."

"Nah. She went to the nursing home for that. This was the gall bladder. I remember now, because she was going off to Roger one day about how she couldn't drink her gin and tonics anymore."

Jean and Roger were the former owners and first occupants of Liza and Adam's yellow ranch house. From what she'd heard, Jean, Cara, and Patty had been inseparable. After Jean had moved out, Cara and Patty simply tucked Liza into the empty space. From what some other neighborhood women had said, Liza, with her auburn curls and brown eyes, even looked a bit like Jean, albeit a younger version with better posture. They'd all been nice to Liza, freakishly so. They'd brought over food and helped with her housewarming party, got her up to speed on the local gossip, but even though Liza and Adam had been living in the neighborhood for three months, there were times, like now, when it seemed like a running joke was going on without her. As if there were a language spoken among the exurban soccer moms that she, childless and undomesticated, didn't understand.

Cara pointed toward Patty with her cigarette. "You're right. You know, I never thought she was that bad. Jean was always making her out to be some kind of bitch-face dragon lady, but I thought she was a hoot."

"She died here," Patty told Liza.

Liza clenched her mug of herbal tea. "Excuse me?"

"In that little room in the back," Patty said. "The one that faces south. With the pink wallpaper and the window that won't open." Quickly she added, "But I'm sure that's not why she died."

"Well, it *was* asphyxiation, according to the coroner's report." Cara was a nurse, at Halloween parties and in real life. The real life version did not employ hydraulic undergarments, at least on the job.

"A woman died," Liza said, "in my house."

"In the ambulance on the way to the hospital," Cara added, "but she was already blue when they found her."

"A woman died in my house." The realtor had failed to mention that. Her neighbors had failed to mention that, and she'd met nearly half of them before she and Adam closed on the three-bedroom, one-and-a-half-bath yellow ranch they'd vowed to repaint one day, because they both hated yellow.

"You guys seemed so cool," Cara said. "And Dan wanted free stock tips. I didn't want you to change your minds and move somewhere else. So do you like her?"

Liza was still thinking about the dead woman. She and Adam couldn't put Estelle into a dead woman's room. "Who?"

"Adam's mother."

Many words popped into Liza's mind in connection with Estelle Trager, but "like" didn't make the list. She thought of Girl Scout words such as honor, duty, and respect. The first time Adam brought Liza home, Estelle had flicked a withering glance up and down and looked, if Liza was not mistaken, disappointed. Liza hadn't understood. Yes, she might have been a bit of a tomboy, but she prided herself on her excellent physical condition, and people told her that she cleaned up pretty well. A trip to the hairstylist and a handful of mousse had earned raves from friends and colleagues. She'd even worn makeup, although the woman at the beauty counter had envied the healthy glow of her skin and confided that all Liza really needed was a bit of lipstick and mascara. But she could almost imagine Estelle thinking, "She'll do until something better comes along." She'd told Adam about this, but he said it was her imagination.

"She likes you fine," he'd said. "She just didn't like that you wore jeans to her house for dinner."

"It was a barbecue," Liza had said. "And they were new."

"It was still dinner."

"She's Adam's mother." Liza sighed, drifting back to the present. "I have to like her."

"Does *he* like her at least?" Patty said.

Liza considered this. "I'm not sure sometimes."

Cara reached for another cigarette. "I got that extra room if you want to run away." She winked at Patty. "The window opens."

* * *

Adam and Dan returned from up the hill with a torque wrench and Patty's husband, Dave, a slightly smaller and paunchier version of Dan. As if the women might not have gathered this from the truck pulling into the driveway and the collective galumphing through the house to get more beers, two of the three men, smelling like burnt leaves, came out onto the deck to announce their presence. Patty quickly dashed out her cigarette.

"Aw, crap," Dave said. "Hen party." He gave his wife a nod, and then looked at Cara. More specifically, he looked at Cara's breasts. "I thought you quit."

She blew smoke out both nostrils. "I did."

"Smoking gives you wrinkles," Dave said.

"Stupid comments get your ass kicked."

He grinned at her. "Promise?"

"Hey," Dan said with mock offense as he knocked his elbow into Dave. "Stop oogling my wife."

"I think it's called ogling," Dave said. He turned to Liza, who was still thinking about the dead woman and starting to get a headache. "It's ogling, isn't it?"

"Depends who's doing it," Cara said.

Their banter went over, around, and through her. Liza

drifted away, her mind revisiting the image of Estelle, so small in her hospital bed. And of Adam, touching his mother's shoulder before they left, his head bent as if in prayer, a soft sweetness to his full lips and in his normally sharp, greenish-blue eyes.

Then Adam popped out onto the deck, his eyes sharp again and seeking hers, and her heart smiled. "Hey, Liza, you seen our tape measure?"

"Top drawer underneath the phone."

The men, purposeful, began to retreat. "Adam?" Liza asked.

He stopped.

"The bedroom in the back? Maybe you guys could get the window open."

* * *

Cara, Dan, Patty, and Dave had gone home to feed their kids and pets and referee the usual weekend bickering about which kids wanted to sleep over at whose houses. As one of the few couples in the neighborhood without children, Adam and Liza were on their own. Liza had dinner on—between her classes and freelance work for the local newspaper, she'd been so busy that Saturday was usually the only night she cooked. The rest was leftovers and assemblage.

"You want salad?" she called out, but her husband didn't answer. "Adam?"

She followed the sound of the radio to the back bedroom. He was chipping away at the window. "Painted shut," he said.

"Maybe we should put your mother in the other room."

"Huh?"

Not only did someone die here, Liza thought, *this wallpaper is truly hideous.* It was comprised of alternating pink and white vertical stripes with a top border of baby blue, repeating ducks. Obliterating the décor had been first on her spreadsheet of the many things they hadn't yet gotten around to fixing. "Maybe this room...is a little too small."

"How much room does she need? She'll just be sleeping in here. We'll give her the run of the house." He grunted and swore as the blade of the too-short screwdriver skipped across the glass and gouged the wood of the jamb. "If she's good."

"But the other room has that really nice view. She can see people coming and going. She can watch the sun set."

His eyebrows darted up and his eyes grew huge. "What, my office? I'll have to move everything. And I won't have high-speed access in this room. You remember how long it took to get that guy out here? I was on dial-up for two months! Dial-up sucks."

"Adam. Someone died in this room."

Adam shook his head. "The house isn't even five years old. Nobody died here."

"It's true. Patty and Cara said Jean's mother-in-law died in this very room."

With a smirk, he resumed stabbing away at the window sash. "Yeah. Right. I wouldn't believe everything those two tell you."

"Why would they lie about something like that?"

"Why does anyone lie about anything? Because they're bored off their asses. They're tired of each other's stories and you're fresh meat."

She glared at him. "And you guys never bullshit each other when you're sitting around drinking beers and trying to fix things you have no business trying to fix?"

"Never," he said. "And we fix stuff. We fixed Ted's ceiling fan. At least the lights work now."

"But not the fan."

"Details."

"You want salad?"

"Whatever."

She felt her jaw tighten. "Not 'whatever.' I want 'yes,' or I want 'no.' 'Whatever' isn't an answer. It's barely a word. It's a passive-aggressive grunt of air."

Adam gave her a cockeyed smile that normally she found adorable but now grated on her. "Maybe you should be studying law instead of nutrition."

Before reacting, she reminded herself that his mother was in the hospital and tried to dial back what Adam's brother endearingly called her "Liza-ness" but what her husband tagged as a tendency toward "holier-than-thou-ness."

"Just tell me if you want salad, please."

"No." He stopped, seemed to be thinking it over. "Yes." Then he returned his attention to the window.

Liza sat on the edge of the old futon, which was propped up on a frame that had seen better times in their last two apartments. "Are you done deciding?"

"Yes," he said finally. "Salad is good."

She watched him work. He wasn't approaching the task at maximum efficiency. She would have chosen a screwdriver with a longer handle for more leverage, would take shorter strokes, and would move the chair out of the way so he didn't have to lean so far over and possibly strain his back. She might be new to home ownership, but she wasn't new to marriage or Adam Trager. Five years in, she knew certain things weren't worth the argument.

"I think she'll be comfortable here," he said.

"No, she won't."

He sighed. "You're right." He looked around the room. "She'll hate the wallpaper."

Liza's shoulders sagged. "She'll hate everything. She's hated this house since the first day she saw it."

"Yeah. But what other choice do we have? Charlie practically lives in a closet, and if she stays by herself she'll never keep her chemo appointments."

Liza turned to him. This was new. So far Estelle had refused to even admit she had the lumps. "She's doing it?"

"Not yet. But she will." He frowned at the chair. "Grab the other arm, would you?"

Liza lifted her side, and they set the chair a few feet to the left. "You can't force someone to take chemo."

Adam picked up the screwdriver. "You'd be surprised."

She watched her husband work a while longer, admiring the way his T-shirt hugged the wiry musculature of his back and shoulders, then said, "Do you think a dead person's spirit can lodge in the place where she died?"

Adam didn't even stop chipping. "Liza. Give it up."

3

The night nurse, a shapeless hulk with dull eyes and a bad bleach job, leaned into Estelle's cubicle doorway. Chomping a wad of gum and looking like she'd been doused with vinegar, she said, "*Now* what?"

The nerve of this one, Estelle thought, staring back. *'Now what?' Is that how you're supposed to talk to sick people?* She made a mental note to complain to her supervisor. *My arm is killing me,* she would have said, if not for the *farshtinkener* tube in her throat. The pain had woken her. She'd tried to move her right arm. It wouldn't budge, and she didn't understand why, so she'd hit the buzzer. Estelle wiggled her hand around, hoping this dolt would take the hint.

"That's for your own protection, Estelle," the nurse said. "You kept trying to rip that ventilator tube out."

Wouldn't you?

"Maybe that is a hitch too tight," the nurse said. *Finally!* "I'll loosen it up if you promise not to rip out that tube."

She nodded. Anything; she'd promise anything. With the adjustment, a new syringe injected into her IV, and that sourpuss out of her hair, Estelle felt more comfortable. But sleep was impossible. As she stared at the ceiling tiles, the water stains formed patterns: ugly, knotted shapes. *Is that what I look like, inside? Is that what my mother's looked like? When I was pregnant with Charlie and those horrible things were growing inside her?*

In those days, no one had dared to speak the name of Miriam's condition. There had been no pink ribbons, no T-shirts, no crowds of people walking in the rain to raise money. No one showed her scars on television. It was called the C word then, usually in a whisper. When she'd found out about her mother, Estelle was already exhausted. Adam was at the age when they start with all the questions, everything why, why, why. Charlie twisted and turned and gave her heartburn, hemorrhoids, and legs that felt so heavy and tired she could collapse any minute. And her husband, Eddie, the schmuck? Useless as always. When he wasn't working, he played pinochle until all hours with his buddies down at the corner. Her mother had gone to the doctor. Just like that. She'd not been feeling well, was tired, had no appetite, and her bones ached. The doctor gave her six months. Estelle raced the four blocks to her parents' apartment in her Cuban heels, leaving Adam with Mrs. Steiner down the hall.

"It's gonna be another boy," Estelle's mother had said, stretching out a hand to pat her daughter's stomach. "I can tell from the way you're carrying. God willing, I'll live to see him."

Estelle had prayed for a boy. Not for the usual reasons. She would have liked a daughter, someone to take shopping, someone to take care of her in her old age, like Miriam had for her own mother. She didn't remember much about her grandmother, but there were whispers. She'd had the C word, too. Estelle didn't want to put another girl through that. Not just the caretaking, watching someone you love waste away, but knowing that your own body was a ticking time bomb.

So what could Estelle have done? She went home, made grilled cheese sandwiches for lunch, numbed over her face, and tried to pretend everything was normal for Adam's sake. The lump of Crisco melted in the skillet. If she pressed her hand on the iron, would she feel anything? What did sizzling human flesh smell like? Someone once told her it smelled like pork.

"Mommy, after lunch can we go to Gramma Miriam's?"

"Not today, Adam."

"Why not?"

May you and your future wife only have boys. "Because she's sick."

"Why is she sick?"

Estelle pressed the blade of the spatula down onto the bread, which made the sandwich flat the way he liked it. "Because sometimes people get sick."

"Why?"

"Nobody knows why."

"Why doesn't nobody know?"

"Anybody." His little face looked pale. Maybe he was coming down with something. Maybe it was just the light in the kitchen. She'd ask Eddie to change the bulb and clean the inside of the glass, if the schmuck would stick around longer than it took to eat and pat her stomach, smirking that fatuous smirk that he was a man, a real man, and twice now he'd knocked her up.

"Why doesn't anybody know?"

"Enough. Nobody knows." She set his plate on the table. "Now eat. After, we'll go to the park and feed the ducks."

Adam appeared to eye the Formica space in front of Estelle, empty except for this morning's coffee, gone cold, and a cigarette wasted in her ashtray. "Where's yours?" he said.

She sighed. Despite his fussy moments, Adam could be such a sweet child, so concerned for other people. *Would this new one be the same?* She wondered if it were true what Dr. Spock and the others said, that unborn babies could sense the world around them. If this one knew his mother's clock was ticking.

4

Holy crap, Cara thought, sinking back against Liza's kitchen counter. Suddenly she was aching for a cig, or at least that the coffee would brew faster so she'd have something to do with her hands. "You mean she never got it checked out…not even to see what she was dealing with?"

Liza, who looked about eight notches up on the tight-ass scale and eight hours down on sleep, shook her head and plucked two mugs from the dishwasher. "Never. Not a single mammogram in her entire life."

"I mean, jeez. Yeah, it hurts for all of two seconds to get your boobs squished, but then it's over."

Liza didn't even rinse the mugs first before pouring their coffee. She usually rinsed everything that came out of her dishwasher, even though she used this fancy organic detergent that probably cost a mint.

"She's never even been to a gynecologist," Liza said.

"No fucking way."

"Not since Charlie was born."

"She just didn't want to know, huh?"

"Well." Liza smiled a flat smile while smacking the dishwasher door closed. "We know now, don't we?"

"Did they stage her? Has it spread?"

"We don't know. They can't test without her permission and she won't give it. She's not talking."

"Still?"

"Yep." Liza tore open a packet of some kind of natural sweetener, dumped it in her coffee and stirred so hard that liquid splashed over the rim. "Well, she's been on a ventilator and really doped up, which makes communicating virtually impossible. And there are all these ludicrous shield laws that prevent her doctors from telling us anything. When she's not so out of it, Adam will work on her. But I'm not very optimistic. She had pneumonia. Pneumonia, for Pete's sake, and wouldn't even go to the doctor until it got so bad she almost died."

Cara crossed her arms over her chest. She'd seen patients like that. She'd seen plenty. There were two or three on her floor right now. "If you want, I'll talk to her."

Liza, gripping her coffee with both hands, looked like she was thinking about it, or maybe considering driving back to Middletown Hospital and braining her mother-in-law with the mug.

"I'm a trained professional, after all." Cara grinned, trying to break the tension. "Heck, if it doesn't work I can always stick her with a tranq dart."

"Just as long as you stick me first," Liza said.

The girl could use it.

5

Later that day, the oncologist appeared, although Liza and Adam weren't supposed to know he was an oncologist. To Liza, he seemed like a reasonable and compassionate man, but despite his initial impression, he shuttled them out of Estelle's ICU cubicle and suggested that "Mr. and Mrs. Trager" (Liza cringed) might want to visit the hospital cafeteria.

"Goddamn privacy laws," Adam muttered, reviewing today's specials with a dismal look on his face. "My own mother and I'm not supposed to know. Even though I already know and she doesn't know I know."

"It's like a sick French farce." Liza eyeballed a platter of something that might have been macaroni and cheese. "Excuse me, what's in this?" she asked the woman behind the counter.

The woman shrugged. "Macaroni and cheese. There's macaroni. And there's cheese."

"Never mind." Liza opted for a box of cereal and a package of trail mix. At least they couldn't screw that up.

"Don't they have people here who help with this stuff?" Adam asked. "Someone who could talk some sense into her?"

"Like a rabbi?"

Adam leveled a tired gaze at her. "Yeah. My mother is going to talk to a rabbi. She hasn't been to synagogue since our wedding and even then it was like pulling teeth."

"She just didn't want you marrying me."

"Will you stop with that? Jesus." He dropped his voice. "You know why she doesn't like synagogues."

Adam's father had dropped dead in synagogue. During the High Holy days, Eddie Trager had a massive coronary while the rabbi was bringing out the Torah. Estelle took two Valium to get through Liza and Adam's wedding. Liza still took it personally.

"Cara offered to talk to her about treatment options." Adam smirked.

"She's a trained professional," Liza said.

"Yeah. Trained at causing trouble."

"Maybe it will be a good thing. Maybe she'll listen to a nurse."

"Or maybe we'll have another Thelma and Louise on our hands." He drained the dregs of his coffee and rubbed his eyes. "Think it's safe to go back and pretend we don't know what's going on?"

Liza sighed. "Adam..."

"This is getting really old."

"I know."

He dropped his gaze to his cup. "So what would Cara tell her, anyway?"

* * *

Liza and Adam got more coffee and started down the long corridor from the cafeteria to the elevators. Estelle's ICU nurse, much nicer than the one who came on for the night shift, greeted them with a smile.

"Your mother's awake now," the nurse said, "and she's got a visitor."

Liza turned toward her mother-in-law's cubicle. The partially drawn curtain revealed the lanky legs and long arms of a man sitting next to Estelle's bed, holding her hand. Liza smiled. *Charlie.*

"About time he got his ass up here," Adam breathed.

Not since her college days had she been so happy to see him.

Liza followed Adam behind the curtain, but apparently neither Estelle nor Charlie had noticed them yet. "This is my other son," Estelle told the female intern checking the dials on her machines. She told the intern, she told the machines, she told the entire fifth floor. Her words slurred together, probably from all the medication, and probably making up for the days she had a ventilator tube stuck down her throat. Her eyes were not quite focused. "A real big shot, big *macher*, this one. A television producer. On that show, you know that show, where the four ladies argue. Look, such a handsome boy. And still single!"

"Mom," Charlie said. His voice sounded patient but amused, as it often did around his mother. "I'm gay. Remember?"

"Nonsense." She mumbled something that could have been English, could have been Yiddish. When she took Valium or was overtired, the Yiddish came out. Adam sometimes wrote the words down and checked the translations on the Internet but often found his mother was speaking a kind of pigeon Yiddish the online search engines usually didn't know. "You haven't met the right girl yet. This is...what's your name, *libling*?"

The intern blushed. "Deanne."

"Deanne," Estelle gasped. "Such a pretty name. You married?"

"No," she said.

"Mom."

"You didn't know you liked Brussels sprouts until you tried them."

It had been a while since Liza last saw Estelle's younger son. The show had just returned from an around-the-world, on-location tour. When he flashed a lazy grin at his mother, his tan intensified his even, white teeth and mostly-blue eyes. Charlie was the taller and more classically handsome of the two brothers and had known Liza first, a set of facts that had always annoyed Adam. Reminding Adam that he was the brother to whom she'd sworn her primary loyalty in the eyes of a rabbi, both their families, and the State of New York mollified things. Sometimes.

"All right. I'll give it a try." Charlie turned to the intern. "Deanne. You want kids?"

"Sure."

"Colonial, split-level, or contemporary?"

"Anything. As long as we can hire a maid."

He made an expansive hand gesture. "Sky's the limit; I'm loaded. Are you Jewish?"

"Catholic."

He shrugged. "Sorry. My mother was hoping I'd marry a Jewish doctor. See, Mom. I tried."

But Estelle had already fallen back to sleep.

"Better luck next time," Liza said.

Charlie smiled, stretched up and gave Liza a hug. She sank into his arms, inhaling the light, masculine scent of whatever he used to sculpt his hair. He was a big hugger. Adam wasn't. When it was Adam's turn, he pretended at it with Charlie, but male embraces always made Adam look pained.

Charlie didn't know about the tumors, because neither Adam nor Liza thought it was right to talk about it on the phone. And apparently, none of the medical staff had broken the code of silence. Charlie was being Charlie and trying to cheer Estelle up. Liza was certain he would have acted differently, been grimmer, and not pretended to flirt with the interns if he'd known the truth about Estelle's condition. Adam had simply told Charlie the pneumonia had been pretty bad, Mom was expected to be in the hospital for a while, and now that he was back in town, he might want to get on a train to come see her.

"So how's she doing?" Charlie asked Adam.

"Let's go for a walk," Adam said.

* * *

Liza stayed behind to be with Estelle. *It's funny, the images the mind constructs about people,* she thought, as she watched her mother-in-law's chest rise and fall. *When they loom the largest in your life, the archetype gets hard-wired. No matter what happens after that moment, this is the version you always remember.* Liza saw her father as a robust, dark-haired man running on the beach or showing her how to bait a hook and swing the line far out in to the northern California surf. Yet she was surprised each time this stooped, gray-haired man came to meet her flight. No matter how her husband aged, she was certain she'd see the clear, green eyes and amused, crooked grin of the Adam who watched her mince down the aisle in her wedding dress and heels, actual high heels, when all she'd ever worn was sneakers or sandals, depending on the season.

And Estelle?

Estelle would always be a force. She would always be a loud, opinionated, pigeon-breasted tank of a woman. She would forever stand on the porch of the house Adam and Charlie had grown up in, her hands on her hips, her dyed red hair glowing like fire underneath the lamp. A cigarette would dangle from her mouth, and she'd lean forward into the night as if to scold it. She'd watch a nervous Adam pull into the driveway, bringing only his second serious girlfriend home to meet his mother. He'd been nervous because Liza hadn't dressed the way he suggested. Because she didn't bring the gift he suggested. And the first words out of Estelle's mouth were, "Schmuck, when are you going to get that muffler fixed already, you probably woke the whole neighborhood."

Not, "Nice to meet you."

Not even, "It's about time you got here."

No. Forever Liza would remember this woman belittling the man who would become her husband.

But not this version of her mother-in-law, this sallow bag of flesh hooked to machines, this woman whose already short legs had gotten so thin she looked merely like a torso and a head, a magic trick.

The head's eyes flickered.

"Estelle?"

"Liza." Estelle's voice was small and raspy.

She leaned closer and tentatively pressed a hand to her mother-in-law's shoulder. "Yes. It's me."

Estelle worked her lips together. They look chapped and uncomfortable. Why hadn't the nurses seen to that? "Can I, uh, get you something?" Liza asked. "Lip balm? Water?"

Estelle's bloodshot eyes lolled in Liza's direction. "I want a cigarette."

Liza didn't know whether to laugh or cry. And knowing Estelle, there was probably a pack and a lighter in her purse right now. Maybe she'd even had one while waiting for the EMTs. "I think you've had your last cigarette."

"Then kill me."

"I know it's hard. But you won't be able to smoke anymore."

"I meant it. Kill me. Pull the plug."

"Estelle."

"You'll do it. Adam won't have the heart."

She was too tired to feel insulted. "I will not..."

"When it gets bad."

"Estelle."

"You'll put a pillow over my head."

"Stop talking like that. They have better treatment now..." Liza looked into Estelle's eyes. The possibility hadn't occurred to her until now. What if Estelle herself didn't know? If the doctors had considered her too incoherent to make rational decisions about her treatment options, maybe she wasn't rational enough to comprehend the scope of her condition.

"You could go on the patch."

"Patch." Estelle laughed weakly. "If they got a patch for this, I'm the Queen of Sheba."

6

To help with the household expenses, Cara Miller supplemented her piddly income from her hospital shifts with an even more piddly one as a home care nurse.

Dan, to his credit and her great relief, had switched to the early shift at the factory so he could take on her former roles as Soccer Mom, PTA Mom, and Be-Home-When-The-Kids-Get-Off-The-Bus Mom. That left her free to focus on being Weekend Mom and If-You-Don't-Get-Out-Of-Bed-On-The-Count-Of-Three-I'll-Kick-Your-Ass Mom.

"Where are the boys?" she asked Dan at the end of one particularly lousy November day, as she flopped onto the sofa next to him and kicked off her sensible nurse shoes.

He handed her a beer. She took a long, lovely slug. "Up the hill at Patty's. They're staying for dinner."

Her first reaction was relief someone else was feeding them tonight, followed by the usual guilt that she wasn't being a better mother. That she wasn't more like Patty, who would soon be serving Cara's boys a meal that didn't come from the freezer section at Sam's Club. "They had their orange jackets on?"

"Bet your ass," he said.

Cara snorted. "Hunting season. I hate hunting season. We always get some big-city asshole can't tell a cow from a deer, ends up shooting his buddy or someone's propane tank."

Dan barked out a laugh.

"It's not funny!" She gave him an affectionate slap on the leg.

"It is," he said, still chuckling. "Kinda."

She couldn't help smiling. "Yeah. Kinda. If they live, I mean."

"Anything you can walk away from, baby." Dan wrapped a big arm around her neck and she snuggled into him, heaving out a mighty sigh.

"Tough day?" he asked.

"Aren't they all?" she said. That wasn't especially true.

She liked what Dan called her "Nurse-a-Go-Go" days, even though the pay was crappy. She liked getting out of the hospital and spending time with her home patients. It was usually their family members who pissed her off. And the paperwork. "Oh, I got a new one today," she said. "Randall Osten. He's this super-smart guy. Was a college professor until the ALS made it too hard to get around."

He gave her a puzzled look. "Lou Gehrig had that, right?"

She nodded. "And he told me about his *daughter*. Holy guacamole, what a piece of work." Just thinking about Randall's description of pinched-face Millicent made Cara's head throb. "*Total* Bible-thumper. Trying to convert her father, who by the way is an atheist."

Dan grinned and pulled at his beer. "You could sell tickets to that train wreck."

"Yeah, right? At least it's more interesting than filling out paperwork at the hospital."

Finally Dan noticed the shoebox Cara had deposited on the side table when she came in. "Jeez," he said, his face wrinkling with distaste. "Tell me you went shopping."

Cara said nothing.

"Can't you at least leave those in the garage?" Dan said. "It's creepy."

"It's not a 'those,'" Cara said. "It's a person. Or, at least, it was a person. And no, I'm not leaving him in your crapped-up garage."

"He's *dead*, Cara. How many times—"

"All right, already! I'll find a different place for him. It's only until tomorrow, and the bag inside is completely sealed. I don't know why you got your tightie-whities in a bunch over it."

"Because my wife brings home dead people." He gestured with his beer in a circular fashion. "None of the other guys in the neighborhood have wives who bring home dead people. It's just not normal."

Cara huffed out a breath. This conversation was making her batcrap crazy. She could never seem to make him understand that this was her calling. When poor people died, and family members could not be located, their remains were often warehoused. With a couple of other nurses and donations from a few charities, she was starting a small foundation to give those lost souls a proper, if modest, burial. Sometimes she had to make a pickup and bring the remains somewhere else. Sometimes that involved an overnight stay in her home, since she thought it undignified to leave a person in the back seat of her Jeep.

Dan looked like he wasn't going to give up. Cara stroked a hand along his thigh and gave him her best dirty smile. "But that's why you love me, honey. Because I'm anything but normal."

7

Estelle had found the first lump by accident on the morning of Adam's wedding. The night before, Charlie had given her a pill and she'd overslept. She'd rushed through her makeup, painting on eyebrows and coloring her cheeks. She'd been zipping herself into a dress she wore to another wedding the previous summer, but it didn't sit right in the bosom. As she slipped it this way and that and adjusted her bra, she felt something hard and uneven in her right breast, like the end of a chicken bone. She thought about all those medical shows, the books she'd read, and the women she'd known who'd gone through such things. They compared the size of their tumors to food: a pea, an orange, a grapefruit. This lump was nothing that familiar and nothing that round. This was like a knuckle, a dagger, a hand grenade. She sat on the edge of the bed and smoked three cigarettes in a row. The phone rang twice and each time she just sat on her damask spread and smoked and smoked.

The first time the answering machine picked up, the caller didn't leave a message. That was Adam. Adam didn't leave messages.

The second time it was Charlie.

"Hi, Mom. Just seeing when you want me to pick you up. Call me at the hotel."

This is meshugge, she thought. *People do this every day.* People got married. Other people dressed up and traveled for hours to see the bride and groom recite their vows and step on the wine glass. They ate fancy food and drank champagne and slipped checks into the groom's pockets. They smiled, wished them well, gossiped about the in-laws, and debated the couple's chances in the car on the way home.

Estelle didn't know about that Liza. She just didn't know. There was something wrong with the girl's family. Liza's parents had turned away from their Jewish faith as if it were an overcoat not good enough to mend. Okay, so Estelle herself wasn't completely by-the-letter observant—she drew the line at the onerous dietary laws, and hadn't kept kosher since the children came along. But there was something wrong with the way Liza was raised by her father, like a boy. Adam needed a woman. He had Eddie's feckless streak and needed a firm hand, someone like herself. She didn't know if Liza was up to the task. But she seemed like a smart girl, a practical girl. They'd make pretty children, most likely, but Estelle hoped to God Liza was smart enough to figure out how to make the marriage work.

The phone rang again. If she didn't answer, maybe the boys would think something was wrong and rush over. She couldn't tell them, not like this, not on Adam's wedding day. Whatever her opinions about Liza, Adam seemed happy. She wouldn't make this the day he found out the time bomb went off. But she prayed it wasn't Adam calling.

It was Charlie, asking how she'd slept.

Fine. She'd slept fine. "Your father," she said, "may he rest in peace, he couldn't drop dead on the golf course like everybody else? He couldn't go quietly in his sleep? No, he had to have a massive coronary in the middle of synagogue on Yom Kippur and make the newspapers and scar the entire community for life."

"I'm sure he didn't do it on purpose, Mom. Although if you have to go, it might as well be memorable."

"Adam could have gotten married anywhere. A catering hall. Or that beautiful park on the river. But no, he had to pick Temple Beth Make-the-rest-of-your-mother's-hair-fall-out."

"You need more Valium?" Charlie said.

Estelle lit another cigarette. "Bring the bottle."

* * *

Charlie came back a quieter man from his walk with Adam, Liza noticed, and he said little as the three of them remained with Estelle until the end of visiting hours. He stayed overnight at Liza and Adam's house on the foldout in the living room, since the window in the guest room still didn't open and they hadn't gotten around to shopping for a proper bed. Liza threw together leftovers, and they sat around picking at food and not watching some brainless sitcom on television. It wasn't too long before Charlie had their wedding album open and Slipper curled up in his lap. Liza's cat was partial to him, another fact that often annoyed Adam. And the album was a kind of security blanket for Charlie; no matter where they'd lived or where they kept it, he managed to dig it out. He liked the comfort of family history. And Charlie liked Nick, Adam's former college roommate and one of his ushers. Charlie and Nick had had a brief fling following the wedding.

"I can't believe I let him get away," Charlie told Liza. Adam had refused to talk about the incident. "That man could have been my happily-ever-after."

He flipped the page to a portrait of Estelle with Adam and Liza. Liza looked starched, she thought, although a few auburn curls looked ready to mutiny from the complicated pile atop her head. Estelle looked drugged, her eyes drooping, her smile crooked.

"How much Valium did you give her?" Liza said.

Charlie shrugged. "Two ... three ... seven?"

"I can't believe my own mother had to take tranquilizers to watch me get married," Adam said. "And don't tell me it was because of Dad. She would have gone off the wall if we got married at Denny's."

"Especially if you got married at Denny's," Charlie added.

As silence fell over the room, Liza quickly did the math in her head. She and Adam had been married for five years. Tumors large enough to be diagnosed from a chest X-ray could have been growing for about that long.

Adam stared into space.

Charlie mulled over the photos.

Tomorrow, the oncologist would return.

* * *

"He looks good," Liza said to Adam's back as they settled into bed later that night. Slipper had settled in with Charlie on the foldout.

Adam grunted.

"Is he seeing anyone?"

"We don't talk about that."

She heard the television in the living room and the rise and fall of half a hushed phone conversation. Liza couldn't make out any words.

"We ought to stop by her apartment tomorrow and get the mail," Liza said. "She might have bills due."

"Whatever." Adam nestled deeper into the blankets.

She adjusted her own position, fitting herself around him. "Do you really think she knew about the tumors?"

"Yes." His voice sounded constrained, a current of barely-controlled anger running beneath it. "She knew and she was too goddamn selfish to do anything about it."

"Selfish?"

"Yeah. Like always, she wasn't thinking about anybody but herself. How everything affects her. She doesn't care enough about us to want to stick around. If she didn't get tripped up by passing out in the hallway from pneumonia..."

Liza thought about the X-rays and the huge, crab-like blotches the emergency room doctor had pointed out with the tip of a ballpoint pen. The ones nobody was supposed to have seen, extending their claws, grasping for purchase in the murky, soft tissue of her mother-in-law's body. She held Adam closer, waiting for his tense muscles to relax, as they usually did under her touch, but her usual magic wasn't working. "We never would have known."

* * *

Throughout that first year, since Estelle's discovery on her son's wedding morning, the lump had grown. Another had formed in her left breast. Estelle resigned herself to her fate. She named them Miriam and Ruth, after the ghosts of her mother and grandmother, who had both died from the C word—slow, wasting deaths. She assigned the lumps wants and needs. *Ruth needs a chocolate bar. Miriam needs cigarettes.* She was smoking two packs a day. What harm would it do now?

Shortly after Adam's first wedding anniversary, he came over to her condo and said, "Ma, the place stinks."

She told him to go outside if he didn't like it, but he stayed. "Where's Liza?"

"Deadline."

"She doesn't like me," Estelle said.

Adam huffed out a breath. "For God's sakes, Ma. She likes you. She's just busy."

Estelle scrutinized his face, bored into it with her stare. He was lying. Ever since he was a little boy she could always tell by a certain set of his mouth, his lips tight.

Apparently, he knew that she knew. He put out his hands in a gesture of supplication. "Look," he said. "It's not you. It's… well… you know. The second-hand smoke. She says–"

"She's *meshuggeneh*," Estelle snapped out, pinching another cigarette from her pack. "She's obsessed with health. That's what growing up in California will do to you. God forbid she puts something that isn't organic into her body. She might go into shock."

8

Estelle seemed consistently coherent to Liza the next morning, or at least coherent enough for important conversations. The oncologist whom they were not supposed to know was an oncologist suggested that Liza, Adam, and now Charlie take another walk to the cafeteria. Charlie and Adam merely looked at each other. Charlie rolled his eyes and turned to Estelle.

"Oh, for God's sake, Mom," Charlie said. "We know about the lumps."

Glassy-eyed, Estelle turned her head toward the window. The blinds were open. Fat, gray clouds appeared to be pasted atop a field of blue. The ochre leaves still clinging to their branches seemed to shiver.

"If there's something you want to tell us," Charlie said, his voice softening, "tell us."

The oncologist whom they were not supposed to know was an oncologist excused himself.

Estelle shrugged. "I have lumps." She said this as casually as if she were reporting a leaking sink.

"Okay." Liza sighed with relief. "Okay, so now it's out in the open and we can start doing something about it."

Estelle glared at her. "I told you what I wanted to do about it."

Adam narrowed his eyes at his wife.

"I thought you were talking about the cigarettes," Liza said.

Estelle lowered her voice but not the temperature of her glare. "You know what I was talking about."

"What?" Adam asked.

"Never mind. She was delirious." Liza turned to Estelle. "You were delirious."

"Fine," Estelle said. "I was delirious."

"Should I get the doctor back?" Adam said.

Liza's mother-in-law turned back toward the window. "If you want."

* * *

"We'll biopsy first, of course," the oncologist said. Liza's initial impression was not shaken, although the doctor sounded a tad overeager, wore plaid, polyester pants of the type her grandfather might have chosen, and had an annoying habit of drumming his pen against his clipboard. "Treatment prognosis depends on what we're dealing with. But if the cancer," Estelle winced at the word, "is as advanced as it looks on the X-ray, we'd have to proceed aggressively. We'll start with chemotherapy, then bilateral mastectomy, radiation, and then more chemo just to be safe."

"No," Estelle said.

The doctor flicked a glance to Charlie and Adam. Charlie's expression softened. The vein in Adam's left temple had enlarged. Liza got a clear shot when he turned a hot glare on his mother.

"Whaddya mean, no?" Adam said.

"I mean, 'no.'"

"You heard the doctor," Liza said, hoping to be the voice of reason. "It can be treated."

Estelle looked at Liza as if she were a bad piece of brisket. "You, I'm not talking to. You know what I want."

"Ma. Don't you even want to know your chances?" Adam asked.

"I know my chances. *Bupkes*."

"But like Liza said. Things are different today." Charlie's voice was low and soothing.

"Not for me."

"Ma," Adam said.

"Enough, already."

"Ma."

"Adam, stop."

"Ma. Liza's pregnant."

Liza turned to him, indignant, heat rushing into her face. "Adam!"

Adam colored. "I'm sorry, honey. I know we were going

to wait to tell people, but—"

"You're pregnant?" Light seeped into Estelle's face. "I'm gonna be a grandma?"

Charlie was grinning. Adam looked desperate. Liza would one day burn in hell, but at least she'd have company. Reluctantly, she nodded.

"You'll do the biopsy?" Adam said.

"I'll tell you what." Estelle ran her gaze over her daughter-in-law, performing, Liza imagined, that Jewish-mother ninja mind trick Charlie had told her about, where they could diagnose a pregnancy and identify the sex of a fetus faster than an ultrasound. "I'll think about it."

* * *

Liza pounded the elevator button. "You're sick. That was sick and cruel. How could you *say* something like that?"

Adam shrugged. "I panicked."

"You couldn't say something like, 'We love you and we want you to get better?' You had to tell your mother I was pregnant? In her condition?"

"You mean you're not?" Charlie said.

They both scowled at him.

"I was looking forward to being an uncle."

"Your brother is sick," Liza said.

Charlie smiled. "Yes, but he's creative."

"So, what, I'm supposed to fake being pregnant now? Excuse myself every so often and pretend to throw up?"

"For a while," Adam said weakly.

"And then what?"

"We *are* trying, Liza. Who knows, we might even be pregnant by then."

She crossed her arms over her chest. "At the rate I'm learning new things about you? I sincerely doubt it."

His face appeared to harden over. "And what was that in there? That she already told you what she wanted to do?"

"Where is that elevator?" Liza jammed her hand on the button. "It was nothing. Like she said. She was delirious."

9

Liza's classes were done for the day. She had a couple of hours before she was due at the county courthouse to cover a zoning board meeting. According to the delicate choreography of their week, this was the slot in which she and Adam planned to shop for a bed for the guest room. But he had a work thing, postponed from Monday when they spent the day in the hospital, a conference call with a couple of young hotshot software developers who were about to go public and wanted counseling on their investments. It could mean a commission large enough to pay for the bed outright (among other things) and Liza didn't want Adam to put it off again.

So she'd asked Charlie to come shopping with her. The show had given him the rest of the week off. He needed to pick up a few things anyway, and like so many people in Manhattan, he didn't have a car or a driver's license. And, he added, as he'd be spending more time on this bed than either Liza or Adam, he had a greater stake in making sure whatever they chose was comfortable.

"This is nice." Charlie patted the pillow top of a queen-sized bed with a brass frame.

Liza mentally measured the distance from the floor to the mattress (too high) compared with the length of Estelle's legs (too short). "We'll have to airlift her into it."

"You have a point."

"And a queen, I don't know. The guest room isn't that big. And then the sheets will be more expensive..."

"Practical Liza," he mused. "But fulls are so small, though. You and Adam aren't that big, so your full might seem fine, but get a couple tall guys in there and ain't nobody getting any sleep."

Liza raised an eyebrow at him. "Sounds like the voice of experience."

He just smiled. Liza tried to picture what Adam's face might look like the day Charlie brought a guy home to meet the family. It had been bad enough when Adam had merely seen Charlie and Nick flirting with each other in a corner at the wedding.

"For example." Charlie motioned her over to a full-sized box spring and mattress set. He lay down, his Chuck Taylors splayed out nearly to the end of the bed. "Try it out."

She lay next to him. Comfort-wise, it felt very similar to the bed she shared with her husband, although Charlie took up more space than Adam. If she were a broad, tall woman like Cara, this might present a problem. Charlie turned on his side and supported his head on a bent arm, a wave of dirty-blond hair falling across his forehead. For one brief flash, Liza's old attraction to him surfaced as a lump in her throat, but she took a deep breath and swallowed it away.

"Am I right or am I right?"

Liza sighed. "Yeah. I think. We might have to go queen."

"Works for me," he said, winking.

"This is dangerous." She felt her eyelids growing heavy, her body settling into the plushy pillow top. "Shopping for beds when I've slept about eight hours over the last four days."

"Yeah. Me, too. This week has been surreal. Wake me when it's over, okay?"

She let the tranquilizing hum of the store's background music wash over her body and felt the words tumble out of her. "Adam and I were at a neighbor's Halloween party the night before Estelle went to the hospital. We'd had an argument. At the moment, it felt like one of those insurmountable turning points. But now it seems ridiculous. Everything about daily life feels so trivial."

"Yet it still has to go on," Charlie said. "Listen to me. I've become a Lifetime special. Fade to black and cue the Vagisil commercial."

"You think we're doing the right thing?" she asked. "Manipulating her into getting the biopsy?"

"I might talk a lot of smack about my brother, but this was actually a pretty brilliant fake. She'll forgive him. Hell. She's been keeping possibly malignant tumors a secret for God knows how many years. I think she's lost her right to judge us."

Liza thought about this.

"Besides," Charlie said. "*My* kids will need a grandma, too."

She turned on her side to face him. "Charlie?"

He blushed. "Well. I mean, eventually. When I find Mr. Right. But I'd like to."

"You'd adopt?"

"Or call Rent-a-Womb. Or..."

Liza lowered her gaze. It was a stupid thing they used to talk about in college: when Charlie found his true love, Liza would have their children. But they were eighteen years old and probably high at the time.

"Yeah. Things have changed." Charlie smoothed his long fingers over the pillow top's surface. "It was a sweet idea back then, but now it would be like a bad tabloid story. Can't you just see us, under the alien mushroom shaped like Jimmy Durante: 'Woman bears gay brother-in-law's love child.' And I guess it is only fair that you have Adam's kids first."

She sighed. "If we can."

Charlie brushed a wave of hair out of her eyes, and she shivered but tried not to let it show. *It's just fatigue,* she told herself. *It's weakening my reasoning abilities.*

"It'll happen," he said. "After we get Mom squared away and we can all get back to some semblance of a normal life. And when it does? You guys will be great parents."

"You think so?"

"Yeah. I can see Adam being really good at the dad thing. He wants to make up for all the stuff our father didn't give us. And you. Hell. Why do you think I wanted you in the first place? You were lying back smoking a joint, reading me the dirty bits from *National Lampoon*. I said to myself, this woman simply has to be the mother of my children."

She smiled at him and kissed his forehead. "You're sweet. Okay. If my uterus is still intact after Adam and I have our two-point-four kids, you're in."

"Why, Liza Stanhope, that's so goddamned romantic I

think I'm gonna cry."

Footsteps sidled up next to them. "Can I help you folks with anything today? All our beds come with a thirty-day in-home free trial. You two don't find it comfortable, we'll get you something else no charge."

"Hey, that's great." Charlie winked at Liza. "'Cause my wife and me, we're planning on having a lot of sex. I mean a *lot* of sex. I mean, scare the dog, wake the neighbors, break the headboard sex. We're gonna need something durable. And we're gonna need it fast."

10

The bed took up most of the floor space in the guest room.

Adam stood over it, hands on his hips. Charlie gathered up the plastic wrappings and said, "At least we don't have to worry that she's going to fall out."

"Yeah," Adam said. "There's nowhere to fall."

Liza folded the delivery paperwork neatly in half and stuck it in a drawer assigned for such things, making a mental note to add it to her spreadsheet. "Did you fix the window?"

Adam smiled, looking pleased with himself. "Watch this." He slid up the sash. It hovered for a moment and chattered back down.

"Nice." Charlie nodded at the bundle of wrappings in his hands. "Where does this go?"

"Kitchen trash." Liza evaluated the condition of the window. "We could brace it open with a block of wood or something."

"Like my brother's head," Charlie said over his shoulder as he left the room.

"Hey," Adam called back. "At least I'm trying."

Liza wrapped her arms around Adam, and he relaxed, ever so slightly, letting out a long, slow breath. "Thank you for trying, honey," she said.

"I'll fix it."

She kissed the side of his neck, felt the scratchy stubble. "I know you will."

"Are you coming to the hospital with us?"

Liza pondered the request. She'd considered skipping her afternoon lecture to go with them but thought it would be good for Adam and Charlie to have some time alone. And if reports were true, the hospital might be releasing Estelle as early as Thursday, so Liza needed to get everything ready. There was cleaning to do, and shopping: curtains for the window that wouldn't stay open and whatever food the doctor would allow Estelle to eat. "I should go to class and do some other things," she said. "But I'll be there tomorrow."

* * *

Her professor was explaining the types of molecules that were too large to penetrate the blood-brain barrier. But even after a double espresso, most of what he'd said hadn't penetrated Liza's own blood-brain barrier. Maybe going back to school had been a horrible idea. Maybe the human brain was only capable of absorbing complex new information during a certain window of opportunity. Like, when she was younger. Was that why most of her classmates were fresh-faced, sponge-brained children and she was...well, not so much that way anymore? She hardly felt thirty-three was old. It just wasn't eighteen. She didn't bounce back like she used to, couldn't drink like she used to, and the last time she smoked a joint, she fell asleep.

But one night last autumn changed everything. A planning board meeting had run late, thanks to a couple of squabbling aldermen, and she'd been racing home to file her story by the midnight deadline for the next day's paper. Instead of watching the road, she'd been crafting the lead paragraph in her head. Every angle seemed duller than the last. She wished she'd been assigned the school board meeting instead, where there was bound to be a much more interesting discussion on nutritional guidelines for the lunch program. Then something flashed into her headlights. She swerved but couldn't avoid the thunk of metal on flesh and ended up in a ditch. A wounded deer dragged itself into the woods.

Unhurt and waiting for Adam to pick her up, she realized her life was headed in the wrong direction. She'd nearly killed an innocent animal and herself because she'd been crazed— crazed by what? The composition of a lead paragraph for a story nobody would read? A story that she'd collected after three-and-a-half hours on a hard metal chair suffering through the blather of self-important people who liked to hear themselves talk, for which she'd get forty dollars and a byline?

"I should have been a dietician," she told Adam in the car on the way home, as she scribbled several alternative leads in the margins of her notes. She had fifteen minutes to file. It didn't much matter what she produced; her editor always rewrote the whole thing anyway.

"That would have kept you from hitting the deer?"

"I'm serious."

"So do it," he said. "Go back to school."

"What," she sneered, gesturing to her steno notebook, her tape recorder, the meeting agenda, and her scrawled bullet points. "And leave all this?"

* * *

"The human brain is very sensitive to fluctuations in body chemistry. It needs glucose as fuel to function at optimal capacity and the molecules are small enough to pass through the blood-brain barrier...is she sleeping? Ms. Stanhope, are you sleeping in my class?"

Titters of laughter surrounded Liza. *Oh, God. He was talking about me.* "No. I'm awake. Just...lost my place for a second."

Her nutrition professor raised his eyebrows. "Perhaps your brain isn't getting enough glucose today."

"I'll work on that," Liza said.

After the lecture, her professor, who also happened to be her faculty advisor, beckoned Liza over as the other students were filing out.

"I'm so sorry," she said. "It's been a rough few weeks."

He nodded. "Returning to an academic environment after some years away can be a difficult transition. If you have a few minutes, we can talk now."

She didn't. Estelle would be coming to stay with them this week. There was simply too much to do, the list of items on her spreadsheets too long and daunting.

"Need I remind you how poorly you did on the midterm? Finals are only a few weeks away, and—"

Liza let out her breath. "My mother-in-law has advanced breast cancer," she blurted, not meaning to approach this so bluntly.

His face softened. "I'm terribly sorry. You're caretaking?"

She blinked at him. "I...um...that seems to be the case."

He folded his arms across his chest. "Have you considered postponing your degree? Your choice, but..."

"No." Liza shook her head. "I need this. I need the focus. I guess I just need to learn how to focus a little better. And...well, do you know anything, I mean, scientific evidence, about nutrition and cancer?"

He held up a finger. "Let's go to my office."

* * *

She left with a bibliography of books, studies, and websites, for which she thanked him profusely, but now she was really running late. The bank had closed, and the ATM wasn't working, so she had to put groceries on her already-groaning credit card. Adam wasn't answering his phone, so she didn't know what to pick up for Estelle, or whether she should even expect him and Charlie home for dinner. And the order she'd placed at the home improvement store for the guest room blinds and curtains, supposed to be ready today, had mysteriously vanished. The teenage boy working in Window Treatments didn't seem overly concerned.

By the time she made the turn off the main road into her neighborhood, the sun had set. Not enough glucose had passed through her blood-brain barrier, rendering her hungry, cranky, and cold. She'd had far too much coffee and each cup had produced diminishing results. Random groceries sprawled across the back seat of her VW bug. Cara and Dan were home, she noticed, as she approached the Miller's house. Part of her wanted to pull into their driveway, grab a beer from the fridge, and stay for dinner. But duty took her the rest of the way up the hill. Responsibility turned her into her driveway. Adam's BMW sat in the carport. All the lights in the house were on. She hoped someone had started dinner, or ordered in, and that they weren't waiting for her to do something about it. As she clicked off the ignition, a horrible thought occurred to her. What if this wasn't a temporary situation? What if Estelle would be living with Adam and Liza for the rest of her mother-in-law's life?

Adam greeted her at the door with an odd, guilty expression. Charlie was nowhere to be seen. A familiar lump was zonked out in the recliner in the corner of the living room, a familiar lump of tabby cat on her lap.

"Guess who got sprung," Adam said.

"But she..." Liza lowered her voice. "She wasn't supposed to be here until Thursday."

"She's out cold; don't worry about waking her. She was doing okay and wanted to go, so they released her early."

"But I don't have her room ready!" The beginnings of a headache pounded into Liza's temples. "The store couldn't find the curtains and I didn't clean and..."

His smile stopped her. "Take a look."

Liza wandered into the guest room. *I must be hallucinating.* She blinked, had to leave and come back in. The blinds she'd ordered, wood-toned slats to match the molding, had been installed tidily, their pull cords trimmed to the perfect length. The curtains, hung, steamed, and gathered behind wrought-iron tiebacks, looked like something out of a magazine. The rug had been vacuumed, the bed made, and the few remaining boxes and miscellaneous crap they hadn't yet unpacked from the move had vanished.

And a vase of flowers sat on top of the bureau. Somehow, all of it together even managed to make the ugly wallpaper a lot less ugly.

Adam, still grinning, came up next to her. "Wait until you see what's in the refrigerator."

"Adam? You...Charlie...you did all this? When?"

He shook his head. "It was the neighbors. Cara and Patty and what's her name, Ted's wife up the hill. All I know is Cara called to check in just after we found out Ma was being released. She said, can I do anything, and I said probably, because you had class and were stressing about finishing the room. Something about curtains and you hadn't been able to pick them up."

"Judy." Even the spider webs in the corners of the ceiling were gone.

"Huh?"

The afghan on the bed looked like the one from Patty's living room sofa. She'd seen the vase in Cara's kitchen. "Judy. That's Ted's wife." To her surprise, one of the first emotions she felt, after disbelief, was a stab of annoyance. Adam probably told Estelle that it was the neighborhood women, not her, of course not her, who had barfed Martha Stewart sunshine all over the guest room. Because Estelle didn't think Liza was capable of anything domestic. She'd once overheard her tell Adam that Liza must have been raised by wolves.

"Yeah. Okay," Adam said. "I'll try to remember that."

She stared at her husband as one particular event from the last few days resurfaced. *Christ, Adam told Estelle I'm pregnant. I'll never hear the end of it from that woman now. She'll follow me around, fret over every move, every stretch, every morsel that passes through my lips, because being "raised by wolves," I wouldn't possibly know how to take care of a growing human baby.* Even if it were only an imaginary one. She needed a drink. She needed a friend. She needed a drink with a friend. "Where's Charlie?"

The briefest flutter of disappointment passed over Adam's face. "Down at Cara's, helping her hang photos. Why?"

Liza worried her tongue across the back of her teeth and felt her brows bunch together. *Why the hell–?* "Hang photos?" she said.

Adam shrugged. "She said she needed help. Dan's out with the kids, some school thing, Ma was asleep and I had work to catch up on, so he volunteered."

Slowly Liza became aware that she was pouting. She quickly tried to rearrange her face before Adam could see. Too late.

"Hey," he said. "For all the work she and the others did up here, I think we can loan out Charlie for a few minutes."

Liza suddenly felt petty and small. Did she truly believe she had the exclusive right to Charlie's company or the temerity to feel ungrateful for the neighborhood women's help? "I was just, you know, thinking about how many people would be here for dinner."

"Probably all of us." Adam checked his watch. "Look, I've got a conference call with the Seattle office in about five minutes. I think Ma's gonna be out for a while. No sense in you hanging around here when you could be having fun with your girlfriends."

"Nice." Liza grabbed her keys. "I'll tell him you said that."

* * *

"Door's open!" Cara yelled from inside. "Beer's in the fridge; make yourself at home."

Liza inched into the entryway of the Miller's split-level, dodging three cats and a nervous beagle puppy that peed a bit, fortunately not on her sneakers. "Is that how you greet everyone who rings the bell?"

From half a flight up, in the middle of the high-ceilinged living room, Charlie flashed Liza a quick smile. "You're lucky she's dressed." He swirled a tumbler of Scotch and seemed quite at home as he watched Cara, on a stepladder, hold various photos up to the wall like a game show hostess. *If her jeans were any tighter*, Liza thought, *they could perform a pelvic exam. What's she doing with Scotch on their beer budget? And how could she just come into my house and—*

"Hey, babycakes," Cara said, blowing Liza a kiss. She felt her indignation starting to defrost. Cara, like Charlie, had a quality about her, an affable charm that made it difficult to stay angry with her for long, no matter how hard Liza tried.

"Up a little on the left," Charlie said. Cara tilted. "Perfect."

Liza let out a long breath. *The girls meant well*, she told herself. *And putting it all together had to have been a lot of hard work.* "Thank you," she said. "That room!"

Cara lit up. "You like it?"

"I can't believe you guys did that."

"That's what we do."

"Not where I'm from." Until they'd saved enough money for a down payment on the house, Adam and Liza had rented a small apartment in Kingston, and before that, when they first started living together, an even smaller apartment in Manhattan. They hadn't even known their neighbors, let alone wander in and out of each other's dwellings doing home repairs and helping themselves to alcoholic beverages.

Charlie must have seen Liza staring longingly at the Scotch, because he offered her his glass. She took two long sips, savoring the warmth trickling down her throat, before handing the tumbler back. "Now, now," he teased, in a voice barely above a whisper, "too much is bad for the baby."

"Funny," she said.

"Is Mom still sleeping?" Charlie asked, resuming a conversational tone.

"Yeah. Adam thinks she'll be out for a while."

"Thanks for letting me borrow Charlie." Cara inched her way down the ladder and snaked an arm across his shoulders. Liza felt a vague pang of jealousy. "I won't keep you guys. This is mainly the one I wanted to get right. I wanted to surprise Dan."

It was Cara's wedding photo. Cara, of course, looked sumptuous and gift-wrapped. Dan looked young, confused, and possibly under the influence.

Charlie gazed soft-eyed at the portrait, an emotion passing over his face that could have been regret, but then his normal state of gentle amusement returned. He said to Cara, "Liza made a kick-ass bride."

"I loved your dress," Cara said. "I only saw the pictures from your album, but it was probably twice as hot in person."

"Yeah. It made her look like she had boobs."

"Shut up." Liza felt blood rush into her cheeks. Hopefully, they would think it was from the Scotch.

"Seriously," Charlie said to Cara. "She was like Porno Bride. I saw guys knock each other over trying to get on line two, three times for dollar dances."

"They were not," Liza said, still smiling.

Cara pointed her pencil at Liza. "There's your next Halloween costume. Except Adam will be Porno Bride. You'll be the groom. You'd look so cute in a tux."

"You'll have to wax my brother's back," Charlie said.

Cara's phone rang. She was back up on the ladder, reconsidering her selections. "You want me to get that?" Liza said.

"Could you, hon? It's probably Dan."

Liza picked up the receiver, cleared her throat and said, trying to sound serious, "Cara Miller's House of Pornographic Bridal Designs."

"Liza?" It was Adam. Her blush pulsed in stronger.

"Sorry. Cara was just, uh, assigning next year's Halloween costumes."

He continued as if he hadn't heard her. "Listen. Ma's up. She wants Charlie. I'm on hold with this call. Think you can wrestle him away from Cara's clutches for a while?"

"Sure." But why didn't Estelle want to see *her*? Okay, she wasn't one of Estelle's biological children, but she'd married one of them. Liza would have thought that would make Estelle stop hating her. Just a little. "She's asking for you," Liza said to Charlie as she put down the phone.

Charlie's face fell. "Again? Okay. I'm on it." He gave his half-finished tumbler to Liza and leaned in close, a hand on her shoulder. "Please tell me you're coming back soon," he said. "We're gonna need a buffer."

After he left, Liza knocked back the rest of Charlie's Scotch. It wasn't top-shelf, but why let it go to waste? She'd emptied her glass, and as Cara stepped from the ladder, dusting off her hands on her shapely, denim-sprayed derriere, Liza considered pouring herself a fresh one for the road.

Cara stood back next to Liza, arms crossed over her chest, admiring her perfectly straight wedding portrait. "Honey," she said, "I can finish up on my own. The boys need you back there. That's a hell of a lot more important than this."

Liza gazed longingly at the bottom of the glass. "Yeah. I should probably get going before they all kill each other. Funny. Separately, Adam and Charlie are two of the smartest, most together guys I know. Add Estelle and they devolve into a couple of eight-year-olds." Liza sighed. "Thanks again for finishing up the room. You guys are the best."

Cara smiled. "Anytime, hon. But someday I'm going to

get the rest of the story out of you."

"Story?" Liza blinked at her. "What story?"

Cara rolled her eyes. "Please, you think I just fell off the truck? I'm talking about you and Charlie. I see the way he looks at you. Like you're the one that got away."

Liza's stomach twisted. "Good night, Cara."

"You'll tell me," she said, grinning impishly and pointing a finger at Liza. "One day. I'll get you stinkin' drunk, and you'll tell me everything."

11

"Half an hour at three-hundred and fifty degrees!"

Liza hadn't even reached her front door, and she could already hear Estelle bellowing from inside the house. Part of her wanted to run back to Cara's. The bag of various things her neighbor had given her for Estelle's convalescence was growing heavier. She hoisted it higher on her hip, plastered on a smile, and walked in.

Estelle, in full makeup including penciled brows and faux beauty mark, shifted her weight in the lounge chair, wincing. "Liza. Sit. Adam's fixing dinner." She yelled toward the kitchen, "Leave the cover on!"

Adam spun around the corner clutching a wooden spoon in his fist. "Ma. I deal with the stock market all day. I think I can figure out how to heat up lasagna."

"You gotta leave the cover on! Or else it's gonna get all dried out on top; you'll break your teeth. You know how much your father, may he rest in peace, paid for Charlie's caps?"

"Ma, we won't—"

"You tell him, Liza, maybe he'll listen to you. Tell him to keep the cover on." Her bloodshot gaze widened at her daughter-in-law. "What are you doing there still with that bag? You shouldn't be carrying heavy things in your condition."

Liza blinked, remembering she was supposed to be pregnant. *Crap.*

"Sit," Estelle said. "Charlie, don't just stand there, take your sister-in-law's bag."

"Of course." He rushed up to take it from her arms and gave Liza a private, exasperated look, the "my mother is driving me crazy" look. She'd seen it on both of Estelle's sons, except that on Charlie, it seemed more amusement and less anger.

"It goes in the bathroom," Liza said, and then, forcing another smile, turned back to Estelle. "My neighbor, Cara, is a nurse. She loaned us a footbath from the physical therapy department of the hospital. Wasn't that nice? It's got heat, massage—"

"Good, and you'll need it," Estelle said. "When I carried these two, my feet hurt like you wouldn't believe."

Liza said, "I meant…she meant it for you."

"What?" Estelle's faux brows arched upward. "She didn't need to fuss for me."

"Really, it was no trouble. She already had it in the house from when her father was sick."

Estelle still looked skeptical.

"I'm sure she cleaned it," Liza said with a sigh.

"They're great, Mom," Charlie said. "You'll love it. Come on, Liza, I'll help you set it up. So you can get off those poor, aching feet."

He followed her down the hall and said under his breath, "Tell me the rest of Cara's hooch is in here."

"Sorry. Just the footbath."

In the bathroom, Charlie frowned at the various plastic parts he extracted from the bag. As he handed her the basin, he said, "How much water do you think a person can drown in?"

She blanched, remembering Estelle's request in the hospital.

"I meant for me," he said.

"If I don't beat you to it."

"Oh, no you don't, Little Mama. You're suffering for two now."

From the kitchen came the groan of the oven door opening and closing.

"Did you leave the cover on?" Estelle said.

Adam yelled back, "Ma. For chrissake. I left the cover on."

"Liza!" Estelle began to cough. "Liza!"

"I'll be right there, Estelle," she called out.

Charlie and Liza exchanged glances. Then out of the corner of her eye she saw a sanitary napkin wrapper that hadn't made it to the trashcan. She snatched it up, balled it in her hand, and was about to stuff it underneath the rest of the garbage. Then she stopped. "What am I doing?" she said. "This pregnancy thing. It's ridiculous. If I'm pregnant, you're straight."

Charlie appeared to think about that. "You know, I'm not sure which she wants to believe more."

"There's been too much pretending around here." She let out her breath. "Did she see her room, at least?"

"She doesn't like it. She says it's too fussy, you shouldn't have spent the money, and the window won't stay open."

Liza crunched the wrappings in her fist. "See, that's what gets me. Stuff like that, she's honest about. She'll tell me she hates my new haircut, she'll tell me if I'm gaining weight, but a tumor in her breast the size of a fucking orange—"

"Liza!" Estelle barked, making Liza flinch.

"Ma," she heard Adam say, the patience in his voice barely contained. "She'll be back in a minute."

"You have that cover on? Liza! Check if he's got the cover on."

Liza closed her eyes and massaged her temples. Charlie patted her shoulder. "Come," he said. "Let's rescue my poor brother."

"Ma," Adam said. "Enough about the cover. You don't like what I'm doing, there's the phone. Call in Chinese."

Liza walked into the kitchen. Charlie went for the refrigerator and a cold beer. She went for her husband. She touched Adam's cheek. Relief seemed to wash over his face.

"Might as well," Estelle said. "It's the only food that tastes like anything."

"That's because you smoke," Liza said. "You'll see, now that you've stopped, soon you'll be able to taste things again."

"Who says I stopped?"

"Ma," Adam said. "You've had your last cigarette."

"You can't tell me what to do. I've been smoking since I'm thirteen years old. And it's not like anything's gonna help now."

"Ma."

"Liza? Is that cover on?"

She gathered Adam in a hug and felt him relax—

slightly—against her. Without turning away, she batted out a hand, groping for the oven door. Charlie stepped in and quickly opened and closed it again to provide the required sound effect.

"It's on, Estelle," Liza said. "No need to worry."

* * *

Estelle was asleep in the guest room with the window that wouldn't stay open. Charlie, installed on the living room foldout, murmured to some mysterious stranger on his cell phone. Liza, already under the covers in her own bed, watched Adam shuck off his jeans and sweater in exchange for a T-shirt and sweatpants. She'd almost forgotten he had such a nice, compact body. She'd almost forgotten what it felt like against hers, and it hadn't been that long ago. "The biopsy's scheduled for when?" she asked.

"Tuesday."

Liza visualized the calendar in her head, the spreadsheet of their week. Charlie would be back in the city Monday morning. Live daytime television, and the four talk show divas he catered to, waited for no man. Or at least could wait no longer. "You want me to go with you?"

"Nah. It's supposed to be a quick thing, in and out. You've had to miss enough classes. As long as one of us is with her."

To make sure she actually goes, Liza imagined that Adam was thinking.

He slipped under the blanket and settled in with a groan. "I've never been so tired. The woman is exhausting. Even when she was healthy she was exhausting. *Did you leave the cover on? Did you leave the cover on?* Jesus H. Christ. And you and Charlie! Sneaking off to the Miller's and leaving me alone. Thanks a hell of a lot."

"You were the one who told me to go down there."

"Yeah, because she was sleeping."

"So I'm supposed to know by my magical remote viewing powers when she wakes up? Adam—"

"And then you were in the bathroom for, like, a half hour."

"Setting up a foot bath. For her. And it didn't take that long. Adam. Stop it. This isn't about me."

He let out his breath and slid a hand along her hip. "Sorry. I'm just tired, I guess. On television, people have cancer and everything happens so fast. There's the diagnosis, there's the chemo, the hair falls out, and then you're done. They don't tell you about the waiting. They don't tell you about sitting around and waiting for doctors and waiting for tests and not being able to do a damned thing about it."

"I know," she said, drawing him closer.

She held him while listening to the rhythmic snoring from the guest room and Charlie's soft half-conversation, punctuated by the occasional seductive chuckle. She slipped a hand beneath the waistband of Adam's sweats. She just wanted to feel something normal, *be* normal, even if it were only for the time it would take to have sex with her husband while no one else was paying attention. Even if it was quick, even she was too tired or too nervous to have an orgasm. She found Adam semi-hard but shrinking rapidly.

"My *mother's* in the next room," Adam said.

She continued working on him but his excitement had fizzled. "We'll be quiet. Remember? When you brought me home for Thanksgiving for the first time? We barely made a sound."

"I thought you were having your period."

"It's almost over."

"Liza. Honey. I'm really tired."

"I'll do all the work." She tugged down her panties, slithered one leg over his and breathed in his ear, "You just relax."

"I just...*can't*."

She rolled off of him, mouthing a silent scream. "But I can't pretend to be pregnant anymore! I could live with myself if there was at least a possibility..."

"Sorry," he sighed.

"She's going to be staying with us at least until we get the results. That could be another week." *Or forever.* "Are you telling me we can't—?"

"I'm not saying we can't. I'm just saying it's not going to happen tonight. Jesus, Liza. It's too much pressure."

She tugged up the waistband of her panties, nearly tearing the elastic. "Fine. But this is all *your* fault."

"What, you're trying to guilt me into having sex? I made a mistake, okay? I said I was sorry. The words just came out." He paused. "I got her to agree to the biopsy, didn't I?"

She thought about this a moment. "So in your view the end always justifies the means?"

"Not always."

"Like if the means are immoral." Yes, Estelle might have been on Demerol when she asked Liza to kill her, but maybe deep down she meant to say it. Like alcohol loosened the inhibitions. *In vino veritas.*

"I'm too tired for a philosophical argument. Besides, I'd hardly call it immoral. It was stupid. It was desperate. But I wouldn't call it immoral."

"So what would you consider immoral?"

"Liza. I'm going to sleep now. I think Charlie's still awake. He works with that Jerry Springer crowd. Go bother him about what's immoral."

12

After the biopsy, Adam helped Estelle out of the hospital as if she were a delicate china doll. *I gave birth to you and your brother, hard births,* she thought, as he guided her to the parking lot. *I'm stronger than that.* But it was such a pleasant change, his being nice to her, so she didn't say anything. And she felt good, too. Better than she had for a while. Maybe it was the crisp, late fall air, which usually gave her a burst of energy. Perhaps it was just Charlie's Valium. She'd taken a couple of the little yellow pills before the procedure.

They reached the car and Adam held open her door. "You need help getting in?" he said.

"Don't trouble yourself." She landed on the passenger seat with a sigh. He tried helping her with the seatbelt, but she waved him off. Her bosoms were sore where the doctor had driven the needles in. *Both! Why do both? A square of noodle kugel taken from one side of the pan has the same ingredients as one from the other corner. Wouldn't Miriam and Ruth also be made of similar stuff?*

"Ma," Adam said. "You gotta wear the belt. We're going on the Thruway. It's not safe. And there's a law."

"I'll take my chances," she said. "I just can't wear that thing."

He took a deep breath, came around to the driver's side, belted himself in, and started the engine. She watched his face, the tightness around his eyes and mouth. It was a terrible thing to admit, that while she loved her firstborn, she sometimes did not like him. She wanted to, so desperately she wanted to, feel that unconditional acceptance many mothers had told her about. Adam had been such a nice little boy, sweet and loving, but something happened when he became a teenager. She blamed it on her husband. Eddie was hardly ever around, and when he was, maybe he would take one or both boys to the batting cages or play a little game of stickball in the street. But he didn't show them how to be a man, what it takes to be a man. Maybe because the schmuck, may he rest in peace, didn't know how.

Well, Eddie knew how to be a little boy, all right. He played pinochle till all hours, and then he would climb on her like she was some kind of amusement park ride, forgetting or not caring that she was exhausted from chasing after the children all day and shopping and cooking meals and doing the wash for them and for her mother and father. But Eddie didn't know from being a man. From being a provider. Teaching your sons how to be good men, good decent men.

She peeked at her firstborn's face while he pulled out of the parking garage and merged into traffic, his eyes steeled for potential trouble. Somehow Adam had figured it out, this "man business," but large chunks seemed to be missing. In Estelle's observation, he had made up for Eddie's shortcomings by being his exact opposite–strict, stern, responsible to a fault, to the point where he could lack compassion, to the point where he had a temper if things didn't go the way he expected. Estelle had hoped Liza would help in that area, but she still didn't know if Liza was the right girl to balance him out. *And what kind of girl drinks when she's expecting?* She wondered if Adam knew. Or if she should tell him.

"There's that place in New Paltz," Adam said. "You want to stop for lunch?"

"Don't spend your money," she said toward the window, watching the worst of Middletown go by. *Oy, this town is ugly. The litter, the closed-up stores, the homeless people...*

"It's a diner, Ma. It's not that expensive."

"We can make lunch at home. There's still some of that lasagna left. Or I'll make grilled cheese. You used to like grilled cheese. Remember, I made it for you after school?"

She saw his face lighten into the faintest of smiles. "Yeah, I remember."

"Does Liza make grilled cheese?"

He hesitated a moment. "Sort of."

Estelle pursed her lips. "Don't tell me. She uses all that organic *dreck*, doesn't she?"

He made an expression she recognized from his boyhood, when he'd told a lie and knew she knew. "It's just different, that's all. She puts in sliced tomato and onions. Then brushes it with olive oil."

"Sliced tomato?" Estelle said. "Olive oil? Fancy-schmancy. What, Crisco isn't good enough for her?"

"She says it's bad for my cholesterol."

She stared at him. "You have cholesterol? Adam."

"Well, not yet, but Liza says—"

"Listen to you. 'Liza says.' Go to the doctor."

"I've been to the doctor," he said. "And I'm fine. Liza is just concerned about our family history. You know, she's going to school for this stuff."

"My daughter-in-law the expert," Estelle said. *Drinking, with a baby. With my grandson.*

She saw the turn coming up for her condominium complex and hoped he would miss it.

"Hey, is there anything you need from your place?" he said. "We're practically going right by."

Feh, she thought. Estelle never wanted to see that horrible little box again and regretted ever selling her lovely home to move there. However, she did need things. "I wouldn't mind some different clothes. And my knitting."

He took the left at the light and Estelle watched the familiar landmarks slide by. The horrible little box was ten minutes from the hospital. Now that she was staying by Adam, any time she needed a medical test, they had to drive over an hour. A big waste of time. Estelle shifted in her seat, finding a place where her back didn't hurt. She missed the comfort of her own car. "If I had known this was going to be such a little nothing thing, I could have driven myself."

Adam's hands tightened on the wheel. "A little nothing thing? Ma, the only 'little nothing thing' about this morning was the needle."

She felt her own hands tightening. "I told you, I know I made an appointment."

"You're just lucky they were able to work you in."

"I spoke to the girl myself. She must have forgotten to

write it down."

He sighed. "It's okay, Ma."

"Those people are terribly incompetent."

"It's *okay*, Ma."

They pulled into the complex and parked in front of her building. The place seemed smaller, older, and more run-down than she remembered from only a few weeks ago. The fallen leaves had been haphazardly removed. A gutter drooped from the north side of Building B. Adam must've seen it, too, because he said, "I don't know why you're paying those maintenance fees. It doesn't look like they're doing much of anything."

"Not like I'm going to be here much longer," she said.

"Ma." He snapped off the engine. "Don't."

* * *

I should never have sold the house, Estelle thought, as she wandered her condominium like a real estate appraiser might, touching furniture and frowning into corners. Several weeks now since her last cigarette, the stale smell of her beloved Marlboros seeping from every pillow, drape, and rug raised her craving for a smoke, although the Valium kept a lid on it, somewhat. Maybe she would ask the doctor for her own prescription. She didn't want to get Charlie in trouble.

She absent-mindedly drew a line in the layer of dust on the Queen Anne side table that had been her mother's. The framed childhood portraits of Adam and Charlie could also use a going over. Staring into their little faces, she felt a void in the pit of her stomach. She had nothing to leave them. Eddie, of course, had no life insurance, and his pension was so meager she'd had to get a part-time job to pay the bills. She had nothing. Nothing but this horrible little box and all its contents.

"You'll take the sofa," she said.

Adam, who'd been checking one of her light switches, turned. "What. Now?"

"Later. Tell Charlie he can have the armoire. It was your

father's. It'll be nice; he doesn't have any closet space in that apartment."

"Ma. You're still here. Stop giving your stuff away."

She held up her hands. "I just don't want any arguments. I've seen people go without telling anyone what's what and the family argues."

"We won't argue."

Estelle wasn't sure. Mostly, Adam and Charlie seemed to get along well. There was that business with Liza, with Charlie knowing her first, but that was old news. "It's human nature," she said.

Even though she vowed to get what she needed and get out as soon as she could, she found herself dawdling. The blinds needed an adjustment. She put away some dishes that had dried on the rack next to the sink. She tested the dampness of the soil in her potted philodendron.

"What are you doing?" Adam asked. "Liza watered that plant a few days ago."

She shrugged. "I'm just checking to see if she forgot. When I was in her condition, my brain was like a sieve."

Adam rubbed the back of his neck. "Ma. I got to tell you something."

Estelle couldn't hold it in any longer. "She's drinking."

"Huh?"

"Liza." Estelle felt vindicated to have this out in the open. "With the baby. I smelled alcohol on her breath last night. After she came home from the neighbors. I knew that Cara girl was trouble, with those tight dungarees and the bosom out to there and the husband never home and the kids running wild. I didn't say anything. I just thought you should know first. As her husband."

"Ma. There's no baby."

Oy, will this one never get it? She stretched out her hands. "Because she's been drinking!"

Adam just shook his head like she was a crazy woman.

Estelle continued. "Didn't I warn you? Properly raised Jewish girls don't drink like fish! It's the father. I told you. Unitarian? What kind of *meshugge* religion is that? With all that coffee, and talk about the origin of the universe, and letting people believe in God or not?" She paused to catch her breath, and then lowered her voice. "You know her father was drunk at the wedding."

"Ma, *I* was drunk at the wedding. So was Charlie."

Apparently her elder son still failed to see the distinction. "No. There's drunk and there's drunk. You were celebrating. He was drunk. It's in the genes. Don't say I didn't warn you when you come home one day and find your wife passed out on the sofa–on *my* sofa–and your son sticking his finger in electrical sockets and eating rat poison."

"Ma." He rubbed his temples with both palms, squeezing his eyes shut. "There's no baby because there's no baby. It was a false alarm."

No grandchild? Estelle thought, feeling her breath catch. "False alarm?"

"She got her period last week. We didn't want to tell you before the procedure."

Estelle let the heft of this sink in for a moment. *So now, once again, the children are the parents, conspiring against me to spare my feelings?* A hot ball of anger rose from her belly. She felt her eyes narrow, and that anger rocketed into her arm and smacked the side of Adam's head. "Schmuck."

"Hey!" He blinked stupidly at her, his hand going to where her palm had landed, and she did not regret having done it. "How is this my fault?"

"It was your fault it was a false alarm. It's bad luck. To go around tempting fate, talking about things when you don't know yet."

"But we've been trying. When she was late, I thought–"

"You thought. You thought you'd get a sick woman's hopes up for nothing? I was gonna make a blanket."

"You can still make a blanket. It'll happen. One day."

She glared at him. "One day. Stop talking already and help me pack."

13

Dr. Phillips, the oncologist whom they could now know was an oncologist, called the house a week later while Estelle napped and while Adam was on a web conference with a client. Liza spoke with the doctor and did not feel encouraged by the grave tone in his voice, although when she pressed him on it, he would not offer details. Instead, he forwarded her to his receptionist to make an appointment.

After she hung up, Liza took a few deep breaths then slipped into Adam's office. His eyes flicked from the computer screen up to her. "Can I call you right back?" he told his client. Slowly he stood, some of the color draining from his cheeks as he held on to the back of his chair.

"The test results are in," Liza said. "He wants us to come to his office."

Adam nodded, exhaling in a slow stream through pursed lips. "If it's good news they tell you on the phone. If it's bad they want you in person. This is bad."

Adam looked suddenly very young and very scared. Liza put her arms around him and rested her head in the hollow of his neck. She thought about clichés people sometimes used in these situations, such as, "It'll be okay," and, "We'll get through this together." But she didn't know if they'd be okay. Or even if they did get through this together, would they ever be the same? Liza's family had been through a crisis and everything had changed. Her mother had slipped on wet leaves while hiking with a girlfriend, fell into a ravine, and hit her head on a rock. She lingered in a coma for a few days and died naturally, sparing her father the agonizing decision about when or even if to pull the plug. Her parents, practical people like Liza, (or she was practical like them) had living wills; they'd made their wishes known. Her father had told Liza— all of twelve years old at the time—the second night in the ICU that her mother didn't want to be kept alive by artificial means if it looked as though she had no hope of recovery. He'd agonized over the potential choice, but in the end, his wife had decided for him. Liza and her father got through it, somehow settling into a new level of normal, but nothing had ever been the same.

Adam pulled back and met her gaze. His eyes were soft and questioning, a quality Liza had not seen in some time. "If it's bad," he said, "I don't want her to go home right away and be alone. You mind if she comes back here for a couple, three days, while we decide about treatment?"

These days, Liza had a hard time saying no to anything Adam wanted. But Estelle wasn't dead yet; she still had free will and wasn't being kept alive by machines. It occurred to Liza that in everyone's distress and confusion, the patient was being ignored. "If that's what she wants."

His eyes narrowed and color flared back into his cheeks. "You *want* her to die? Is that it? I know you've never liked her, but—"

"Adam!" She felt like she'd been hit by a truck, the blow so strong she clutched her belly to reassure herself she was still whole. She heard Estelle stir in the living room and lowered her voice to a strangled whisper. "Oh, my god, are you *insane*? You actually think I want her to—?"

He rubbed at his temples. "Well, no, I didn't mean…just that if we don't all get on board about this, she won't do it. I know her."

Liza's heart pounded faster, and she took a steadying breath, knowing that again, he wouldn't like what she was about to tell him. "She's an adult, Adam. She can make her own decisions about her health and her treatment."

"Her own decision was to stick her head in the sand and let this thing fester for years. Is that what an adult does? Is that what a mother does to her children? Just…lets herself…as if we…as if she doesn't…" His voice faded out. He swallowed, and slashed his right hand across the air in front of them. "No. If it's not too late, we're getting treatment and that's that. She's done with making decisions. That privilege ended the minute we saw that X-ray."

* * *

Liza came with Adam and Estelle to the oncologist's. Charlie couldn't get away—a crisis on the set—but they brought him in on speaker. When he talked, Liza watched the phone as if she were looking into his face. She imagined him here, nodding, asking questions, taking it all in with clear-eyed pragmatism. Occasionally he might even reach out a hand to touch his mother, then Adam, then Liza.

"The tumors have all the typical signs," the oncologist said. "I've been at this a long time, and one thing I've found is that if it looks like a duck and quacks like a duck, it's probably malignant." He appeared to be a down-to-earth, experienced man, which Liza could appreciate, and she was almost willing to forgive what happened in the hospital. Almost. He had several diplomas on his office wall, from important schools. On his bookshelves were photographs, Liza assumed, of his wife and children, all shiny, dimpled smiles, freckles, and perfect hair. On the corner of his desk sat a little house made of Popsicle sticks, spray-painted gold, with a tiny, crookedly painted sign on the front that read, "Dr. Phillips is in." He seemed like a decent guy. If he'd withheld the truth from her and Adam, if he'd been cagey on the phone, it was because he felt a duty to protect Estelle's rights, and the value and dignity of the patient always came first. Liza had made no headway with her husband on this account. They'd had several harshly whispered arguments over the last few days about morality. Most ended with Adam glowering back to his computer in a huff and Liza off to class, Cara's, or a zoning board meeting.

"But now that we have the biopsy results," the oncologist continued, "at least we know what we're dealing with." Adam sank deeper into his chair. "And I'm not seeing metastasis on the preliminary brain or liver scans. So I think we have a shot at this."

Some of the color returned to Adam's face. "You're kidding."

"That's excellent," Charlie's voice crackled from the speaker. "See, Mom? We have a shot."

Estelle said nothing.

"But it's going to require aggressive treatment," the doctor said. "We start with chemo. Then I'd proceed with a bilateral mastectomy. Then radiation. A few more hits of chemo in case we missed anything."

Estelle said nothing.

"When can we start?" Adam asked.

Dr. Phillips estimated that they could start chemo the first week in January. More tests were required first. Blood work, scans, and they needed to test her heart, to make sure it was strong enough to withstand the barrage of chemicals. They'd install a port for the chemo so they wouldn't have to stick her with an IV each time she came in for treatment.

"That's great, Mom," Charlie said. "No IVs. You'll have a porthole."

"I'm gonna lose my hair," Estelle said.

Adam sighed. "So we'll buy you a wig."

"I hate wigs. They make my head sweat."

"You could wear a scarf," Charlie said. "I've seen them around the city, very elegant."

"I'll look like a gypsy. I'll look like one of those Hassidic women walking through Ellenville on a Sunday."

"Ma. So wear a bandanna. You'll look like a biker."

Estelle shot Adam an evil glare. Liza bit her lip.

"Hair loss is a possible but temporary side effect of the chemo," the doctor said. "It grows back after treatment."

"See, Mom, you'll grow new hair," Charlie said. "You never liked your hair anyway."

Estelle wailed, "What if it doesn't come back at all?"

Adam had that look Liza had come to know well, the "my mother is making me crazy and I'm about to lose it" look. She put her hand on his arm. It didn't seem to help. "Ma. For crissakes. Would you rather have hair or be dead?"

Estelle's mouth formed a flat smile. "At this point, I'm not sure."

"Well." Dr. Phillips tented his fingers atop his desk. "It sounds like you four have a number of things to talk about. Call if you have any questions."

Before they disconnected, Charlie promised to come up on Friday night. Liza and Adam took Estelle back to the car. They were halfway home before anyone spoke. Adam started.

"See, Ma? It wasn't as bad as you thought. He thinks he can cure this."

Estelle snorted toward the window. "Cure, what cure? There's no cure."

Liza, unsure of what to do at this juncture, touched her mother-in-law's shoulder. It was softer than she'd imagined. "Maybe that was true years ago, but Estelle, the doctor said, that if you follow the course of treatment, he's confident—"

"That what? That maybe it'll be gone for a couple of years and then it will come back?"

"How do you know that?" Adam said.

"I know. I read things. I watch those women on Charlie's show. People almost die from the treatment and they have their bosoms cut off and then it just comes back and they have to lose their hair all over again."

"Ma, enough about your hair. It's not a big deal."

"Says you. You're a man. Men are supposed to lose their hair. Not women."

"Ma."

"I'm not doing it."

"Ma."

Estelle clamped her arms across her chest. "I don't care what you say. It's my business."

The tips of Adam's ears were turning red. He sucked in a breath and forced it out. "But you were right there in the room with us! You heard him, the doctor said that if we—"

"We? What *we*? You're not the one getting your bosoms cut off."

Liza closed her eyes, meaning only to briefly absent herself from this argument, but she drifted toward imagining how she would feel if her breasts hung in the balance, so to speak. She would probably let a doctor cut them off, if it meant saving her life. "At least read the literature the doctor gave you," she said. "At least think about it for a little while before you decide—"

"I've been thinking about it for the last five years." Estelle turned toward the window, fingers digging into the paperwork the receptionist had given her, and said in a voice barely above a whisper, perhaps not meant for Liza or Adam to hear, "I've been thinking about it all of my life."

14

No one had talked about Miriam's condition. At least not out loud. There had been whispers; neighbors with kindly smiles appeared at the door with casseroles, milk, and clean laundry. Adam spent a lot of time with Mrs. Steiner. And Charlie continued to grow in the womb.

Her mother had patted Estelle's belly. "How are my grandsons?" It seemed the only thing that lit up her face, hearing about Adam's latest precocity and the progress of his developing brother.

Estelle had watched her mother's thinning hand with its yellowed nails curve over the circumference of her baby. The soft, elastic skin Estelle had loved to stroke as a child was now stretched tight over her mother's knuckles. She couldn't wear her rings anymore; they slid off and she didn't want to lose them. "You'll take them," Miriam once said to Estelle, but she couldn't bear the thought, so they sat at the bottom of her mother's jewelry box. It was black lacquer painted with red Chinese letters. Everything was Chinese design that year: the teapot in the kitchen, the silk kimono hanging on the back of the bathroom door, and the black slippers at the side of her mother's bed. Estelle wondered what Dr. Spock would say about the situation. Could unborn Charlie absorb this misery? Could he measure the progress of the C word through her mother's hand? Sense the spread of the gnarled cells through her body? Could he hear the neighbors at the door, the hushed status report she gave Eddie in the dark of their room when he finally came home?

Estelle took the bony hand off Charlie and wrapped it up in hers. So cold. "He's fine, Mom."

There was no question in Estelle's mind that she was having a boy. He must be a boy. She couldn't have a girl. She would never have a girl and make her go through this, too.

* * *

In between bouts of studying for her final exams, Liza hunted down books on cancer. She cruised the Internet sites on her professor's list, and bought the healthful things they suggested: dark green, leafy vegetables for their antioxidant powers, nutrients shown in blind studies to preserve cell wall integrity, minerals to boost Estelle's immune system, infusions to flush toxins from her body. So far, Estelle had refused anything Liza couldn't hide in something else, but Liza was still trying.

"More Unitarian voodoo?" Estelle said with a lifted brow, when Liza came home from a trip to the health food store.

Why are you making this so hard? Liza plopped the bag on the counter with a sigh. *And where's Adam? He used to defend me.* When Estelle first got sick, and Liza wanted to cook for her, Adam had told his mother that Liza was going to school for nutrition. That Liza wanted her to feel better, and it had nothing to do with religion or lack thereof. Now, he'd metaphorically thrown her to the lions.

But Liza refused to let her discouragement—and disappointment in Adam—show. After hanging her coat in the hall closet, she walked her latest find, a little paper sack of herbs, to where Estelle was planted in the recliner, knitting and watching television, with Slipper, that traitor, curled up on her mother-in-law's stubby legs. "You brew this into a tea," Liza said. "It's supposed to help your immunity and increase your circulation. If you decide to try chemo, it's supposed to reduce nausea. And it'll help the drugs work by protecting healthy tissue, leaving the cancer cells more vulnerable."

Estelle sat up and leaned toward the bag. "It smells like compost," she said, wrinkling her nose. Even the cat jumped away. "No dice."

Liza bit back her words and took another in what felt like a lifetime of long, steadying breaths. She knew Estelle had at least been perusing the copy of *Cancer and Nutrition* she'd left on the coffee table. The bookmark had been moved, and she knew it wasn't by Adam. Yet she had to tread carefully with her mother-in-law, couching her language in terms of Estelle's personal choice and not talking in absolutes, like Adam and Charlie. Respecting her as a grown woman who had borne two children and buried a husband. But still—? "Maybe if we add some almond milk and stevia," Liza forced a bit of a smile, "it will taste less like lawn clippings."

"No, thank you," Estelle said. "Next time, save your money and just buy some Lipton's."

Liza retreated to put away groceries. She heard the upholstered groan of Estelle resettling in the recliner. "It was just an idea," Liza said under her breath. *All I can do is fill our home with good food and positive energy, and hope for the best.*

She took two glasses of water—one thing Estelle never refused—into the living room, setting them on the small table between the recliner and the sofa. "Adam's in his meeting?" Liza asked.

"Where else?" Estelle said with a shrug. "It's the Atlanta people, I think."

The television in the living room babbled away, tuned to the show Charlie used to produce, with the two women who seemed to talk only about sex and shopping, before he'd moved on to the one with the four women who seemed to talk only about sex and shopping. One of the women, a loud brunette with so much collagen in her lips she looked like she'd been French-kissing a hornets' nest, asked the panel which Prada bag went with her shoes so she could tell her husband what to buy her for Christmas. *What a waste of electricity*, Liza thought, and then announced she was going to make soup.

Estelle looked up from her knitting. She'd been at this project, it seemed, every waking moment for the last three days, but she would not disclose the intent of the final product. All Liza knew was that it was very large, very yellow, and it kept her mother-in-law from wanting to smoke. "What kind of soup?"

"Lentil." Iron to build the blood. Fiber to cleanse Estelle's colon. And, mostly, because there was not much else in the house. Busy with her classes, freelancing, taking care of Estelle, and hunting down the elements of the perfect cancer-killing diet, she'd neglected to keep up with their customary level of what Adam called "normal food." Which meant white bread, American cheese, hamburger meat, and Doritos.

"What are you serving it with?"

Liza stopped, puzzled, mid-way across the kitchen, holding a bag of organic kale in one hand and an onion in the other. "A ladle?"

"I meant dinner. The main course. What are you serving it with?"

"Well, this sort of will be the main course. It's a meal, with salad and bread. The soup has kale and sweet potatoes." More antioxidants. "It's filling."

She got a skeptical grunt from her mother-in-law. The needles clicked.

"Adam likes it," Liza said.

The needles clicked.

With a sigh, Liza resumed chopping onions and garlic. The rhythm calmed her, as did the satisfaction of seeing results. Soup, she could control. She could chop the onions as fine as she desired. Add celery or not, add potatoes or not, pour in a little wine or not.

A puddle of olive oil shimmered at the bottom of the pot. The two women on television debated the merits of pointy-toed shoes versus round as seriously as if they were members of the UN Security Council. She grew disappointed all over again at Charlie's choice of career. He knew back in college that he wanted to work in television, but he wanted to do something relevant. Bring important issues to the fore. Ferret out the truth and make poetry out of the struggles of the common man. She doubted that when they were sitting in Professor McClure's Media and Society class, he'd hoped one day to bring to the daytime viewers of America a lipstick that wouldn't stain your coffee mug.

A voice rose over the television.

Liza came around the corner, wiping her hands on a dishtowel. "Did you say something, Estelle?"

"I said we'll have chicken soup. Not tonight. Just some

night when I'm here. I'll show you how it should be made. Adam likes that, too."

* * *

Lentils, feh, Estelle thought, starting another row of stitches. Lentils were what you cooked when you couldn't get meat, like during the war or when money was tight. Her mother had made mock chopped liver with them, but it wasn't the same. She'd vowed never to eat lentils again and never to serve them to her children, no matter how little Eddie was earning. Why make lentil soup when you could get a whole chicken from the market for only a few dollars? She blinked a few times. Her eyes felt tired from the television and from knitting for so long, or maybe from the cat hair, and she let her lids close. Her mind wandered back until she could almost smell the chicken soup she used to make for her mother.

Estelle had left five-year-old Adam with Mrs. Steiner that afternoon. She'd dropped her son off with the patient, matronly neighbor so often lately Estelle had feared that Adam would start calling her Mommy. In her silent prayers she'd asked her child to forgive her, forgive her absences, her distraction. She'd promised herself to always be there when Adam came home from school. Other than that, she went to her ailing mother.

On the way to the Flatbush Avenue walk-up her parents called home, Estelle stopped on the corner and got a nice chicken from the butcher. He winked at her, asked when the baby was coming, and gave her a little discount. He knew the family. Everybody knew the family. She stopped at the greengrocer and bought celery, carrots, two parsnips, an onion, and a bit of fresh dill. As Mr. Silverman weighed out her produce, Charlie woke and stretched, kicking her low and to the right. She braced a hand against him, and all the women in the shop smiled a knowing smile. Charlie had been giving her trouble all week. In bed, she felt a foot, an elbow, a knee. The women on her mother's block all had their theories, those Jewish ladies who could tell if you were pregnant, (*shvanger* or something like that in Yiddish), just by the way your face looked, and knew its sex by the way you carried or how well or poorly you felt. They knew what it meant when a baby gave you heartburn, when he kicked, when certain foods made him act up or calm down. But later, as she was skimming fat off the top of the water in the soup pot, as she was tapping the spoon into the empty coffee can beside the stove, as the steam curled the hair around her face, Charlie stopped fussing. The ladies found something prophetic about that, too.

He liked when Estelle cooked.

Not everything, though. Pot roast made him press some knobby appendage up into her diaphragm in protest. He liked the lighter things. Soups. Breakfast. He loved breakfast. Eddie was gone too fast in the morning for breakfast, because he liked to sleep as late as possible. So she'd make for herself and Adam. Eggs, pancakes, French toast.

Pearl, Eddie's mother, said, "So much food? You're spoiling my grandson. And you're going to give some poor woman a headache; he'll always expect the royal treatment."

But Estelle didn't care. The only happiness, the only comfort she'd had since her mother got sick had been in the company of her son. Eddie ate and ran. Her mother's appetite had been waning. Her father picked. Estelle had to remind herself to eat for Charlie.

Adam, however, ate enthusiastically, and it was such a pleasure.

When she was pregnant with Adam, he didn't show a preference like Charlie. Or, perhaps, she'd been so overwhelmed by the idea of her first pregnancy that she'd failed to notice these nuances.

But Charlie liked her chicken soup.

Estelle's father came into the kitchen. Miriam wanted a glass of water. "You're making her hungry," he said, and kissed his daughter's cheek. "She keeps asking when it's going to be done." Then he made some weak protest about Estelle being on her feet in her condition, but she said she didn't mind. She didn't mind at all.

15

Cara swung her Jeep into the lot assigned to Randall Osten's townhouse, got her satchel, and knocked on his door. He had ALS and was in a wheelchair. According to Visiting Nurse policy, if no one answered after what was called "a reasonable attempt" to announce her arrival, she could use the key they provided. She was just about to knock a second time when the door swung wide to reveal a pinched-faced woman in a candy-striped waitress uniform. Her disapproving stare warned Cara against crossing the threshold.

Cara smiled, hoping to defuse her. Randall had warned her about his daughter, who had moved into the area for a few months to "take care" of him. Truth was, she depressed the hell out of him, and he would have rather she'd stayed in Wisconsin. "You must be Millicent."

"You must be late." Millicent pulled the door shut behind her so they were both standing outside. "I was supposed to be at work fifteen minutes ago."

That explains the ugly uniform, Cara thought. *But how weird is this? She'd come to take care of her father but got a job?* "I'm a nurse," she said. "Not a babysitter."

"You were supposed to have been here at two o'clock. That's what it said on the calendar. Cara, two o'clock. And it's two-fifteen."

"I think you and I have a misunderstanding about the service I provide. I check in on your father twice a week, Tuesdays and Thursdays."

"At two o'clock."

"Approximately."

"Two-fifteen is hardly an approximation of two o'clock."

"Well." Cara forced out a smile, even though she was itching to smack the mousy-haired bitch. "Now that I'm here, I guess you'll want to be on your way."

"But I need to talk to you. That's why I stayed."

This should be good. "All right," Cara said. "We'll talk. Can I come in?"

"I'd rather talk out here." Millicent looked left and right, as if scouting for eavesdropping neighbors.

"Sure," Cara said. "But maybe we can talk in my Jeep? It's wicked cold out here."

Millicent shook her head, although she seemed to be shivering in her polyester uniform and thin coat. She reached into a pocket and extracted a Ziploc bag containing a vial of clear liquid and a disposable syringe. "I found this in my father's refrigerator. Is this what I think it is?"

Cara examined the vial. It was morphine. The dosage was probably large enough to kill a person about Randall Osten's size. "Probably."

Millicent's eyes narrowed. "Get rid of it."

"Because...?"

"Only God can decide when it's time to call him home. It's not up to us. It would be a prideful sin to do His work."

Perhaps this was one of the reasons Randall didn't want his daughter to come. Randall Osten was an atheist and pretty set in his ways about it. "I'm not sure that's your father's viewpoint."

"My father has lost his way. Now, I won't accuse you of bringing this into his home, but I will ask you to see that it's removed."

"All right."

Millicent smiled. She was actually a pretty girl, when she took the stick out of her ass. "Thank you. You can see to my father now. He's been looking forward to your visit. I'm so glad we had this discussion."

And then she left.

Cara found Randall in the living room, half-dozing in his reclining wheelchair. His voice was raspy and tired. "From the look on your face, I can see you've met Millicent."

"Nice girl."

"Pain in my ass. God this and God that. Bunch of crap if you ask me."

"Randall?" She held up the bag. "Is this yours?"

He attempted a shrug. "Might be."

"Millicent asked me to get rid of it. Should I?"

"No. I'd like to keep my options open."

"So I'll put it somewhere Millicent won't look?"

He appeared to think a moment. "Put it in the brass urn on the bookshelf."

Cara turned toward the gorgeous, wall-to-ceiling, built-in bookshelf and spied the urn, second shelf down, next to a series of thick tomes about Winston Churchill. Unlike those who put weighty books out for show, trying to convince people they were better than everybody else, she knew that Randall had read all of them, and somewhere in his library were a few he'd actually written. He'd offered to loan Cara anything that might "pique her interest," as he'd said, but Cara wasn't much for books. When she did manage to have a few minutes to herself, she was usually too tired to do anything that required serious thought. But she loved listening to him talk about history. He must have been one awesome teacher.

"She won't find it there, say, when she's dusting?" Cara said. "She seems like the dusting type."

"She won't dust there. It's her mother's ashes."

A grin slid across her face. "Creepy. But smart."

"Yes. She thinks having her mother cremated was a sin. Still hasn't forgiven me for it. So I sincerely doubt she's going anywhere near that urn."

16

Adam carried the shopping basket. "She said not to forget the parsnips." He looked lost and frustrated and kept checking his watch. He had a conference call with a client in Eugene, Oregon at five. Also, Liza knew that he hated this store because they didn't sell Doritos and white bread, but the result would be his mother's chicken soup, so he was trying to be patient. Not hard enough, in Liza's opinion. "I don't even know what a parsnip is let alone where to find one," he said.

Amazing, Liza thought. He'd lived with Estelle Trager for how many years, eating her chicken soup how often, and he didn't know what a parsnip looked like? But then again, he didn't spend too much time in the kitchen. When she'd met Adam, he'd been living on take-out food, beer, and care packages from his mother. "It's like a big, white carrot. It's probably near the radishes." As he left to root among the roots, Liza ticked off in her head what else she needed. More garlic. Onions. Sweet potatoes. Also, she wanted a couple bags of fresh cranberries for their vitamin C and phytochemicals; she'd make sauce and cut down the sugar.

Looking pleased with himself, Adam came back holding a chunk of horseradish in a plastic bag.

"Close," Liza said.

His face fell. They hunted around and finally found them next to the cilantro. "Why don't they label things in this store?" Adam said. "For the prices they charge, they could make some freaking signs."

"They have signs," Liza said. "They're just really, really small. And, apparently," she pointed out the one that read 'parsnips,' "invisible to the male eye."

"Very funny," he said, and watched her hands as she deftly snapped a plastic bag from the roll and worked it open. "Please tell me you're not going to make the matzo balls with whole wheat flour and bird seed."

He looked truly worried that this would be his fate. But she'd learned her lesson with the grilled cheese sandwiches on whole wheat bread. Her free-spirited parents had shucked the conventions of their youth, but through Charlie, and then Adam, Liza had learned that sometimes tradition trumped common sense. She let out her breath. "I guess the occasional glob of white flour isn't going to hurt. Much."

* * *

As fall turned into winter, the diagnosis permeated their day-to-day lives, and most of Liza's energy went toward gently nudging Estelle to at least consider chemotherapy. But it was easy to forget that her mother-in-law was still regaining her strength from the pneumonia, and the battery of antibiotics, narcotics, and steroids her doctors had her on during and following the course of it.

"Sit, don't strain yourself," Liza said. "I can handle the cooking." But when she'd turned her back to wash carrots at the sink, her mother-in-law was up. Wincing in apparent pain, Estelle cradled her right breast as she ferreted around in the cabinet beneath Liza's stove.

Her stomach clenching with fear, Liza rushed to her, hands extended. "Estelle, I'll get that, don't, please don't—"

But Estelle ignored her. "Where's the eight-quart?"

"You shouldn't be—"

"The eight-quart. The big pot. Where do you keep it?"

Liza let kind of Zen resignation flow over her. *This is Estelle's choice. If she wants help, she'll ask. You can't force someone to take your help.*

She still had her head in the cabinet. "Didn't I buy you and Adam an eight-quart?"

Estelle had bought them an entire set of aluminum pots as a wedding present, but Liza didn't know how to tell her mother-in-law she'd thrown them all away. Aluminum pots? With all those studies about Alzheimer's? It wasn't worth the risk. Adam had gone nuts when he'd found out—he hated waste—but she'd rather have him get a little steamed now than forget where he lives when he's fifty. Eventually he saw her point or decided it wasn't worth the argument.

"Funny thing," Liza said. "I haven't seen them since the move." Which was, technically, true. While Adam and Charlie loaded the truck, Liza had thrown the pots in the dumpster behind their apartment building. Some homeless people were probably roasting a pigeon over a flaming oil drum and giving themselves Alzheimer's right now. She wondered if they could hunt Liza down one day and sue her.

"You don't have anything big?" Estelle said.

Liza held up the stainless steel pot she'd bought to replace it. It had been sitting in the dish drainer. "Can we use this?"

Estelle sniffed. "We'll just have to make do."

* * *

The pots were a problem—Estelle promised to buy them a new set off the Home Shopping Channel—and the kitchen didn't have nearly enough counter space, but at least her daughter-in-law had sense enough to own a good, sharp knife. Estelle quartered the onions, the parsnips. It had been a while since she held a knife but the body remembered. She watched her own hands and in her imagination they became the hands of her younger self. They were unlined and smooth, and she wore her wedding ring while she chopped onions for her mother's soup. Then suddenly Estelle felt so tired she could barely stand.

"Estelle?"

"I just need to get off my feet for a few minutes." She fumbled her way along the counter toward the dinette and a waiting chair, and fell into it with a long, heavy exhale that set off a coughing fit.

Is this is the start of it? Estelle wondered, trying to catch her breath. *Is this what it feels like when the cells start eating you alive?* Liza had gone white. *Will they all look at me like that, later? Is that how I looked at my mother?*

"Keep going." Estelle waved a hand toward her daughter-in-law, feeling the spasms subsiding. "I'll talk you through it."

Liza stared at her.

"Keep going. Don't worry about me. I'll be fine."

But Liza didn't look the least bit convinced.

"What? Stop it. This is from the pneumonia."

When Adam was four years old, five maybe, did he see the same look on Estelle's face that she saw on Liza's right now? When he came home from school and asked if he could go see Gramma Miriam? Did Charlie feel what she'd been feeling? Could he have absorbed her fear and worry via her bloodstream? No. That couldn't be. Charlie had been such a happy child, a sunny disposition, always trying to make her laugh. Adam was the serious one, the worrier. He fretted over everything. What to wear to school. Which college to choose. If Liza would want to marry him after knowing Charlie first. "If she doesn't, then she's not the girl for you," Estelle had told him.

Maybe Liza was the girl for Adam after all. So she had her problems. She'd been raised by hippies, still dressed like a college girl and couldn't keep her hair combed, but there was potential. Estelle hadn't smelled alcohol on her breath since that last episode. Except for the cat hair, she kept the house fairly clean. She knew how to cook. It was odd food, poor people's food, things you might feed to a rabbit, but neither she nor Adam seemed to be starving. She wondered if they would raise her grandchildren to be vegetarians. She supposed it could be worse. They could be Catholic. They could be Republicans.

Liza stood there with a cup of hot water and a Lipton's teabag, and she continued to stare at Estelle. "Go on," Estelle said, secretly pleased that her daughter-in-law had made a fuss and even brought her real tea instead of twigs and bark. "It's just a little cough."

Liza went back to the cutting board and picked up the knife, hesitant about what to do next. "The carrot?"

"Quarter it. Like I did the parsnip." Estelle craned her neck for a better look. "Watch your fingers. Keep them away from the blade."

"I know how to use a knife."

"Just in case. People slip."

Estelle didn't realize until she wrapped her hands around

the mug just how cold she had been, how steady it made her feel to hold something as ordinary and domestic as a cup of tea. If God forbid Estelle had had a daughter, maybe she'd be like Liza. Bringing tea, making soup. Except maybe if she were Estelle's daughter, she'd be a little more feminine. But that's not Liza's fault; she was raised mainly by her father, during the years that counted at least. There had been no one to show her how to put on makeup or do her hair or keep her legs together. No one to tell her that a good girl doesn't drink beer out of a bottle with men or go to the market in sweatpants. She watched Liza's efficient strokes, plus the concern in her daughter-in-law's brown eyes when she occasionally looked up to make sure Estelle had not keeled over.

This will be the mother of my grandchildren.

Then she thought about the chemotherapy. So maybe it wasn't too late. Maybe it was like Adam said and wouldn't be so bad. Other people had done it. They'd been on Charlie's program, those women who'd survived for five, ten years. Of course, they were all much younger than Estelle. And they'd probably started much, much earlier. Instead of taking Valium, smoking cigarettes, and hoping one day she'd wake up to find the tumors had magically dissolved during the night.

"So what did that doctor say, how many chemo treatments?"

Liza sucked in a breath.

"Did you cut yourself?" Estelle said.

"No," Liza said. "Just…no, I'm fine. And that would be eight to twelve treatments, depending on how your body responds to it, possibly more."

"And I'd have to give up sugar completely?" Most sweets she could take or leave, but the thought of a life without chocolate seemed impossible.

"It's not a medical requirement, but it would help. And it's your choice. But one of my professors told me how cancer cells thrive on sugar. You stop it, and essentially you starve them. Sugar also compromises your immune system. Chemo does a number on your immunity, which is why it's important not to do any more damage to the healthy tissue."

Estelle tried to take this in. Liza said more about cell wall integrity and mitochondria and a bunch of other things she didn't understand.

"What about coffee? Do those cells like coffee?"

"I haven't read anything that says they care one way or the other."

"How long until I lose my hair?"

"It could be a while."

Estelle thought about that. "All right," she said with a nod of finality. "We'll start, we'll see how it goes."

The knife slipped off the carrot. Fortunately, it didn't seem as if Liza had cut herself. Her eyes widened. "Really? You'll try it?" Liza said. "I'll tell Adam—"

Estelle waved a hand. "Leave him be; he's got work. Yes, I'll try it. But under one condition. If it gets too bad I'm going to stop."

* * *

Liza, having just sheared off the tip of her fingernail, put down the knife and gave Estelle her full attention, arranging her face to neutral non-judgment. She'd hoped Estelle would choose to try chemotherapy of her own accord and not from her sons' demands. "Of course. It's your body. It's your treatment."

"And like I said, when it gets bad, I don't want to suffer."

"But you don't have to. There are drugs—"

"No. You don't understand." Estelle lowered her voice and emphasized each word. "I said, 'I don't want to suffer.'"

Liza felt her skin prickling against the back of her shirt. The nape of her neck went damp. She opened her mouth but nothing came out.

"I want what we talked about in the hospital," her mother-in-law said.

"Estelle. You had pneumonia. You were barely conscious; you were on six kinds of medication. Surely you didn't mean...what you said."

Estelle pulled herself up to her full, seated height, which wasn't much, and shot Liza a clear-eyed glare. "I meant every word of it."

"That you wanted a cigarette?"

"Yeah." Estelle smirked. "That I wanted a cigarette."

Liza stared at the partially quartered carrot, the knife, the flakes of onion skin sticking to the cutting board. She'd completely lost her appetite and her desire to ever make soup again.

"You'll do it," Estelle said.

"Me?" A fist tightened around Liza's stomach. "Oh, no. I'm not—"

"Adam and Charlie won't. They're too softhearted. Good boys, but weak-willed, like their father. May he rest in peace. So you'll have to do it."

"What are you saying?" Liza glared at her. "That I'm cold-hearted enough to...kill a person? Is that what you're saying?"

"Oy, no, of course not. I'm saying you're practical. You're a practical girl. At least that's what Adam says about you. You'll know how to do it."

Liza threw up her hands. "So what do you want me to do? Push you out a window? In front of a bus? Hold a pillow over your head?"

Estelle appeared to consider her options. "The pillow would work. I saw Cary Grant do it in a movie. Or you could get me pills. People take pills. Marilyn Monroe took pills. Some people think it was the Kennedys, but I know it was pills."

This is ridiculous, Liza thought. "Or, how about I poison you? Feed you the wrong kind of mushrooms? Put rat poison in your coffee? Hey, I read a book where the killer stabbed someone with an icicle. No evidence."

"No," Estelle declared, after seeming to take a second to think about it. "That might be good for you, but it will probably hurt too bad. What kind of mushrooms are you talking about?"

Liza raised her eyes to the ceiling. "I can't believe I'm

having this discussion. Estelle. I'm not going to—" She lowered her voice. "*Kill* you."

Estelle went on as if Liza weren't even in the room. "Maybe Charlie knows someone. People in the city, they won't care. They do these kinds of things all the time."

"Yeah, the streets of Manhattan are filled with people killing each other. All the time. Estelle. The chemo might work. The doctor said. At least it will help the swelling go down, and you'll be more comfortable. And then you might feel differently."

"You won't go to jail," Estelle said. "They're more lenient these days. Especially for a woman. You say you're sorry. It was a mercy killing. You say you did it out of the best of intentions. Then you write a book, and Charlie will put you on his show."

Liza picked up the knife and pointed it at her mother-in-law. "We're not talking about this anymore. We're making soup. How should I cut the celery?"

"Big chunks. And I'll sign a paper."

"A paper."

"The paper will say that I asked you to do it. You know, like Dr. Kevorkian. We'll get lawyers; we'll make it legal. So you won't get in trouble."

Liza whacked at the celery. "I really doubt a bunch of lawyers are going to sign on to you agreeing to let someone kill you—"

"Well, they should. Wait till one of them gets...gets *this*. Wait till one of them watches his mother waste away to nothing. Miriam, my mother, couldn't even wear her slippers, beautiful silk slippers we bought her in Chinatown, they were falling off her feet! You could see her skull underneath her face. She was in so much pain and so weak she couldn't get out of bed to go to the toilet! If we could have...done something about it, we would have! No one should have to live like that, if you can even call it living!"

Liza could only stare. Adam and Charlie had both told her, on separate occasions, that their grandmother died from heart failure, not cancer. Had Estelle been trying to protect them? Was that why she'd kept her own tumors a secret?

She lowered her voice. "And you never told the boys...?"

Estelle threw up her hands. "Would *you* want your children to know that your mother's a ticking time bomb? That she's going to die a horrible death, with her skull sticking out and her rings falling off?" She stabbed a finger into her own chest. "My grandchildren could have those genes. They could be in this position."

Liza swallowed hard. She hadn't really considered that. "Things are different now," she said, but the words sounded weak to her own ears. "The chemo's going to work, the doctor wouldn't say he thought he could stop it if he didn't think—"

"He doesn't know! He doesn't know!"

Adam stomped into the kitchen, red-faced. "What the hell's going on in here? I'm on the phone and I can barely hear my customers!"

"Your mother—" Liza set down the knife and roughly pushed her hair out of her face. "Your mother—" She glared at Estelle. Estelle turned away. "Wants a cigarette."

Adam turned on Estelle, pointing a finger. "Ma. You're not smoking. End of discussion."

17

Liza worried that her and Adam's hushed bedtime strategy sessions about Estelle's treatment plan would replace sex as a form of communication between the two of them. After a few weeks' hiatus, they *were* making love again, but it had become something to get out of the way so they could talk. It was all a hurried, silent process performed with one ear open, like parents of a newborn.

So this is what it's going to be like to have a kid, Liza thought.

Adam rolled off her and rearranged his pajama bottoms. So what if she went a couple times without an orgasm; the world would still turn around. And that wasn't really the part that mattered to her. Mostly.

"Tomorrow, we have to schedule all those tests," he said. "What is that, blood work...?"

"And the heart scan."

"I hope we can do them all in one day," Adam said. "Save us all that running back and forth to Middletown."

"Funny, when she sold the house and bought the condo there, you were grumbling because it was too close, that she'd be over here all the time."

"That was then," Adam said.

"And now it's too far." Liza stared at the ceiling, a checkerboard of reflected panes cast by a neighbor's floodlights. They highlighted the terrible paint job done by the previous owners. She mentally added it to the dozens of other things on the spreadsheet that would have to be redone and at this rate never would. "You know, I don't like the idea of her going back to her place now. I know the two of you talked about that. But she'll be starting chemo soon, and she might not be able to do things for herself. She'll be tired, nauseated— I can hardly see her doing laundry or grocery shopping."

"So we'll come by on the weekends and help. In between, Charlie and I can chip in and hire someone to look in on her. Buy groceries, do errands—"

"You'd trust your mother to a stranger?"

"Liza, this is going to take *months*. You'd rather have her here the whole time?"

"If that's what it takes to get her through this." She had visions of Estelle downing all her medication at once with a fifth of Scotch, a toaster in the bathtub, sticking her head in the oven. No, wait, she had electric, but still...

"I thought you didn't like her. She's always judging you, you said, telling you how to dress, what to cook—"

Family is family, even if she hates me. She tried to see the situation from Estelle's point of view. "But she's your mother and she's all alone. She talks a good game, but underneath she's probably scared. I don't want to even think about her going through this process an hour away in a second floor apartment in a complex where she knows three people, two who barely speak English and one who gets around with a walker."

Adam huffed out a breath.

"It's not right," Liza said. "We have the room. One of us is always around..."

"We'll all end up killing each other."

Liza just stared at the horribly painted ceiling.

18

Estelle didn't like the sour look on Adam's face (which looked so much like the sour look on his father's face) or the number of antacids he'd popped since they'd settled into what the hospital called their "Chemo Lounge." She paused at her knitting. "You don't have to stay," she said, but hoped he wouldn't leave.

Adam glanced up from the *Wall Street Journal*. "So what am I supposed to do, go all the way home and come back?"

She shrugged and added a few more stitches. "Go to the movies. Go shopping. I'm just gonna be sitting here dripping for another couple hours. It's gotta be like watching grass grow."

"I didn't come here to be entertained."

Various pieces of equipment hummed and wheezed. Adam turned his attention back to the stock market report. *My poor bubeleh*, Estelle thought. *He shouldn't have to see me like this, connected to machines, a porthole for the IV, like something out of a science fiction movie. I used to make the entire Thanksgiving dinner all by myself, including three kinds of pie. Now, I'm on my feet fifteen minutes and have to sit down.*

She tried to lighten the mood. "Maybe with this cockamamie thing I can get cable, you think?"

Adam rubbed the back of his neck and took another antacid. "I'm glad one of us finds this funny."

She pursed her lips. "Charlie would find it funny."

"Charlie's not here."

"What are you getting all upset about? I just said—"

"Forget it, Ma. Just forget it." He returned to the stock market page.

"What are you reading?"

He didn't look up. "An in-depth analysis of which market sectors are expected to have the best P/E ratios for the rest of the first quarter."

The unfamiliar words buzzed around her head like flies. "I'm sorry I asked." Estelle clicked away for a while, then said,

"I've been thinking about your living room. You gotta do crown molding. I saw it in a magazine."

"Ma. We got eight-foot ceilings. I'm not doing crown molding. It'll make the place look like a cave."

"It won't, you'll see. It really pulls a room together."

"It's a ranch. It's not gonna work. Now, if we had a colonial, maybe. But not a ranch. It doesn't go."

"It'll go."

"Ma."

"It'll go!"

"Fine. Whatever. We'll do crown molding. I'll put it on the list."

The needles clicked. *Health care,* she thought. On the news that morning, they said you should put your money into health care and drugs. *Why the hell not,* she thought. She'd seen the first of her medical bills. For what hospitals and insurance charged, they were probably rich as Rockefeller.

She took a deep breath and let it out, gazing at the thick brush of her elder son's hair. So handsome. Both her boys were, in different ways. *It's time,* she thought, biting at the inside of her lip. "Your grandparents had crown molding," Estelle said. "In that apartment on Flatbush Avenue. You remember?"

"Ma. I was four years old."

"You remember."

"I remember that the place always smelled like soup and Grandpa pretended to pull pennies out of my ears. Does that automatically mean I remember the crown molding?"

"You don't have to be smart. I just asked."

The needles clicked. Adam glowered into his newspaper.

It's time he knew the truth. He'll get angry, but better to have it out in the open. "I was making soup," she said. "All those days when I left you with Mrs. Steiner. I was making soup for Gramma Miriam. Toward the end it was the only thing she would eat."

She had his full attention. "What do you mean, 'toward the end'?"

* * *

Adam and Estelle were not due home from the "Chemo Lounge" for another hour, so Liza, having just returned from her first day of spring semester classes, took advantage of the free time and walked down to Cara's. Her conversation with Estelle about suicide methods had been roiling around in her mind for days. A nurse's perspective—especially from a nurse like Cara, who seemed more reasonable and compassionate than the others she'd met lately—might be exactly what Liza needed. Plus, the house felt extra frosty when no one else was home. The furnace was acting up. For three days now, they hadn't been able get the thing to crank higher than fifty-five degrees. Fortunately, Adam had taken one look at the complex wiring and gas intakes and decided to leave it to the professionals. Unfortunately, the professionals couldn't give them an exact date of service. She also hoped that Cara might have a spare quilt for Estelle's bed.

After the various house pets had skittered through their legs at the front door, Cara pulled Liza into a hug. For a woman who routinely lifted and transferred sometimes very large people, Cara's touch could be extraordinarily tender.

"Hey, babycakes, great timing. The kids are playing video games in the basement and Dan won't be home for another couple hours. Union stuff." She pulled back and met Liza's gaze. Her eyebrows drew together. "You look like crap. Want a beer?"

"Please." Her feet feeling suddenly leaden, Liza followed Cara up the five stairs to the kitchen and plopped into one of the Miller's dinette chairs.

Cara fished out two bottles, opened them, and did not as much sit in the opposite chair as occupy it. She leaned back and crossed her legs. "All right," she said, nudging a hearty-looking winter ale in Liza's direction. "Talk."

After stammering for a bit, feeling blood pulse into her cheeks, Liza summed up the conversation she'd had with Estelle.

"Holy shit." Cara lit up a cigarette, blowing the smoke out the side of her mouth. A cacophony of children's voices rose from the Miller's downstairs playroom. She turned toward the stairs and yelled, "Hey. Knock it off!" Then she said to Liza, "Does Adam know?"

Liza shook her head. "Don't tell him. Please. He's on edge as it is."

"You gonna do it?"

"Of course I'm not going to do it." She eyed Cara. "Would you?"

Cara shrugged. "Depends. If someone was really suffering and they wanted out, maybe. I've taken care of some of these people. A little too much morphine might have been a lot kinder than letting nature take its course."

"That's what you'd use? Morphine? Theoretically, of course."

"Yeah." Cara leveled a gaze at Liza. "That's what I'd use. Theoretically. Of course."

* * *

Adam had to go out for meeting—or at least that's what he'd written in the note he'd left for Liza on the kitchen counter. He came home so late that Liza was already in bed, attempting to read, snuggled under several layers of blankets. The book was a bestseller Patty thought she would enjoy, but Liza was so mentally saturated she had to scan each sentence several times before moving on.

"The hell's this," he said, almost tripping on Cara and Dan's electric space heater.

Liza gave up pretending she could still absorb the written word. "Dan brought it up for your mother's room until the heat guy comes to fix the damned furnace."

He shot a dark glare at it and shook his head. "Don't tell me. She said it costs too much to operate and she sleeps better in the cold."

"Something like that. We went a few rounds. I told her to keep it in there in case she changed her mind, but she insisted we use it." She didn't add the part where Estelle said that sleeping in a cold room was bad for conception.

"Doesn't feel like it's even working," Adam said.

"It works. If you're six inches away." So far, the greatest beneficiary had been her cat, curled up in front of the blower like the Sphinx guarding Pharaoh's tomb.

Adam quickly changed into sweats, and he and Liza huddled under the covers for warmth. The blankets smelled like onions and garlic and everything she'd been cooking for the last week and a half. Adam smelled like Adam, a wonderful smell she couldn't describe except for the fact that it made her feel normal and safe. Then they were on each other, kissing, pulling at clothing, making love with a ferocious hunger she vaguely remembered from when they were dating. Afterward, she locked her legs around his back and refused to let him go.

"You can't still be cold," Adam said, in his voice a hint of the playfulness that she'd so desperately missed.

"No," she said. "Just gathering you up for strength."

His arms tightened around her and he kissed her neck. "I can give you some more strength in a few minutes."

The sound of muffled coughing from across the hall startled her and silenced Adam; for a few minutes, Liza had almost forgotten someone else was in the house. She coughed twice more, then stopped. When Adam spoke a few seconds later, his voice was hushed but still had a hard edge. "My grandmother died from breast cancer."

Liza sighed. Finally, Estelle had told him. The weight of one less secret fell from her shoulders. "I know."

A longer silence stretched uncomfortably between them. The heater cycled off with a tinny rattle. Finally, he said, "She'd always told me and Charlie that her heart stopped."

"That was the official cause of death. Caused by the cancer."

"But I didn't know that! I had nightmares for the longest time when I was a kid, that you could be sitting around, fine and dandy, playing with trucks or eating cereal out of the box or watching Scooby Doo, and boom, your heart would stop and you'd die."

"And that would have been better than malignant cells eating your body alive?"

"Back then, I probably would have thought that was cool."

She nudged him with an elbow. "That's sick."

"I was five years old! My friends and I dared each other to eat dried worms off the sidewalk, for chrissake."

"If we have a boy and he eats dried worms off the sidewalk, I'm blaming it on you."

"I made Charlie eat a worm once."

"Somehow that doesn't surprise me."

The coughing resumed. Liza and Adam didn't speak again until the fit stopped.

"She told me all this stuff today during her chemo." Adam's voice was barely above a whisper, but still, it quavered with anger. "How it was when Gramma Miriam was sick. I think she thought it would help me understand why she waited so long."

Communication, Liza thought. *This is a hopeful sign.* "Did it?"

"I walked out."

So much for that. Oh, Adam. "You walked out?"

"I was just sitting there listening. And she told me all this stuff about soup and Chinese slippers and rings that didn't fit. And all the time I'm thinking, goddamn it, you *knew*. You knew this could happen to you. They know it runs in families, yet you never went to the doctor, never got the mammogram, never cared one good goddamn about me and Charlie. And I just…snapped. I got up, grabbed my stuff, and walked out the door. I didn't come back until the treatment was over. We didn't say one word to each other the whole trip back."

That explains a few things, Liza thought. Why Estelle had been so quiet during dinner and went straight to bed afterward, armed with the extra sweaters and blankets Cara had loaned them. Why Adam hadn't been home. "You didn't have a meeting tonight, did you?"

He huffed out a breath. "I went to the movies."

"What did you see?"

"I don't know. Stuff blew up. That's all I remember."

* * *

By Saturday morning, the furnace had been repaired and they no longer needed five layers of clothing just to stay moderately warm. Charlie was due, and Liza felt the mood in the house sparkle as if touched by a magic wand. She'd bought the blend of coffee Charlie liked and changed the sheets on the foldout. Estelle put on makeup and did her hair; the noxious cloud of hairspray mixed with perfume normally made Liza gag, but somehow it didn't seem so bad that day. Adam fetched his brother from the train station. Charlie arrived with a sack full of goodies from Zabar's, a Lindy's cheesecake, and dirt on the four famous ladies.

And just as the coffee finished brewing, he also had Cara's riveted attention. She'd stopped by to pick up the space heater before taking her kids ice-skating. While Charlie talked, she leaned forward as if she were eating up the gossip with a spoon. "So that's your job?" she said. "Keeping those bitches from each other's throats?"

Feeling useless and vaguely usurped, Liza ducked into the kitchen and wiped down counters that didn't need wiping.

"That. And occasionally producing a television show." He sniffed. "It's a living."

Cara said, "I read in the *Star* that Jessica had so much Botox she can't even blink."

"Close to it. It's pretty freakish." Liza heard the clunk of someone setting down a coffee mug. "Mom?" Charlie said. "You're looking kind of green. You okay?"

Liza rushed out. A film of sweat shone on Estelle's forehead.

"It's probably the nausea," Cara said. "From the chemo."

Estelle nodded.

"Can I get your Compazine?" Liza said.

"Doesn't work," Estelle said in a gasp. "I took three."

"You're not supposed to take that much, Estelle." Cara turned to Liza. "Does anything else work?"

Liza shrugged. "We tried ginger tea. She threw it up."

Cara smiled gently at Estelle and patted her knee. "I got something for you, hon. I'll bring it by tonight."

* * *

Later that evening, Patty helped Liza clean up from dinner, a simple Saturday meal consisting of several pizzas and a variety of leftovers. While Liza was answering Patty's question about how to get her kids to eat more vegetables, Adam, jaw tense, came into the kitchen with a fistful of paper plates and shoved them into the trash.

Oh, no. Liza knew the expression on her husband's face. It was about four notches short of the one that preceded whacking an inanimate object.

"She gave my mother pot," Adam said.

That's what you're freaking out over? "It was just a little," Liza said.

"Cara gave my mother pot. You know she's not supposed to be smoking."

"It's not like she whipped out a bong, Adam. We made tea. And it helped."

"I don't care."

Patty jumped to Liza's defense. "You don't care that your mother is no longer puking her guts out?"

"Maybe you can do that in California, but here it's still against the law."

"I hardly think they'll bust our door down for a tiny bit used for medicinal purposes," Liza said.

"She has kids," Adam said. "What's she doing with pot in the house?"

"Where do you think she got it?" Liza said.

"She found it in Jason's book bag," Patty added.

"Oh. That's nice," Adam said. "He's what, ten? Real nice message she's sending."

"And the Valium you and Charlie have been pushing on your mother for years?" Liza said. "That's okay?"

He said nothing.

Cara sidled into the kitchen and took two beers from the fridge. She smiled at Adam. For a second his gaze dropped to her breasts, emphasized in a clinging sweater. But Liza, when she was sober, could hardly fault him. They were like a total eclipse of the sun. Sometimes Liza found herself staring. "Don't give my mother any more pot, okay?" Adam said in a softer tone.

"But she's feeling better." She squeezed Adam's shoulder. "Maybe you could use some, too, hon. You're wrapped a little tight. Have a beer."

He took it from her. If she'd offered him hemlock he would have probably taken it.

"And that's different." Liza gestured toward the bottle. "That high can be legal, but a tiny bit of pot—"

"It's not the same, Liza."

"People who smoke pot don't get into cars and kill people," Patty offered. "They mostly want to eat junk food and watch TV."

Charlie wandered in, beaming pearly whites, dazzling the ladies with his good looks and near-celebrity status. But that was what usually happened when Charlie entered a room. "So the party's in here. Mom's starting to wonder if it's something she said."

Adam grabbed Charlie's arm. "Charlie. Talk some sense into my wife."

Charlie winked at Liza. "You married her."

* * *

Adam followed Cara's beer with several more. By the end of the evening, he was sleeping like a bear in January, and Liza stared out the bedroom window at a gentle snowfall. Estelle had been asleep for hours. She heard the television in the living room and slipped out of bed, hoping to find company. Charlie was watching an old black-and-white movie. A fast-talking dame with dark lipstick was holding a gun on a guy trying to be as smooth as Bogie. Charlie's cell phone was propped on the arm of the sofa. He watched the device intently, as if he could will it to ring. Liza made a show of scraping her feet along the carpet, to alert him.

He turned and smiled. "Come sit. The bad guy's about to buy it for being a Nazi sympathizer. Or a bootlegger. I'm not sure which."

He stretched out a corner of his afghan—Cara had brought another one—and she curled up beside him as three shots rang out. The Bogart wannabe winced, dropped to his knees, and continued a slow descent to the floor.

"I miss the days when people in movies died in tidy, choreographed heaps," Liza said.

"I miss hats." Charlie turned a sly look on her. "I bet you'd look good in a hat."

"Hardly," she said. She'd missed this. Late nights with Charlie. Talking through the movie, mocking the cheesy dialogue and bad acting. Discussing the movie they would write one day. But things change. She wondered if he ever thought about what he gave up to work for daytime TV divas.

"Sleeping Beauty turned you out into the cold, dark night?" Charlie asked.

"Snoring like a buzz saw. It's not pretty."

"So stay up. *Dark Victory*'s on next. I love watching Bette Davis die. She's the best."

Charlie's phone rang. He glanced at the ID then back to the screen.

"Waiting on someone?"

"I'm playing hard to get." He looked tired. "Actually I'm playing, 'there's very few people I want to talk to right now.'"

"But there's someone you do want to talk to."

Charlie didn't answer.

Liza felt slightly miffed. He'd never kept secrets from her before. "Is this classified information?"

"It's a problem."

A romantic problem, Liza surmised. "Closeted?"

"Worse." He let out his breath. "Politician. And closeted."

"Is he important?"

"Could be. He's on everyone's short list to run for Congress."

"So what's the big deal? You live in New York. Who would care if he came out? It might even enhance his caché."

"His wife and kids might have something to say about that."

"Oh, Charlie..."

He sighed. "I know. I'm the poster child for 'Gay Men, Stupid Choices.' We met when he came to do a segment on the show, and we just clicked on so many levels. He reminded me of Jimmy Stewart in *Mr. Smith Goes to Washington*. You know, that earnest belief that he's in this thing to save the world? It was *so* hot. Ah, but who am I talking to? Liza the Practical. You always made sure they were attainable before you fell for them."

Not always, she thought. But she was over Charlie. About ninety-nine percent of the time. "Maybe he'll get divorced."

"I doubt it. She's very religious."

"Too bad," Liza said. "You'd have made a great First Lady."

"You think?"

"Absolutely."

Charlie's face sagged as he turned toward the window, where the snow was piling up against the pane. "Is there any cheesecake left?"

19

At first, Estelle had to admit the chemo treatments weren't as bad as she'd imagined. She'd take her drip, knit, watch a little television—Charlie's show was on during that time—then go home. It was almost like a little party. People brought lunch. They brought games, something to do while you're hooked up to the IV bag. The other patients had warned her what to expect, especially about the "window." *Count on having a couple, three good days after the first treatment*, someone told her. *Then you get tired.* If you needed to do your shopping, get the laundry done, the oil changed, or take a weekend trip, you were supposed to do it in the "window."

"After that, it ain't like the ads on television," one man had said. "You know, the guy takes the iron shot and he's out conga dancing. It don't work that way. Everything just gives you more side effects. Some you never even dreamed about."

The man had been right. For instance, last night she took off her mascara and a sweep of lashes came with it. No one told her she'd lose her eyelashes.

Sometimes Adam took her to her chemo appointments. Sometimes Liza did. Liza was better company, although her daughter-in-law had never been much for casual conversation. When it was Adam's turn, he scolded Estelle and glowered out the window like a sourpuss. But luckily for Estelle, today was some kind of federal holiday and both of them came. Adam behaved better when his wife was around.

Both kids looked tired and Adam was a grump; he said he hadn't slept well. Right after he and Liza checked her in, they went out to get coffee. Liza gathered orders from the nurses, with Adam carping at her that she didn't always have to take care of the whole world. *It's that house*, Estelle decided. *He'd never been that grumpy when they rented.*

Not even five minutes after they left, Dr. Phillips came into her cubicle. Several days ago, she'd had another scan and some blood work. When no one had called, she'd assumed there was nothing to report, that everything was going as planned.

"Estelle." He pulled a chair up next to hers and patted her arm. She felt her muscles tighten, felt herself getting smaller, shrinking away from him. *It's not good when the doctor sits down and touches you. When they call you by your first name.* What had her mother's doctor done? She remembered a nurse. Nothing like that Cara, but a nice, patient woman in a little cap and white shoes, who'd taken Miriam's pulse and temperature and massaged her swollen legs. Estelle didn't remember seeing a doctor at the house. Maybe her mother's illness had progressed too far for him to bother. "How are you feeling?" Dr. Phillips asked.

She glared at him. "How do I feel?" *You've ruined food for me,* Estelle thought. *Everything tastes like dirt. I'm nauseous; I have diarrhea; sometimes there's blood. I'm trying my son's patience. Some days I just wanna die already.* "How do you think I feel?" she said. "I'm hooked up to this cockamamie thing like a car at a gas station and my eyebrows are falling out."

The doctor smiled. *Putz,* she thought. *Wait till you get sick. Then we'll see if you're still smiling.*

"I was looking at your tests," he said, his nose in the file. "And frankly after five treatments I usually see better numbers."

Estelle swallowed. "It's not working? After all this?"

"On the left side. That tumor is shrinking. But the right one isn't responding. In fact, it's getting larger."

A hollow feeling bored into the pit of her stomach. *I can't go like her. I don't have the strength. I can't put the kids through that.* "If this isn't working, I want to stop."

He closed her chart. "That's your decision, although I'd recommend—"

"Is it spreading?"

"We won't know unless we do more scans."

"So it could be spreading?"

"That's always a possibility. It's like when you bring your car to the mechanic. You ask them to check the brakes, they check the brakes. If there's a problem with the transmission, they won't know unless they check that, too."

She looked out the window. Adam and Liza would be back soon. They wanted to stop for lunch after the chemo; God knows why they should waste their money.

Dr. Phillips scribbled on a piece of paper. "Tell you what. We'll do another CT, liver function, bone scan. Then we'll see what we're dealing with."

But am I strong enough to die? Estelle swallowed and turned back to him. "No. No more chemo. No more tests."

* * *

Liza was working so hard to stay positive her face hurt. The morning had been horrific. Adam and Estelle were like oil and water. Actually, more like vinegar and baking soda—tolerable enough separately, but together, Vesuvius. "Anything you like, Estelle?"

"I don't know." Her mother-in-law put down the luncheon menu. "Maybe just a little soup."

"Ma."

Liza narrowed her eyes at her husband. "If your mother wants soup, leave it alone. She's supposed to be eating lightly after chemo anyway."

"She needs her strength. Ma, get a steak. You gotta build your blood."

"Oy, don't talk to me about steak," Estelle said. "And why even bother eating? It all tastes like crap anyway."

"Fine," Adam said. "Get soup. But please, just try to eat something."

They ordered. The waitress brought hot beverages: tea for Estelle and Liza and decaffeinated coffee for Adam. Liza slipped Estelle some natural sweetener from her purse. But Estelle was already dumping in the contents of the pink packet from the tray on the table. They sipped in silence, and for those few moments when Adam's and Estelle's mouths were occupied with something other than attacking each other, Liza was thankful.

Then Adam put down his coffee and said, "Hey, what happened with those tests you got last week?"

Estelle's fingers tightened around her mug. "They were fine." She cut her eyes from Adam to Liza and back again, as if she were testing whether they believed her. "In fact," Estelle said, "the doctor liked them so much, he said I could take a break."

Adam's eyebrows scrunched together at the exact moment Liza felt her face make the same gesture. "How much of a break?" he asked.

"A month, two...who knows? He wants me stronger for the surgery. Later I'll go in for more tests and we'll take it from there. So I could probably go back home. Getting this out of my system, I'm sure I'll feel better and maybe do for myself for a while."

"It's no trouble having you, Estelle..." Liza said.

Estelle waved a hand. "You got enough to do. Adam has his customers, you've got school, the newspaper, I'll be fine, you don't need—"

Adam cut her off. "I want to talk to that doctor."

"Why bother?" Estelle said. "He'll only tell you what he told me."

"I want to hear it from him."

Liza pressed a hand to her husband's arm. She could almost feel his blood pressure rising. "Adam..."

Estelle raised what was left of her eyebrows. "What, you think I'm lying to you?"

"Why would I think that?" Adam said. "Because you've never lied to me before?"

Estelle was up, looking unsteady on her tiny feet, oblivious to the stares of the other diners. "I don't have to take this from you. I'll be in the car. You can get my soup to go."

"Estelle, you don't have to..."

"This isn't about you, honey. This is about my schmuck of a son. Just like his father." And then she was gone.

Liza turned on Adam. He just glowered.

"Was that necessary?"

Adam lowered his voice. "She lied to me about the tumors. She lied to me about how my grandmother died. Why should I trust anything she says?"

* * *

Too angry even to put on her gloves, Estelle fumbled her increasingly cold fingers through her purse and dropped two quarters into the pay phone outside the restaurant. The receptionist answered.

"I need to talk to the doctor."

"I'm sorry, Dr. Phillips is with a patient."

"This is Estelle Trager. T-R-A-G-E-R. I'm a patient, too. You tell him that privacy agreement I signed? The one where he has my permission to tell my children about my condition? I'm taking it back. I know my rights. He's not to tell them a thing. Do you hear me? Not one word. Not a test result, not a diagnosis. Nothing. Or I'll sue his cheap, polyester pants off."

* * *

Liza stared glumly at the space where Estelle had been sitting. "Do you think she'll be okay living on her own?"

"At this point," Adam gulped the last of his coffee and plopped the empty mug on the table, "I don't care."

She wrapped her hand over his. She knew he loved his mother. But anger was flavoring everything he said, everything he thought and did. Adam continued, color rising in his cheeks. "A sudden illness, that's different. Even if she had the cancer, found it early, and decided to get treatment. I'd do everything I could for her. But this? Some days I never want to see her again."

They sat together for a few moments in silence. He pulled his hand out of Liza's and rubbed his eyes. The waitress asked if they needed anything. He shook his head as if rousing himself from a trance. "Just the check," he said. Liza peered out the window and saw Estelle on the pay phone at the corner of the building. *She shouldn't be outside so long in this cold.*

"You think she's calling a cab?" Liza said.

Adam craned his neck to see where Liza was looking. "Nah. Probably calling Charlie to complain about how we're mistreating her."

* * *

When they came home, Adam claimed that Dan needed help moving something heavy and took off down the hill. *Just as well,* Liza thought. *Let him cool off.* After cooling herself off with a couple minutes of meditation and a prayer tossed in for good measure, she went in search of Estelle. She found her mother-in-law in the guest room, packing her suitcase. Estelle looked unsteady, fogged over even, as she hunted for various articles of clothing. *It's too soon to let her be alone.* She had visions of Estelle falling in the shower, leaving the stove on. Or harming herself more intentionally. Liza picked up a flannel nightdress patterned with tiny roses and folded it in quarters. "You don't have to do this," she said.

Estelle's neck stiffened. "I'll be fine."

"Then we'll come up. At least a couple times a week. On Saturdays we'll pick Charlie up at the train station on the way."

"It'll be nice to see you." She pursed her lips and nodded toward Adam's office. "Him, you can leave at home until he learns how to behave. I don't like to talk bad about Eddie in front of the boys, may he rest in peace. But sometimes I think Adam is becoming more and more like his father."

Liza sighed and dropped the folded gown on top of the other things. She tussled around in her mind for the right words for the situation. *Why can't I be more upbeat and compassionate, like Cara? She always seems to know what to say. Maybe that's why she's a nurse and I'm...what was that Adam once called me? The Food Police?* "He's still a little angry," Liza said finally.

"Well, so am I." Estelle cast a glance around the room until it landed on a tote bag in the corner. It contained the clothing Estelle had worn when she was first admitted to the hospital; Liza had picked it up when they released her. Liza knew its contents well—a nurse had shoved the clump of it at her when they transferred Estelle from the emergency room to ICU. Then she'd taken pity on Liza and given her a bag. Into it, Liza stuffed the old white bra, the giant white underpants, the nylon nightgown, the terrycloth robe that stunk of cigarettes. Adam and Liza had bought her new nightclothes, so Liza wondered why they had held on to the bag.

Estelle was now fumbling through this paper sack, muttering to herself.

"Are you missing something?" Liza asked.

"Where is it? I know he took it from me."

"What?"

"My lighter."

Liza let out her breath. "Estelle..."

"I'm not gonna smoke. Honestly, most of the time I don't even feel like it anymore. I just want the lighter. It was my mother's."

She evaluated Estelle's promise. Although if Liza were true to her convictions, then allowing Estelle to smoke was not Liza's choice, either. But still... "You know what they do to you," she said.

"Who doesn't?" Estelle said, not looking at her.

"No. Not the cliché stuff. Not just the cancer. They ravage your body, they'd sabotage all of your efforts to heal." Because of Liza's studies, she could run down all of the physiological effects of nicotine and the nutrients it destroyed. Vitamin C, the whole B family, blood calcium levels. "They leach the calcium from your bones."

Estelle appeared unmoved. Liza gave up. If her mother-in-law wanted to smoke herself into asphyxiation, if she wanted to smoke until she shrunk to the size of a garden gnome (she was already well on her way), then Liza had nothing to say about it.

She retrieved the lighter from the top drawer of Adam's desk.

Estelle wrapped her fingers around it as if it were a touchstone. "Thank you," she said. Liza couldn't remember

Estelle ever thanking her for anything before. She carved it into the place in her mind that kept unexpected kindnesses.

Then Estelle tossed the lighter into her purse as casually as a set of car keys.

"You'll return the afghan," her mother-in-law said. "And that foot whatchamajiggie."

Liza nodded but felt they'd be borrowing them again.

"You'll give me her phone number," Estelle said.

"Cara?"

"She said I could call. If there was anything I needed."

Probably more marijuana. Liza forced a smile. "Great." Adam would hate this. Liza wasn't too wild about it herself, mainly because of the legal issues. She had visions of reading about her mother-in-law in the newspaper: *Sixty-five-year-old local woman and nurse busted in pot ring.* Liza hoped that if Estelle needed bail money, she'd call Charlie first.

"I never knew you could make tea," Estelle said. "I always thought you had to smoke it."

"And you know this for a reason?"

Estelle shrugged, gave Liza a coy glance. "I tried. Once. At a party. Just to see what the fuss was all about. I never told the boys."

Big surprise. "And?"

"I didn't see the big deal. But this time...I don't know, but I don't remember the last time I slept so well."

"I guess that's something."

Estelle folded a bra in half and nested one cup into the other. Liza imagined Estelle was thinking she might never need that or any bra again. She tried to envision what it would be like to wake up from surgery minus her breasts. If that would make her less of a woman, if Adam would no longer find her attractive. She thought of Estelle's wedding portrait: a beautiful, busty young thing. Eddie grinning at her like he'd just won the lottery.

"You know," Estelle continued, "I don't think I've slept a full night since I found the first lump?"

It must have been so frightening, Liza thought, but then felt a surge of anger for what Estelle had put her sons through. "It didn't have to be like that."

Estelle waved a hand. "Water under the bridge. I got what I got and I made my peace."

"That may be, but Adam and Charlie haven't."

Estelle picked up her knitting. She examined the most recent row of stitches and frowned. "This will go in your bedroom. You need some color in there, with all that beige. And maybe a lamp, for that side table."

"They've only had a few months to get used to this, Estelle. You've lived with it for years...you have to give them some time to catch up."

Estelle gave Liza a clear-eyed glare. "You think this is easy?"

"I never said..."

"The throwing up? The pain? The diarrhea and everything else? You think that's been a picnic? I love my boys. I did the chemo for my boys. I'd never want to see them hurt, but all this talk, talk, talk about what it's like for everyone else except the person who's actually going through it." Liza started to protest, but Estelle stopped her. "No. Not you. You've done so much already. You. And Cara. A total stranger! You and a total stranger are the only ones who really care about what *I* want."

Liza couldn't think of anything to say. It was the closest thing to a compliment Estelle had ever given her.

"And what I really want is to go home." Her shoulders sagged as if just the thought relaxed her. "I just...want to go home. I want to sit in my own chair, sleep in my own bed, drive my own car to the supermarket. I want to finish this afghan. You like the yellow?"

Liza hated yellow. Adam hated yellow. "We love the yellow."

"You'll put it over the bed. You'll see, how it will brighten up the whole room. And the cat hair will blend right in. Less to clean."

"I'm sure it will be lovely."

Estelle dropped her gaze to the pile of wool. Stroked her fingers into it. "My husband, the schmuck, may he rest in peace. He went like that. Sometimes I think he was the lucky one."

* * *

Adam grabbed a cart and started pushing it toward the freezer aisles while Liza tried to orient herself in the unfamiliar supermarket down the road from Estelle's condominium complex.

Strange how they lay these places out, she thought. *Why are the rice cakes next to the beef jerky? So someone bent on choosing the less-healthful alternative can simply look to his left, and say, 'Oh, look, something with less crap in it.'* This, she decided, was the problem with America. Most people automatically turn toward the right, and food marketers knew it.

"We'll get easy things," Adam said. "Frozen dinners and stuff."

"You know she won't eat them."

"If she can't get out and doesn't feel up to cooking? She should have something in the house."

"But Adam, they're full of chemicals. Artificial colors, too much sodium...no nutritional value whatsoever! She needs the best food she can get into her body right now."

"So *you* can drive an hour here and back every day and cook for her. You can bring seaweed and wheatgrass and force it down her throat."

She stopped and glared at him, her hands on her hips. "You're being a jerk again."

"Sorry." He glowered into the freezer door. "Shit. The rest of the soup. I left it on the kitchen table at the house."

"I took it," Liza said. "I put it in her fridge." Right now it was the only thing in Estelle's refrigerator that was still edible. Which was why after they brought her back to the condo, they went shopping.

But mostly they stumbled around plucking things off shelves and arguing about their nutritional merit. Adam was pale under the fluorescent lights; Liza hoped she didn't look as bad as she felt.

"I hate what this is doing to us," she said.

Adam snorted. "Tell me about it. I wasn't like this before. Or was I always a jerk and you were too polite to tell me?"

"I don't have the energy to be polite anymore." She sighed. "You think it's right, letting her go home?"

"She'll be fine." But Adam didn't sound convinced, or convincing.

"You saw how she got out of the car."

Adam let out his breath. "Liza. You heard her. It's what she wanted."

"She wanted a cigarette when they took her off the respirator, too. Would that have been okay with you if I let her light up?" Liza knew she was being unreasonable and frankly couldn't even follow her own line of logic. Yet she couldn't stop defending it. "This is different and you know it."

Adam contemplated a wall of candy. "We should get her some chocolate. It's her favorite."

Chocolate? Liza frowned. *For what it's going to do to the cancer cells, we might as well buy her a carton of Marlboros.*

"You gotta let her have something," Adam said.

"She can have fruit if she's got a sweet tooth. Not too much. And not raw."

Shaking his head, Adam grabbed a bag of Snickers bars off the shelf and threw it into the cart.

* * *

After they stocked Estelle's pantry, changed her sheets, cleaned her shower, took out her trash, sorted her mail, and said hello to all of Estelle's neighbors including the ones who didn't speak English, Liza and Adam left. They went home to their little yellow house where they hadn't changed the sheets, cleaned the shower, or sorted their own mail. They fell atop the dirty sheets, the rumpled blanket, and the discarded clothing. Liza stared at their poorly painted bedroom ceiling.

"Oh, my God," Adam said.

Mentally, Liza cringed. What now? Mice? A hole in the roof? The clang and wheeze of the furnace, breathing its last?

"What?" she said.

"Nothing. It's quiet. No phones. No arguments. No Mom. No Charlie. No neighbors. Just us. It's been so long since it was just us."

"Yeah," Liza said. "Just us."

It was too quiet. In this quiet space Liza thought of all the things Estelle might do now that she was alone. Smoking wasn't at the top of the list. Liza had a bad feeling, an awful feeling.

She climbed over Adam for the phone. "I'm calling her."

"We were just there..."

"Just to make sure she's okay."

"She's probably asleep already," Adam said. "Call her in the morning."

Who knew what might happen by then? "But—"

"It's after midnight! You call now, she'll think someone died. You want to give my mother a heart attack?"

"No, I mean, all right!" Liza put down the phone and flopped back beside him. "I'll call tomorrow."

He reached a hand up to lightly rub her arm. "Can we just have a few quiet moments so we can at least try to pretend that everything isn't going to hell?"

She tried. She truly tried. But she kept thinking about razor blades. Broken shards of glass. Vials of medication. Tequila borrowed from a neighbor who didn't speak English.

"You're worrying," Adam said. "I can smell it."

"Sorry. I feel guilty leaving her alone."

Adam pulled in a deep breath and slowly let it out. "Yeah. Me, too."

20

Cara never took her purse on "nurse-a-go-go" days. In and out of so many houses, it was too easy to leave behind and too tempting a target. She'd had things stolen. Cash, a credit card, smokes. Instead she bundled the few personal items she needed—lip gloss, tissues, keys, nicotine gum—into the pockets of her denim jacket and locked the rest in her car. But she was off-duty now, in Estelle's neighborhood yet again, between a dialysis patient and Randall Osten, so some of her self-enforced personal rules could be ignored.

Estelle had made them coffee. When Cara drank coffee she wanted a cigarette and automatically reached into her purse. She got as far as setting the pack and the lighter on the table before seeing the longing on Estelle's face.

"Sorry." Cara started to put her cigs away.

"If you want to smoke, I don't mind," Estelle said.

"But you've been doing so well."

"Most of the time I don't miss it. Tell you the truth, I've lost my sense of smell. If you lit up now, I doubt I would even notice."

"All right," Cara said, but blew the smoke the other way.

After a few beats, Estelle smiled impishly and said, "I want to show you something." She turned and reached for what appeared to be a large photo album from the small bookcase next to her chair.

"Need a hand?" Cara asked, but Estelle had already plopped the album onto the table and opened the cover. She leaned over Estelle and pointed to the picture on the left-hand page. "That's Adam?"

Estelle nodded. "From the summer we spent with my brother-in-law and his wife in the mountains. He must have been about six months."

Cara smiled. "Look at the little baseball cap! It's adorable!"

"He hated it."

"I had a feeling Adam was a fussy baby."

"Fussy?" Estelle pressed a hand to her chest. "You have no idea. Everything had to be just so."

She could see that about Adam. "Show me Charlie."

Estelle beamed and started flipping through the pages. "Now Charlie, he was a beautiful baby. A perfect little angel."

"They are perfect when they're little, aren't they?" Cara sighed. "Before they can walk and talk and get their asses into trouble." Cara had, on previous visits, told Estelle about her misbehaving older son.

"Is that situation getting any better?" Estelle asked.

Cara shrugged. "The school wants me to send him to a shrink. I told them, he's ten. Ten-year-old boys do stupid shit, especially when they want to impress their friends. The jerk who gave it to him said it was oregano. Shrink. Please."

"Don't waste your money," Estelle said. "All they'll tell you is that you have to keep going until they have enough money to pay off their summer homes."

"They're not so bad. We went a few times, Dan and me."

Estelle's eyes widened. "You and Dan? And it helped?"

"Yeah." Cara pulled at her cigarette. "I think. We're still together, and that's something."

Estelle appeared to ponder that. "Maybe Liza and Adam should see somebody," she said. "I don't like the way they argue."

A half-smile of surprise froze on Cara's lips as she blew out the smoke. *Thank God they argue.* She felt a pang of sympathy for her neighbor, who appeared at times above all the petty emotions of mere mortals. "Better out than in, I always say."

Estelle turned another page. "Here's Charlie."

She immediately recognized Charlie by his big, blue eyes and sunny smile. "What a cutie."

"Like I said, never a minute of trouble. Which is why I don't understand why he hasn't found some nice girl and settled down."

"Probably because he's too busy looking for a nice boy."

Estelle's lips tightened. "He says that, too. But I don't

believe in that sort of thing. When he meets the right girl, he'll change."

"I don't think it works that way," Cara said.

"It's his father's fault."

"I don't think it's anyone's *fault*—"

"No. They always say it's the mother, but not this time. Eddie called him a sissy because he wouldn't go down the sliding board. He made Charlie wear a dress and stand in the corner."

Cara sighed. "People just *are*, Estelle. They are what they are." But still, poor Charlie. If Dan ever did something like that to either of their kids, she'd kick his ass to China and back.

"It was the cancer," Estelle said, her mouth turning down at the corners.

"I don't understand—"

"When I was pregnant with Charlie, I was taking care of my mother. I don't know, maybe he absorbed what was going on and it changed him. Maybe I should have taken better care of myself..."

"Estelle. Please don't blame yourself. You didn't do it."

She cradled her head in her hands and moaned. "We *all* smoked back then! We didn't know!"

"It doesn't make sense to beat yourself up about this. The horse is already out of the barn. Look. Is Charlie happy?"

Estelle sniffed back tears. "I think so. He has a good job, he seems to have a lot of friends..."

"Is he in jail? On crack? Doing dirty things to support his addiction to hair products?"

"No!"

Cara turned up her hands in a gesture of finality. "Then you did okay."

Estelle fingered her coffee mug. She'd only had a sip. "He had a girlfriend once, in college. He used to date Liza. Maybe that's when it started. But I don't understand. Okay, she's a bit...unconventional, but she's such a *good* girl..."

"That's it!" Cara said with a smile. She knew it wasn't nice to tease Estelle, but it was the most fun she'd had all day. And boy, would she bust Liza for not telling her about this. "She was *too* good. Liza ruined him for other women."

* * *

As Liza stared out the kitchen window, admiring the first crocuses and daffodil shoots to poke through the rapidly melting snow, she saw the Jeep pull up to the house. Moments later, the back door burst open and in strode the full glory of Nurse Cara, wearing the cagiest smile. "You slept with Charlie?"

Liza felt the blood draining from her face. Thank God Adam wasn't home. "He told you?"

"Nope." Cara's grin spread. "So it's true. Ha. Works every time."

Damn it. "How did you...?"

"I stopped in on Estelle today. I was in the neighborhood, wanted to see how she was doing. You little slut," Cara said with a teasing twinkle in her eye.

Liza's back tightened. Why would Charlie have told his mother? The official story was that they dated for a few weeks but decided to remain friends—strictly Platonic. Adam didn't know about her one, fumbling, drunken, humiliating attempt to seduce his brother.

"So was it any good?"

Liza glared at her neighbor, who was awaiting her response with a cocked eyebrow. "He's still gay, isn't he?"

Still grinning, Cara plucked two beers from the fridge, opened them, and handed one to Liza. "I think I have a little more respect for you now. Welcome to the dirty bitch club."

"Please don't tell anyone." Liza slunk into a chair. "And please don't tell Adam."

"He doesn't know?"

She picked at the foil label on the bottle, wondering which way to go with this. If she could trust Cara. "It's just too weird and Biblical. Charlie and I both decided to forget it ever happened. It was a long time ago. We were drunk, it was a big, stupid mistake, and I want it to go away."

"I did the UPS guy once. Before I met Dan." *Great*, Liza thought. Now Cara was going to spill *her* sex secrets. This, from a woman who did it with her husband on the Miller's front lawn after their Halloween party. Next to Cara, Liza felt like the Virgin Mary. "It was those brown shorts," Cara said. "They made me crazy. Except after that he kept bringing flowers. I had to move."

* * *

If not for Bette Davis, Liza wouldn't have talked to Charlie at all. He was in a few of her classes, but he was just too handsome, and such good-looking men seemed always to look past her as if she were invisible. Missing her father and overwhelmed by the college experience—the noise, the people in her face everywhere she turned—Liza spent her first few Saturday afternoons at the retro cinema. She whiled away the hours watching Bogie and Bacall, Tracy and Hepburn, and the magical Bette Davis. One Saturday she noticed Charlie, sitting alone—and the next, and the next. Each week she sat a little closer, daring herself to take another glance at his perfect profile: the carefully styled thatch of blondish hair, falling just so around his brow and ear, the chiseled cheekbone, the strong jaw. One week, when they were showing *All About Eve*, she got up the nerve to speak to him. One stumbling word about the movie led to the next. One exchange led to the next, and it was like a dam had burst. They became fast friends, sharing class notes, coffee, and their lives. Liza had never had a serious boyfriend in California but had plenty of male friends who treated her like a sister. Charlie was different. It took her a while to realize just how different, but by then she was already in love and never told him. What would her admission accomplish other than make him feel badly that he couldn't return her feelings? She told herself it was hopeless and tried to make it go away. Then they both broke up with their boyfriends on the same night. It was a full moon, and she should have known better. They drank tequila shooters to blunt their pain, and she should have known better. She sat in his lap and kissed him and he let her, and both of them should have known better. She didn't tell Cara all of it. The truth? It was good. The truth was—and maybe it wasn't quite the truth but the magic of being eighteen and in love for the first time, which carried its own kind of truth—that in her memory, Charlie was a better lover than Adam. That was what she didn't want to remember, and sometimes couldn't forget.

"So, how's Estelle," Liza said to Cara, trying to shake the memory of Charlie's drunken, tender embrace out of her head.

"She doesn't look good."

"It's the chemo."

"No. I know how chemo looks. This is something else."

"But the doctor..." Liza's voice sounded tinny and far away to her ears, as if she were speaking through a tunnel. "He looked at her scans, her blood. He said she was doing well enough to take a break."

Cara's eyes narrowed. "He said that? Or *she* said he said that?"

Adam, and now her, too? "You think she would lie about something so important?"

"Honey." Cara sucked at her beer. "I've heard it all. One guy I saw at home told his family the doctor said the cancer had gone into spontaneous remission. He died a week later. I had one dude at the hospital slip into the nurses' station and change his release date on his chart. People walking out, like, a day after major surgery..."

"Maybe we should call her doctor."

"Probably a good idea. If you're doing well on the chemo, doctors don't usually want you to stop. You hear about chemo breaks if someone's been sick. Has pneumonia, an infection. If your immunity is already down, they don't want to give you chemo on top of it."

"I'm calling him." Liza grabbed the cordless handset and punched in the number seven. Never in her life did she think she'd have an oncologist on speed dial. Maybe this time he'd be in. Adam had tried twice already. He'd been with a patient, he'd been on rounds, and he never called back.

"Dr. Phillips' office."

"Hi, this is Liza Stanhope. I'm calling about my mother-in-law, Estelle Trager. It's important. Is the doctor available?"

"I'm sorry. He's just left for the day."

Damn it. "Will he be in tomorrow?"

Cara gestured for the phone. After a moment's hesitation, Liza handed it over. "Hello. This is Cara Miller. I'm a visiting nurse affiliated with County General. Estelle Trager is my patient. She tells me she's refusing treatment? I just wanted to confirm that before I get her on the waiting list for hospice."

Cara put her hand over the receiver. "She's putting me through."

"Hospice?" A knot tightened Liza's throat.

"Pretty good, huh?" Cara smiled. "Gets a doctor's attention every time. Nobody wants to get sued. Hello? Dr. Phillips. Hi. Yeah." Her eyes lit up and she did a quick victory dance before saying into the phone, "Of course I'll wait while you get her chart."

There was a lot of nodding and listening from Cara's end. Finally she hung up, all traces of her celebration gone. Cara pressed a hand to Liza's arm. "Honey, she's refusing treatment. And the latest test results weren't that great."

Liza swallowed, her mind jumping right past the lie about "going on chemo break." "What do you mean, weren't that great?"

"One of the tumors is shrinking. The other is getting larger. He can't tell if it's spreading without getting her in for more scans, but she won't do it."

"Shit."

"And another thing. You, Adam, and Charlie aren't supposed to know any of this, so you didn't hear it from me."

Liza dropped her head into her hands. "Adam's gonna freak."

"If you tell him."

She peeked out from behind her hair. "I'm not supposed to tell my husband that his mother's cancer is getting worse and she doesn't want us to know?"

Cara dug her cigarettes and lighter out of her jacket. "Repeat the last phrase in that sentence."

"She doesn't want us to know?"

"She has that right," Cara said.

Liza drew in a breath. She knew that. She'd always known that. Choosing to stop treatment was Estelle's prerogative. But once again, lying to Adam and Charlie about it? Somehow that didn't fall into the same moral plane of thought. "If this were Dan's mother, would you feel the same way?"

"If it was Dan's mother I'd get on a plane and kick her ass until she begged for chemo."

"So it's okay for me to help perpetuate a lie."

Cara smirked. "Like, you and Charlie were just friends?"

She knew she shouldn't have told Cara about Charlie. Liza shook her head. "Don't you even suggest to me that's on the same level. We're talking about a human life. We're talking about Adam's mother."

"I think I know how we can do this," Cara said. "You hold tight for a little while."

Tight? If Liza were any tighter, she'd snap.

* * *

Later that evening, Liza was attempting to read about sports nutrition and electrolyte replacement when she heard Adam pull into the carport. Every muscle in her body contracted. She stared at the book, the charts and graphs swirling around in her head, re-forming themselves into the claws of tumors, extending their reach into her mother-in-law's body. Breaking away and regenerating more limbs like a horror movie monster.

"Hey," he said, pressing a hand to her shoulder. "Jesus, I'm supposed to be the tense one. You could crack walnuts on these things." He began kneading her muscles.

She lowered the book. "Long day." She was about to add a couple of details but figured the less said, the better.

"Did the doctor call back?"

"No." Before that word escaped her lips, Liza merely felt queasy about her collusion with Cara. She now officially hated herself.

"Self-important son-of-a-bitch. That's twice now, I've left messages. Charlie said he called, too, and got the same song-and-dance."

With two sentences, she could end the subterfuge immediately. Then another tactic occurred to her. "Maybe we should just go there."

"Yeah. Just show up and refuse to leave until we get some answers."

"Your mother would be furious."

"Why?"

Liza stammered, "For not trusting her."

She could plainly see the anger in his face, reflected from the kitchen window. "Like she ever trusted me."

21

Liza hadn't completely lied to her husband. She did plan to go into the city to interview the New York Knicks' team nutritionist for a paper. But she omitted her intention to visit Charlie. Away from her house, away from Estelle, and most importantly, away from Adam.

A security guard checked her name against a list and called someone to escort her onto the set. She found Charlie sitting cross-legged on a square of fake-looking wood flooring, twisting the leg of a stool. Under the lights, his ever so slightly receding hairline shone more prominently. She tossed a Knicks' jersey at Charlie's head. Unflappable, he watched as it slid down his body and landed next to him in a polyester heap.

"You promised me a point guard," he said.

"Next best thing?"

"His sweaty uniform? And all I have for you are stale donuts."

"It's clean," Liza said. "What are you doing?"

He rolled his eyes. "Diva wars."

"What now?" She sat down beside him.

"Melanie thinks she looks too short on camera. I'm making her stool taller."

"I didn't know you could do that to a stool. I thought they just came in one size."

"Not ours." He forced a smile. "They're special, *magic* stools. They can also hold a lot of weight."

One of the divas was a super-plus-size model. "Maybe *you* could get through to her," Charlie said. "Explain that being 'big and beautiful' might be a political statement, but that extra fifty pounds is choking off her coronary arteries."

"I'm not going there with her," Liza said. "Didn't she throw a chair at some guy because he wouldn't bring her a Danish?"

"He only needed a couple of stitches." Charlie looked up at Liza. She'd let her guard down and was momentarily stopped by his blue eyes: their magnetic attraction heightened when he smiled. "The scar would give you character. Plus you could sue her and make a mint."

She shook those old feelings away and focused on why she had come here. The set was crisscrossed with crew, barking instructions, laughing, and attacking things with tools. "Can we go somewhere quiet?" she asked him. "It's about Estelle. I really need to talk."

* * *

Charlie opened a door bearing the name of one of the more famous divas. "Don't worry. She's cutting a new album; she leaves skid marks getting out of here after the show. Sit. You want coffee? I do. I have a killer hangover. Saint Patrick's Day is a conspiracy, I tell ya." He tapped a number on his cell. "Anything?" But before Liza could answer, he added her usual—decaf latte with unsweetened soymilk and cinnamon—to his order and flipped his phone closed.

"So what's up?" he said.

Just over Charlie's shoulder, in one corner of the dressing room, a stuffed penguin sat in a little chair, staring at her accusingly. *You should be telling Adam this*, it seemed to say. Liza took a deep breath and said, "She did it again. She shut us out. She told her doctor not to tell us anything."

"You're kidding me."

Liza shook her head.

"That explains why Dr. Polyester's not taking my calls. Adam must be ripshit."

She dropped her gaze into her lap and focused on the stillness of her intertwined fingers. "I haven't told him yet."

"Honey..." Liza could imagine the disappointment in his eyes.

"I know." She was reluctant to meet his gaze but needed it for strength. She took a slow, deep breath and glanced up to find his expression not scolding but encouraging. The words came easier then. "It gets worse. She's not improving. One of the tumors is getting larger. And she's refusing treatment."

Charlie, her verbal sparring partner, never at a loss, was suddenly speechless. Finally, he found his voice. "Shit. I had a feeling it was bad. But I'd hoped." He let out a long sigh. "How did you find out? If we're not supposed to know?"

"Cara. She pretended to call for information as her nurse."

Charlie nodded his approval. "Conniving. I knew there was a reason I liked that woman."

"So." Liza's voice came out in a squeak. "What are we supposed to do with this? Confront her, even though she'll know we went behind her back? Accept her choice? Or cruise along in denial until something happens to land her in the hospital again?"

"Denial has always worked so well for me." He shook his head. "Honey. I'm kidding. We have to get Adam on board. Knowing my brother, he'll want to drive over and read her the riot act, no matter how we got the information."

"She can't hate all three of us."

"Good point. She needs one of us at all times so she can have someone to say nasty things to about the others." He rubbed the back of his neck. "Damn. Where's that coffee?"

* * *

Well. That *was useless,* Liza thought, as the train pulled away from Grand Central. Charlie was usually a good distraction, but after leaving his studio, she'd realized that her problems had only multiplied, reproducing like the one-celled organisms she watched under the microscope in the lab. She should have just gone to Adam in the first place. Let him vent his rage over his mother's decision, and then call Charlie.

For a while, she reviewed the notes from her interview, but her mind kept pulling her toward the men in her life, their differences and similarities, and how she ended up between them. Adam and Charlie. Sometimes the brothers seemed like mostly-matching bookends. They had a way of standing, sitting, tilting a head, lifting an eyebrow, or even holding a drink that was uniquely Trager. Both of them liked white meat. Both of them liked basketball but hated football. Both of them liked her.

Then there were the differences. She'd never seen Charlie truly angry. Yes, he'd been upset; he'd been disappointed, heartbroken. But he didn't blow up like Adam. Adam was a yeller, a door-slammer. That purged the anger from his body and then he would be done, getting a beer from the fridge or wanting to make love. Charlie, however, looked like he didn't have a care in the world. At least that's what most people saw, especially Estelle, who beamed at his sunny, infant face after many months of her own sorrow and pigeonholed him for the rest of his life. Charlie's "happy child" label had stuck in Adam's head, too. And Charlie, so eager to please for so long, because on some level he felt he owed it to his mother, only showed his true face to a select few.

But he and Liza connected in a much deeper place. She knew about the disappointments, the men who got away, the friends who'd betrayed him. It was difficult to explain their connection to Adam, to make him see that her staying close to Charlie wasn't a fault with their marriage.

"I suppose it could be worse," Adam had once said. "At least he's family. If you kept hanging out with some guy you had a serious relationship with, it would be different."

Liza's gut clenched, remembering her one time with Charlie, the one wonderful, awful, drunken time. Afterward, she and the Trager brother she hadn't married only mentioned it twice: first, during an awkward, hung-over exchange at brunch the next morning where they vowed never to speak of it or drink tequila again. Then he brought it up a few years later at a small gathering at Adam and Charlie's childhood home, before Estelle sold the house and moved to her condo in Middletown.

Everyone had left except Liza and the Trager boys. She'd hoped to get in a little better with Estelle, as up until then, there seemed to be no pleasing the woman.

Liza had been just about to ask Estelle if she could help with the dishes when Adam rather awkwardly wrapped an arm around Liza's shoulders and cleared his throat. *Oh God,* she'd thought, her pulse pounding in her ears. *He's going to do it. He's going to tell her. Not now*, she'd tried to think at him. *Yes, we talked about telling her tonight, but wait until we clean up, make some coffee, have a few minutes to sit together, talk.* However, typically Adam, he forged ahead.

"We're getting married," he said. "Liza and I..."

Charlie beamed. After the smallest of hesitations, Estelle smiled, looking as if it pained her. "Mazel tov," she said dryly. "We'll open that bottle of sparkling cider my neighbor brought and have a toast. I'll get the nice glasses. Adam, come help me. They're in a box on the top shelf of the pantry closet."

Adam's face fell as his arm slid off Liza.

That left just Charlie and Liza in Estelle's living room.

"Welcome to the family," Charlie said.

"What did I ever do to her?" Liza said. "I'm always nice. I never come empty-handed." She'd even bought Estelle a present for her last birthday, a chenille scarf she'd picked up from a craft collective the last time she was out to see her father in California. But she'd never seen Estelle wear it.

"Look." Charlie shrugged. "Let me give you a tip from 'The Guide to Jewish Mothers.' You're taking away her oldest son. They're a bit codependent, in case you haven't noticed."

Then Adam and Estelle started yelling at each other. Liza might have heard something to the effect that he was about to jettison a brilliant future for a godless hippie who was raised by wolves and might or might not be the reason that Charlie thinks he's gay. But that could have been her imagination.

Charlie stretched an arm across Liza's shoulders. Fortunately, he didn't tell her everything was going to be all right. He just watched her face. His eyes softened and a faint smile played on his lips.

"For the record," he said finally, "I think the wolves did an excellent job."

"Thanks."

He kept his gaze on her, steady and growing more deliberate. "This is going to be weird, isn't it?"

"Weird because my future mother-in-law hates me?"

"Weird because..." Charlie lifted a brow.

Liza flinched, remembering. "Oh."

"We were both rebounding," Charlie said softly. "And very, very drunk." He smirked in a kind of wistful, defeated manner that had always made Liza want to smooth away the sorrow. He addressed the floor. "If I'd known one day you'd be marrying my brother, I would have never suggested doing tequila shots."

"You introduced us," Liza reminded him.

"Yeah." Charlie sighed. "My loss, his gain."

"This isn't going to change anything between us," Liza said. "We can still be friends. If Adam doesn't like it, tough. You're part of the package."

He gave her a level look. "You say that now, Miss Bravado. But I've played this scene. You and Adam will become a 'we.' You'll become this insular little unit. 'We went to the movies, we went to Tahoe, we saw this amazing art exhibit'...watch. And then you'll start having kids, and you'll become a different species altogether. And poor Uncle Charlie will come up on holidays and sit in the corner quietly getting drunk while you talk about Mommy and Me classes and diaper genies. Then one day you'll take pity on me because we never spend any time together. We'll take a long walk in the woods, and when you come home, Adam will want to know what he can't give you that I can."

She'd glared back. "That was a beautiful speech. Truly inspired. Schmuck."

"Why am I a schmuck? It's true."

"Bullshit. You can't stick me in a box. You can't tell me I'll become some Stepford Wife just because I'm getting married. A ring on my finger doesn't mean he's the only man I'll ever be able to talk to again. Jesus. For someone who claims to know me so well you don't know me at all."

"So prove me wrong," he'd said. "I can't wait."

22

Adam held the groceries. Charlie held the flowers. Liza had the bag from the health food store, a sense of dread, and the beginnings of a terrible headache. They stood at Estelle's front door on the first evening of Passover, rang the bell, and waited to hear movement from inside. When nothing happened, all three looked at each other questioningly. "Ma," Adam yelled, punching the buzzer four or five times. "It's us. Open up."

"All right, already," came the hoarse voice from inside. "Don't knock the door down."

She let them in and each pecked her on the cheek in turn.

"Hang up your things then come sit," she said. "I have to check something in the kitchen."

Liza didn't like Estelle's pallor. She didn't like how her mother-in-law pressed a hand to the wall when she walked, or the way she walked, with a bit of a limp. She didn't remember Estelle ever limping before. While other people Estelle's age were grabbing for painkillers, or in Liza's father's case, the fish oil, she'd never heard Estelle admit to even the slightest twinges of arthritis. And if possible, she looked even shorter.

The apartment smelled like soup. And cigarettes. Adam, his jaw tight, flashed Liza a hard look. They'd had a conversation on the way to pick up Charlie from the train station. If Adam found out she'd been smoking, he would turn around and leave. To hell with her. She could die there, for all he cared, puffing away, if she didn't care enough about her body—and the three of them—to even attempt to quit. Liza had stopped short of calling him an insensitive ass but perhaps she should have. "The smell lingers for a while," Liza said next to Adam's ear. "And Cara's been visiting."

Adam started. "Cara? Why the hell has Cara been here?"

"She's a nurse. Remember? She has a patient nearby, and she's been checking in on your mother before she goes home. I'd think you'd be grateful."

Ignoring Liza's last comment, Adam did a little swirly

gesture with his finger indicating the space in which he was standing. "She smokes here? In front of my mother?"

"She probably goes outside, at least I hope so, but it's all over her clothes, her hair—"

"She better not be bringing her dope—"

"Adam."

"Ma," Adam yelled toward the kitchen. "Did Cara bring you more pot?"

"No," Estelle yelled back. "Why? I still have from the first time."

A vein in Adam's forehead bulged. Charlie was trying not to laugh, which irritated Liza. Was everything a joke to him? "Here?" Adam said. "You keep it here?"

"Where else would I keep it?" Estelle said. "A safety deposit box?"

"Ma."

"I only used it one more time, when I couldn't sleep. I don't see the big deal. What, the police are going to put a sick woman in jail? Now come sit. I hope you're hungry."

Adam, Charlie, and Liza filed in, but none of them sat. Three pots were going on the stove. Estelle frowned while stirring one of them. Another was full of water, and she tried to transfer it to a different burner.

"Stop, what are you looking at?" Estelle said. "I'm fine. Sit."

"Ma," Adam said. "Don't lift that pot. It's too heavy. I'll do it."

"Get off my back already. I've been lifting pots since before you were born."

But clearly Estelle struggled. She didn't have a good grip. She winced in apparent pain. Water sloshed over the edge of the pot and Liza started for the stove.

"Let me do that, Estelle," she said.

"Sit. Relax. It's nothing. It'll never boil on that burner. I forgot it's the one that doesn't work so well."

Charlie stepped up and eased the pot from his mother's hands. "You didn't even have to cook, Mom," he said. "We could have brought in dinner. Not that anything else would be as good as your cooking, but at least you wouldn't have had to work so hard."

Estelle made a dismissive gesture. "What, it's nothing. Just like I make every Passover. A little soup, a little roast, a potato. Except you'll have to let me know how it's coming. I can't taste a thing."

"Still?" Liza said.

Charlie dipped a spoon into the pot. Adam, helpless in kitchens and especially his mother's, skulked around the dining room looking for something to fix.

"The doctor said it could take a while to come back," Estelle said.

"Did you try that herbal tonic?" Liza asked.

"It gave me gas." Liza was amazed she'd even opened the bottle.

Meanwhile, Charlie swirled the soup around his mouth like a consummate oenophile. "A playfully insouciant bouquet. Woodsy top note. Bad day for the chicken, but otherwise, perfection."

Estelle beamed at Charlie and swatted his arm. "Oh, you're such a kidder."

"Yeah, my brother, the comedian." Adam peered up at the ceiling. "Ma. How long has this bulb been out, over the table?"

"A while." She asked Charlie, "Are you sure it maybe doesn't need more salt?"

"It's fine, Mom."

"How hard is it to change a light bulb?" Adam said. "It's not even that high."

"I haven't gotten to it. You sure it's okay?"

"It's great," Charlie said.

Estelle shoved another spoon in Liza's direction. "You taste. You're the cook."

Liza blinked. Was that almost another compliment? A swell of magnanimity rose in her chest as she dipped the spoon into the pot and brought it to her lips, letting the gorgeously dill-infused broth seep across her tongue. "It's perfect. Just like you always make it."

Estelle shrugged. "I guess some things are automatic."

Adam was standing on a chair and had the chimney off the light fixture.

"What are you doing?" Estelle said.

He frowned into the inside of the chimney, which Liza imagined was coated with a patina of dust, dead bugs, and years of cigarette smoke. "I'm initiating the launch sequence for a Saturn Five rocket. What does it look like I'm doing?"

"Don't be smart."

"That's right." A couple of dead bugs fluttered down onto the table. "Charlie's the only one who gets to be smart. You got any forty-watt bulbs?"

"If I got, they're in the pantry."

"I'll go," Liza and Charlie said at the same time.

"No. He'll go. You stay." Suddenly Estelle looked pale and held the edge of the stove. "I need you to watch the potatoes."

"Estelle?" Liza said. "Are you all right?"

Her mother-in-law crumpled to the floor.

* * *

It was nothing, Estelle said, as Adam and Charlie helped her onto the sofa. No need to call the doctor. She'd just been feeling a little faint, a little light-headed. It was probably because she hadn't eaten today. Since nothing tasted good, she didn't want to bother.

But sometimes, her senses of smell and taste returned, not evenly but in rushes, like a breeze through an open window when the wind changed. They came with memories. They came with no warning. The soup did it to her this time. She'd put in the water and the cut-up chicken, skimmed off the fat, dumping spoon after spoon into the coffee can next to the sink. Still she could smell nothing. She added the quartered root vegetables, the salt, and the dill. Nothing. Then she looked over and saw Adam's face, and Charlie's face, and the different ways they looked like Eddie and like her parents, and it was as if someone had broken down a door. She smelled the simmering chicken, parsnips, and onions and saw her mother's sickly face, the hollowed eyes and the skin stretched tight across the bone. Estelle saw her father's hand raising the spoon to her mother's lips. And then Estelle felt weak all over as the floor rushed up to meet her.

* * *

"You have to eat, Estelle." To Liza, it seemed like a hypoglycemic reaction. She'd had them herself, when she went too long without food. If eating made her mother-in-law feel better, problem solved. She looked up. The first human she spotted was her husband, standing a few feet away. "Adam, quick, can you fix her a slice of bread with some peanut butter?"

But he just blinked at her as if Liza had asked him to whip up Baked Alaska.

She glared at him. "Bread. Peanut butter. It's basic. Ask Charlie to help you."

"I know how...you don't have to—"

"Go, then," Liza said through clenched teeth. She prayed nothing serious happened to her when no one else was around. She could be lying on the floor for hours before Adam figured out what to do.

"But dinner will be ready soon," Estelle said. "Are the potatoes boiling?"

"Not yet," Charlie called from the kitchen. *So that's where he'd gone, to check the stove. Good thinking.*

"Is the burner on high?" Estelle asked.

"Medium," Charlie said.

Estelle looked confused. "I swore I had it on high." She tried to get up, rocking herself to and fro without success. "Lemme go look."

"Charlie's got it." Liza put a hand on Estelle's shoulder. "You just need to sit for a while and try to eat something."

Just as Liza started wondering what was taking Adam so long, he'd returned, holding out a peanut butter sandwich. It was on a plate. With a napkin. The crusts had been trimmed, the way Estelle used to make them for Adam.

* * *

The pot roast came out dry. The matzo balls were tough. But the soup was perfect. Adam took a second bowl.
"Everything's great, Mom," Charlie said.
"Yeah?" Estelle picked at her plate. "I wouldn't know."
"We'll clean up," Liza said. "And won't take no for an answer."
Estelle gazed at their faces, seeming to judge if it were safe to let them take over. "Fine. Then if nobody minds," she pressed a hand against the table, "I'm gonna go lie down."
Charlie helped Estelle down the hallway. Adam and Liza did the dishes, put away the leftovers in Tupperware containers. They said nothing, but Liza could tell by her husband's body language—shoulders sagging forward in defeat, a sort of deadness in his eyes, a particular set to his jaw—that they were both in agreement: Estelle Trager could no longer be left alone.
Then Adam threw a serving spoon onto the dish rack, the noise rattling the silence.
"Adam—"
"What if we hadn't been here?" he said in a loud, angry whisper. "What if she pulled that whole boiling pot over onto herself? Or started a fire?"
"I don't even want to think about it."
He flung down his dishtowel, determination hardening his face. "I'm gonna tell her she's coming back with us."
Liza pressed a hand to his chest. "You know your mother. If you give her an order, she'll only refuse."
"I don't see that she really has any choice."
Charlie came back into the kitchen.
"We're taking Ma back with us," Adam announced.
"Not unless you want to carry her," Charlie said. "She's out cold."

* * *

Liza made coffee. Charlie produced a fifth of Sambuca from his jacket and dumped a healthy splash into his and Adam's mugs. Liza declined. She hated the taste and had a sense that she ought to keep her head clear. The three of them sat around Estelle's dining room table, not talking much.

"So Adam and I will come get her in the morning," Charlie said at one point, stifling a yawn. "Let Mom get some sleep. She needs it."

Estelle's loud, rhythmic snoring seemed to corroborate the point.

Liza sipped her coffee. She couldn't keep her mind from thoughts of Estelle's future—all of their futures. The acute phases, after the pneumonia and when they were waiting for tests, were short, finite periods. This move could be for the rest of Estelle's life. "But moving in with us?" Liza asked. "Is that what she really wants?"

She was answered with silence, until Adam said, "You saw what happened before. She can't live alone. I want her where I can keep an eye on her."

"While I'm in school?" Liza said. She'd already registered for the summer semester and the three required classes that were not offered any other time. "While you're working fifty hours a week?"

Adam shrugged. "So we'll look at our schedules, make sure one of us is always around. Like before, after the pneumonia."

"This isn't exactly pneumonia," Charlie said.

"No kidding," Adam said.

"He's right, Adam. What if it gets bad, and she needs more care than we can give her?" *Or is still determined to kill herself before then.* Liza cringed.

"We could hire a home health aide. You know, someone like Cara." Charlie topped off his and Adam's mugs with Sambuca, again offering Liza some. Again, she declined, but put up a fresh pot of coffee. She thought better on her feet, anyway.

"We're not hiring Cara," Adam said.

She could almost hear Charlie's eye-roll. "Listen much? I said, 'like Cara.'"

"So someone *like Cara* would come to our house?" Adam said.

Liza measured grounds, poured water. "Why not *her* house?" she offered. "Can we do this and not take her out of her condo?"

"A total stranger," Adam said. "In *her* house. Yeah, that makes me feel even better."

"Because everyone knows it's all about making *you* feel better," Charlie said. "Mom's Little Prince can't bear a moment of discomfort."

"Oh, please. She thinks the sun shines out your ass."

Liza spun back on them. "Stop it, both of you. This isn't helpful. So, what if we let her stay here? We can come up two, three times a week, Charlie can come on weekends, and Cara can stop in on her home-visit days. She doesn't mind."

"And she does have that client nearby," Charlie added.

"Cara's a flake," Adam said. "She's not taking care of my mother—"

"*Our* mother," Charlie said. "And Cara's a sweetheart. Mom adores her."

Adam's jaw tightened. "She's coming to stay with us, and if it's more than we can handle, we'll figure out what to do when the time comes."

"Figure out what to do...?" Liza blinked at him as she returned to the table with a fresh mug. "We can't wait until then. If Cara's not available, it could take days, weeks to get a home health aide."

"Let's just get her home first," Adam said.

"Well, she...is home."

Adam's jaw tightened harder. Liza feared one day he would break a tooth. "You just don't want her with us."

"That's not true!"

"You've always hated her—"

"Adam, for God's sake... I do *not* hate your mother, and you know it. Okay, we've had our rough patches. Like when she said you were throwing your life away on a godless hippie—"

"Raised by wolves," Charlie added.

She ignored him. "But we're family now. This is what families do for each other." She would have done it for her own mother. Or at least she liked to think so.

Adam continued to stare at his wife. "You said yourself. We have the room. One of us is always around."

"I'll come up weekends, give you guys a break," Charlie said. "And kick in for groceries."

"So we're covered," Adam said to Liza. "What's the problem?"

Liza groaned with exasperation. "The problem is that it's *her life*. And maybe she doesn't want to live out the rest of it like an invalid. With you giving her that face—yes, that face right there—and scolding her and making her feel guilty for not having had the courage to do something sooner. Adam, all the yelling in the world isn't going to change that. It's too late and we just have to deal with what is."

Adam looked like he wanted to put his fist through a wall. "Damn it. It's not too late. We've got to give her a reason to keep going. I don't care if she's only doing it to shut me up. As long as she takes the rest of her chemo and keeps fighting. That's it. We'll just have to get you pregnant. For real."

Liza stared at him for a moment and dropped her head into her hands. Charlie tipped the Sambuca into Liza's coffee. She didn't stop him. *What the hell*, she thought. Maybe a couple of shots would make it easier to handle Adam right now. She took a big slug, wincing at the nasty taste but enjoying the feel of dull warmth spreading throughout her body.

"I'm serious," Adam said. "It would be like before, except no faking it this time. We'll give her a grandchild to look forward to. Then she'll have to take the chemo. She'll have to stay with us, because she'll want to look out for you."

She glanced up at him. "In her condition? Look out for me? What, our lives aren't complicated enough right now?"

Adam's cheeks tinged with red. "We...*want* to have a

baby, right?"

Liza dumped more Sambuca into her coffee.

"Liza?" Adam's eyes darkened.

"Maybe we should talk about this later."

"Uh-oh," Charlie said with a sneer. "Someone's in trouble."

Adam glared at his brother. "Someone should mind his own business."

Charlie sniffed. "Someone is being a colossal ass."

"Someone should shut the hell up."

"Oh, for God's sake," Liza said. "We're supposed to be helping Estelle, here."

"Yeah, Adam. We're supposed to be helping Mom."

Adam's hand tightened around his coffee mug. "We *are* helping her. We're taking her back to our house, and I'll do whatever it takes to see her through this, back on the chemo, the surgery, the radiation..."

Enough, Liza thought. "Adam, *please* try to think about this from her point of view. If I were her and feeling crappy and scared and guilty and someone I hoped I could count on for support was treating me like a two-year-old, I wouldn't want to live with him." She paused, steeling herself to tell Adam the worst of what she'd learned. What's that proverb her father once told her? *Many hands lighten a burdened heart?* Somehow, that didn't help. *Just tell him.* She swallowed. With her voice barely breaking into sound, she added, "Maybe that's also why she decided to stop treatment."

Adam and Charlie were now both staring at her. Finally, Charlie said, "I could come here just as well."

The color drained from Adam's face. "She stopped her chemo? *She* did? Not the doctor?"

Liza shook her head. "Not the doctor," she repeated, nearly a whisper.

Adam's chair scraped backward on the linoleum and he was up, storming the hall closet.

Liza went after him. "Adam. Adam, wait. I know you're angry, I know you're scared. But we all love her. Let's talk about this."

"We're done talking. We're going home."

He already had his jacket on. Liza tried to appeal to his sense of compassion, the horror he'd expressed over the boiling pot on the stove. "Adam, you can't leave your mother alone. You saw what happened before."

"Then she can deal with it." A muscle in his jaw twitched. "She wants to shut us out of her life? Fine. If she wants help, she can get it herself."

"Are you even listening to yourself? How could you be so—?" But Adam was already out the front door and pounding down the stairs. Exasperated, she turned toward Charlie. His face betrayed nothing but a slightly raised brow and a tightening around his mouth that only she might be able to conjugate.

"Stubborn?" Charlie supplied. "Pigheaded? Truculent? Am I getting close?"

"You're not helping."

Charlie's face softened. "I think sometimes you forget that she's my mother, too."

It was so easy to forget. Charlie looked and acted so little like Estelle. She let out a long breath.

"Look," Charlie said. "You have her house key?"

Liza nodded.

"Make sure she's all tucked in and safe, no trip hazards around. Leave her a note that we're coming back first thing in the morning." He tossed on his coat. "Then lock up and meet us downstairs. I'll see if I can talk some sense into my caveman brother."

"Don't you dare let him drive."

"Wouldn't dream of it," he called over his shoulder as she watched him leave.

With a mission, she felt somewhat calmed and switched into Practical Liza mode. She did a quick survey of the hall, the bathroom, then nosed her way into Estelle's bedroom. Her mother-in-law seemed to be in a deep sleep, still snoring away, and Liza stood at the door watching the blankets rise and fall with her breathing. Worried about leaving the boys alone for too long, she quickly tidied up, plucked clothes off the floor, and gently rearranged the excess blanket so Estelle would have an easier time getting out of bed. Before she left, Liza wrote the note, begging Estelle to call her if she needed anything, and underlined "anything" several times. There was more she wanted to do, more she wanted to write, but hearing raised male voices from outside made her hurry.

She couldn't say exactly what happened next. The voices grew angrier, the taunts sharper, the volley faster. Adam accused Charlie of something; she knew the tone but couldn't make out the words. There were sounds of a struggle. After taking the stairs two at a time, the next thing she saw was her husband's fist flying toward Charlie's face.

"Adam—?" She rushed toward them, ready to peel her husband off his brother. But Adam had already missed—or Charlie had dodged—and the momentum carried Adam forward. He tripped over his own feet, landed palms first on the asphalt and rolled onto his side, where he remained, grumbling a string of curses.

Liza dropped to her knees. "Adam…are you okay?"

"Sure." He let out a loud groan. "Peachy. I think I'm bleeding. Little bastard."

She turned toward Charlie, who merely threw up his hands in a gesture of defeat. "Hey, I just moved over. He fell all on his own."

"You're such an asshole," Adam said. Slowly, he got to his feet. He shook bits of snow and parking lot grit off his hands, examined a scrape on his palm.

"Pot, kettle," Charlie said.

"You could have told me," Adam said, glaring at Liza.

"So you're taking it out on Charlie?" Liza said.

"Oh, spare me," Adam said. "He knew, too."

"So you try to start a fistfight with him, like a couple of eight-year-olds?"

"Well, if he hadn't moved, I could have…"

Charlie retorted, "Well, if you weren't being such a giant jackass, we could have—"

"You're *both* being giant fucking jackasses!" Liza said.

The Trager brothers stared at her in bleary confusion as

her words dissolved into the cool night, words she rarely used. Well, at least she had their attention. Now what? She could stay with Estelle and send them home, but Adam wasn't fit to drive and Charlie didn't know how. Let Charlie stay? No. Knowing how Adam devolved around his brother, and especially following this stupid stunt, he would probably insist on staying himself out of some ludicrous, unresolved sibling thing. The boys would end up fighting again, which would surely wake and upset their mother. Begging a neighbor to keep an eye out and an ear open didn't exactly thrill her, but she was running out of options. Yet she didn't see a single light on in any of the condos surrounding Estelle's. That left one option. It would be a lot to ask. Even if Cara agreed to come babysit, it would cost her so much in gas...

"How much money do you have on you?" she asked Adam.

"Huh?"

She stuck out her hand. "Wallet. Please."

He slowly complied. She extracted a couple of twenties and handed the wallet back.

"Now the keys."

Grumbling something about being mugged by his own wife, he reached for those, too.

Liza hit the button that unlocked the BMW's doors.

"Okay, both of you idiots, into the car and behave yourselves. I need to make a phone call. Then we're going home, and we're coming back in the morning."

23

Liza's living room smelled like popcorn. Charlie, seemingly unfazed by the drunken, one-sided brawl in Estelle's parking lot, lay on the unfolded foldout, watching *All About Eve* with Slipper and his cell phone next to him. Bette Davis blew cigarette smoke out the side of her mouth. Liza wondered how many young girls she seduced into the habit. She wondered if Estelle had been one of them.

We shouldn't have left her, Liza thought. *I should have insisted we all stay. Or at least taken Adam home and left Charlie there. Cara had readily agreed to drive to Middletown, but what a thing to ask on a Saturday night. I wasn't thinking straight. Damn it, Adam. Why does everything with you have to be so black and white? Why do you have to make it so hard?*

Charlie must have sensed her standing nearby. "He's still not talking?"

Liza shook her head. "I don't know what he's more angry about." There were so many angles from which Adam could choose: Liza for not telling him, Cara for interfering, the doctor for not having the compassion to tell Adam what was going on, his mother for stopping her treatment and ordering the doctor to shut them out, or himself for acting like such an ass. Hopefully, he didn't know that Liza had told Charlie first. Charlie, the king of discretion, had kept that to himself? Or, perhaps Charlie told him in the parking lot. Maybe that's why Adam threw the punch that completely missed any part of his brother's anatomy.

"Plenty of room here." Charlie patted the mattress. Slipper walked across his lap, and with a tiny mew, rubbed her forehead against Liza's outstretched hand.

They'd invested in a queen-size for the foldout, but it felt too weird to bunk in with Charlie. Just what she needed, another thing to drive up Adam's blood pressure. "It's okay." She scooped the tabby into her arms and stroked her soft fur. "We'll sleep in Estelle's room."

Charlie let out a long sigh. "If you want."

She didn't want. Neither, apparently, did Slipper, who squirmed out of Liza's arms and settled back next to Charlie. She didn't want to change another set of sheets; she didn't want to be around Adam, and she didn't want to be alone. "How are *you* doing?"

"I think I'll live. Fortunately, alcohol gives my brother lousy aim."

"Did I miss Marilyn Monroe?"

"Nope." He shook the paper microwave bag. "And we saved you some popcorn."

* * *

It was after ten when Liza finally woke, alone in the middle of the foldout, to the sound of men's voices and the thump and scrape of tools. When, still half-asleep, she stumbled toward the source of the commotion, she found three men huddled around the broken window in the guest room. Actually, only two men were huddled. Adam and Dan were bracing up the sash and apparently attacking it with screwdrivers. Charlie sat on the bed drinking coffee and providing the entertainment.

Something is wrong here, she thought.

"Uh-oh." Dan's broad face split into a grin. "It's the wife. And she looks pissed."

"Sorry," Adam grunted. "We're almost done."

"Lizabelle!" Charlie said. "Come join us. Let's see how many more people it will take to fix a window."

Why is Charlie in such a good mood? His own brother nearly decked him last night.

Then Adam, smiling, told Charlie what he could do with himself while sitting around doing nothing.

She blinked. *And why is* Adam *in such a good mood?*

"Hey," Charlie said, mocking defensiveness. "I made breakfast."

I missed breakfast? Liza attempted to make words to that effect but nothing happened.

"There's coffee," Adam said. "And we saved you some pancakes."

"I slept through pancakes?" she managed to say.

Charlie shook his head. "Honey. You slept through a lot of things. Must have been the Sambuca."

"Yeah," she said. "Must have been."

Ambling into the kitchen, Charlie padding after her, she found a stack of pancakes and topped them with ricotta cheese. She started on the half-cup of coffee that remained in the pot, and while he made more, Charlie filled her in. "So first, Mom's fine. Cara's a total angel; she's coming by later. Then Adam and I talked. Well. I talked, he yelled. He's still plenty pissed and that's understandable. But at least I got him out of the place where he wanted to rearrange my face, then drive to Middletown and start on Mom. That's not going to do anybody any good. And you know her. If you nag at her about something she'll do the opposite, for spite."

"You have to make it seem like her idea," Liza said.

"Exactly." Charlie grinned, refilled her cup and then his own. "You must be married to her son or something."

She wrapped her hands around the mug, inhaling the aroma. Charlie brought the good stuff. "Survival of the fittest." She listened to the sounds coming from the guest room, the clank of tools and the back-and-forth of their task. Adam and Dan worked well together. Adam had had buddies when they lived in Manhattan, guys he played basketball with, guys he had beers with. And Liza? She had acquaintances, people she worked with whom she found companionable, but mostly she had Charlie, and by extension, Charlie's friends. When she stopped to count her blessings, which was more and more often these days, she was thankful for her neighbors, especially Dan and Cara. Over the past six months they'd become good friends. And Cara. Liza owed her big. Hopefully, one day Adam would show a little gratitude.

"So you think he's really okay?" Liza said.

Charlie shrugged. "Hard to tell with my brother. He can be okay enough to get the job done. What's going on underneath has always been a bit of a mystery."

She'd thought so, too. Sometimes she could crack the code but not always.

Dan left, bidding the two of them goodbye with comforting words and a hug for Liza. Seconds later, Adam came into the kitchen with his mug. His mood seemed a hundred and eighty degrees from the black snarl he'd been in last night. "Girl talk?"

"Fuck you," Charlie said with a smile.

"And the horse you rode in on," Adam added.

Oddly, the exchange warmed Liza's heart. She felt jealous of them for having each other. Her parents were zero-population-growth advocates who felt it would be irresponsible to further tax the natural resources of the earth by producing more than one child.

"Window's fixed," Adam said. "We no longer have to fear asphyxiation *or* decapitation."

"My hero."

He slurped coffee. "Although I almost decapitated my brother this morning. Again."

"He told me."

"Well." Charlie conspicuously checked his watch and raised an eyebrow. "Will you look at the time? I need to call my congressman. You two kids kiss and make up."

He disappeared from the room. She looked at Adam. "Subtle," Liza said. "Did you guys work that part out, too?"

"Nah. I think he was improvising."

Liza stared into her cup. "I'm sorry I didn't tell you sooner."

Adam crossed his arms over his chest. "You were afraid I'd put my fist through a wall."

"Or your brother."

"I apologized to him. And I'm…I'm sorry I said all that stuff to you. It really wasn't your fault. At least you were trying to find out what was going on."

"But I should have told you right away."

"Look." He rubbed the back of his neck. "I know now, so let's move on, okay? Charlie and I are going down there in a little while. We'll lay it all out on the line for her, nice and calm. We'll give her a choice. She can stay by herself and arrange for her own help, or she can come here. But if she comes here she has to be straight with us. No more bullshit about what we can and can't know."

"And you think that's going to work? What if she gets defensive?"

His face sagged. "I don't know. I have no idea what to do then. But I can't think of anything else."

He looked so…lost. She crossed to the sink and folded him into her arms.

"So we're okay?" he said. "You and me?"

She didn't know. It wasn't that easy. Maybe she just needed him to say they were, so they could get through this. Liza kissed the soft patch of skin beneath his ear. "We're good." *For now.* She absorbed the smell of him, the Adam smell, infused with coffee, pancakes, and fresh, clean air from sitting in the open window. "You want me to come with you?"

"No. I think it would be better if it's just us."

* * *

Liza had intended to clean the house while Adam and Charlie were gone, but an hour later, she still hadn't mustered the energy to do more than absent-mindedly flip through the Sunday paper. Just as she was trying to will herself into action, Cara rapped on the back door, eyes widening when she saw Liza.

"Wow, you weren't kidding," her neighbor said. "That must have been one rough night, 'cause honey, you look like something the cat drug in. They were really throwing punches?"

Liza flopped into a kitchen chair and rested her head in her hands. "Like a couple of drunken sailors."

"Like a couple drunk idiots, more likely." Cara sighed and helped herself to the rest of the coffee. "You did the right thing. Patients are great, for the most part. Usually the families are what cause the trouble. I don't mean you, though. Oh, before I forget. Here."

The twenties Liza had taken from Adam sailed into her

view. She looked up at Cara. "I can't let you…the gas alone must have cost…"

"Forget it." She occupied the chair opposite Liza, languidly crossing one leg over the other. "I had to check in at Randall's this morning, anyway."

"On a Sunday?"

Cara emptied Charlie's unfinished coffee into her mug. She tasted it, made a face, and added more sugar. "Millicent went away for the weekend. Some church thing. She paid me double, plus mileage. Total bonus, because I'd hang out with Randall for nothing. He ordered in a fancy lunch for us, including caviar. God, I love the stuff—well, if I don't think too long about what it is. So don't sweat it. I'll take it out in coffee."

Liza felt a little better about dragging Cara away from her family on a weekend. "Still. Thank you. What you did, that was huge. Above and beyond."

Cara waved a hand. "No need. Estelle's a riot. Boy." She grinned over the rim of her mug before taking a sip. "Was she surprised to see *me* when she woke up."

Liza's stomach sank with guilt. "Was she mad that we left?"

"She was more mad that you forgot the leftovers."

"It figures." Liza paused, studying Cara's face, hoping to have their decision corroborated as a professional and as a friend. "Is this right, what we're doing? Taking her from her home, if she'll even agree to it…?"

"Look." Cara set the mug down. "Keep her here or put her in assisted living, but getting Estelle out of that apartment is the best thing for her. I can't imagine sitting there alone day after day. It's depressing as hell. So dark, and with the dust and the dead bugs and crap in the light fixtures."

"Adam cleaned most of those out."

"Didn't help much." Cara shuddered. "Even if I was healthy I might be going for the morphine if I had to stay in that dump every day."

Liza thought about Estelle's request. Christ. She couldn't imagine having *that* conversation with Adam. Last night had been bad enough. Still— "If she were to theoretically ask me again about theoretically helping her...end it..." Hearing the words out loud made her cringe. "How would I theoretically get some morphine?"

Cara raised an eyebrow. "She can theoretically get a prescription from her theoretical doctor."

"Just like that?"

"Well. Not just like that. Some doctors won't. Sanctity of life and mental state of the patient and all that. But from talking to her doctor, who's kind of a dick, if you ask me, it sounded loud and clear that he'd hold out on her for both reasons."

Maybe Estelle was a little...*unreasonable* at times, but— "It's not fair to make someone suffer like that. She's obviously in pain."

"I know, honey." Cara drummed her fingers on the table. "But I'll see what I can do."

* * *

It was six o'clock. Cara had gone home to have dinner with Dan and the kids. There'd been no word from either Trager brother, and Liza didn't know what else to do but clean. The kitchen floor was spotless. She'd washed all the sheets, the towels, and made a vat of stewed fruit for Estelle. If Estelle didn't come back with Adam and Charlie, she'd bring it over the next time they visited. She'd reorganized her cabinets and her spice rack; she'd dusted, vacuumed, and cleaned the dried glop from the produce bin.

Tired out, she flopped onto the living room sofa and stared at the streaky paint on the ceiling—another badly done job, another thing for the spreadsheet. Maybe taking Estelle in this time was a mistake. The short-term convalescences they could weather. But this could go on for months. Years. If Estelle indeed had chosen to stop chemo, would Liza have the strength to watch her die, little by little, day by day? Would Adam? Cara said it didn't have to get to that point; hospice could give her the care that she and Adam couldn't. But by then, what would it do to their marriage? What would it do to them? Already they were short-fused, arguing and apologizing with equal frequency, ignoring the little rituals that had been part of their life together when they used to be normal. She didn't remember the last time they went to the movies, or had coffee in bed, or did much of anything else in bed. People had envied the trappings of their life: no children, a nice ranch house, flexible careers that kept them home, often together, during the day.

If they only knew what it was really like around here.

She waited for the sound of Adam's car pulling into the driveway. But another half-hour went by, another, and nothing. Turning on the television to distract herself, she flipped around until she found Tracy and Hepburn sparring. At seven-thirteen, the phone rang. It was Charlie. He sounded awful.

"We're at the hospital," he said. "Mom might have had a heart attack."

Her own heart started thumping harder. "She's okay?"

"Yeah, we think. They just want to keep her overnight. But Liza. Honey." His voice cracked. "Honey, the cancer. It's spreading."

24

It was in her lungs. It was in her liver. While Estelle lay in her hospital bed being monitored, scanned, and medicated, while Charlie took the week off from the show to stay by her side, Liza and Adam drove to the dark, dingy apartment with the sticky walls and the dead bugs in most of the light fixtures. They took all the clothes that would fit into her suitcases. They took her cosmetics and her television. They took her knitting and the framed photographs from the Queen Anne table.

Then they drove home, and set the framed photographs on the bookshelves, Adam's picture next to Charlie's. They put the television on an old rollaway stand Adam used for his computer when they lived in their tiny apartment in the city. They hung her clothes in the closet and drove to the hospital to pick up Estelle.

* * *

If the questions on Liza's Organic Chemistry II final were based on practical knowledge of the effects of metastasized cancer on healthy cell walls, she would ace it. Otherwise she had serious doubts of passing the spring semester. Instead of studying, she'd spent most of the evening sitting with Estelle, listening to stories about when Adam and Charlie were babies. Finally, she realized the time. The exam was scheduled for first thing in the morning.

"There's an extra blanket in the closet if you get too cold," Liza said. "And fresh towels. And—"

Estelle waved her away. "Please. Like I'm a stranger? I know where you keep the linens."

Next to her nightgown, Estelle's cosmetic kit was spread out on the bed, along with a toothbrush, toothpaste, and the cream she used for her face. "Do you need any help in the bathroom?"

"I've been going to the bathroom for sixty-five years." Estelle struggled to her feet, ignoring Liza's supporting hand. "I think I can manage."

* * *

Liza developed a set of rules for visitors. She thought them prudent, under the circumstances. Why make Estelle feel even worse for the time she had left? Those with an active respiratory illness were discouraged from stopping by. Those with iffy symptoms were given a disposable mask from the stash Cara swiped from the hospital. All visitors had to wash their hands before seeing Estelle to reduce the possible introduction of germs. And they had to bring chocolate. Even if it compromised Estelle's immunity, Liza had relented on that count because sweets gave her mother-in-law a welcome bit of pleasure. And why shouldn't she have that? But neither Liza nor Adam would budge on the cigarettes. If guests absolutely could not control themselves, they decreed that smoking must be done as far away from Estelle as possible.

Cara made an effort, which Liza appreciated. From studying the physiological response of addiction, and from watching the smokers in her life, Liza knew what a nicotine fit looked like and how long Cara had refrained.

One particular day, the two younger women and Estelle sat out on Liza's deck, soaking up the June sunshine. When Cara could take the deprivation no longer, she moved to the edge of the deck and lit up, leaning the length of her sumptuous self against the railing. As she puffed away, Estelle watched her with longing in her eyes. And unlike half the men in the neighborhood (Adam included, most probably) Liza knew it wasn't Cara's body she desired.

"Give me one of those."

"Estelle!"

She rolled her eyes at Liza. "What's it going to do, kill me?"

"I'm not about to sit here and let you do it…that way."

Estelle put up her hands. "All right, fine. I won't smoke."

Liza stared harder.

"I promise."

Liza sighed and again told herself there were many things out of her control. "I'm going for a grocery run. Can I get you anything?"

"Beer," Cara said.

"More chocolate," her mother-in-law added.

* * *

Estelle waited a few minutes while listening to various doors inside open and close. "Is she gone?"

Cara craned her neck toward the carport. "Yep. The coast is clear."

"Where's Adam?"

"Went to the hardware store with Dan. Then they're going to try to fix our lawnmower. I wouldn't expect to see them any time soon."

Estelle crooked her fingers toward Cara's Newports.

For a few minutes they puffed in silence, enjoying the warmth of the afternoon, listening to the birds and the rustle of leaves buffeted by a light wind. The nicotine rush didn't feel as good as Estelle would have thought, after so long, but it wasn't bad. Her mind filled with pleasant memories of coffee klatches with the neighborhood women, or having a cigarette or two while Adam and Charlie played in the park.

"Eddie hated when I smoked." Estelle fumbled for Cara's ashtray. Cara slid it closer. "So do my kids," she added. "Maybe that's why I do it. You should have seen me when I found the lumps. I was up to two-and-a-half packs a day. Puffing away like a chimney."

"It's the last one you're getting from me, hon. I feel bad enough about this as it is."

"We don't have to tell anyone, do we?"

Cara smiled. "I can keep a secret."

Estelle had Cara pegged all wrong. In her day, a girl like that would have been a cautionary tale. It would have started with her getting on the back of some tough's motorcycle and ended in a Puerto Rico abortion clinic. But even though she talked dirty, Cara was a decent girl. Human. Reasonable. She probably was a very good nurse. Better than the fussbudgets she had at County. None of them would have let her smoke.

"Adam doesn't talk much about his father," Cara said. "What was Eddie like?"

Estelle shook her head. "Eddie. Eddie was a schmuck. Whaddya call it these days? Not a very nice person."

"Schmuck still works." Cara took a long pull, eyes closed, her lips pursed around the filter, then exhaled. "So why'd you marry him? Were you knocked up?"

"Perish the thought. No. It's what we did back then. You graduated high school and got married. You didn't, and you got to be twenty-one, twenty-two, people started to talk. Would think you were maybe one of those funny girls."

Cara grinned slyly. "What, like Barbra Streisand?"

"You know what I mean." Estelle dropped her voice. "Those girls. The ones who dress like men, walked around the Village holding hands."

"Oh." She flicked Estelle an amused look. "*Those* funny girls."

"People weren't all over the news having parades back then. They kept to themselves. It was a private matter."

"Really." Cara kicked off her sandals and sat cross-legged in her chair. Her toenails were polished a shade of green Estelle had never seen in nature, and she wore a silver ring on her left second toe.

"Oh, yes," Estelle said. "And there weren't all these divorces. You made your bed and then you had to lie in it. Not like today. It's too easy today. You don't like the way he chews with his mouth open, you divorce him."

"Did Adam's father chew with his mouth open?"

"Did he ever. And he snored to beat the band."

"Was the sex good, at least?"

"Sex." Estelle snorted. "Sex is overrated. Five minutes while you're staring at the ceiling making out the next day's shopping list in your head."

"Damn." Smoke trailed from both of Cara's nostrils.

"Guess we're doing it wrong, then."

"You girls," Estelle said. "All this brassiere burning and what did it get you?"

"I'll tell you what it got us." Cara stubbed out her cigarette. "Saggy tits."

Estelle laughed despite herself. Which became a bit of a cough, nothing major, and soon she felt the spasms lift.

"You all right there, hon?" Cara said.

"Fine." Estelle sank back in the chaise lounge and listened to the birds. So many. She liked the back deck. Her Adam did a good job staining it. The house wasn't one she would have chosen, but when the babies came, they could trade up to something nicer, like she and Eddie had. What did they call it these days? A starting house? Start-up house? Lately she couldn't remember a thing. "But my head's all fuzzy. Is that normal? After chemo? I can't even read a book. Charlie brings all these movies and I can't follow the plots."

"Your body's had a bit of a wallop, Estelle. All kinds of stuff happens."

She dropped her voice. "And the blood?"

Cara looked straight at her. "Blood?"

"In the toilet. I don't remember if my mother had that." She was starting to forget what her mother had gone through, except for the horrible wasting away. But she clearly recalled how toward the end, Estelle had made soup while she held the ball of Charlie and cried.

"Well, I'd watch that one," Cara said. "Did you tell the doctor?"

Estelle shrugged. "Eh. It was just a little. Nothing to get excited about. Don't tell the kids, okay?"

"Sure, but if it gets any worse—"

A door slammed inside the house.

"Oh, shit. Estelle. Put it out. Someone's here."

"What—?" Before Estelle could tie the thoughts together, Cara snatched Estelle's cigarette and ground it into the ashtray.

The glass door opened. Liza stood behind it. "Did you see my checkbook? I thought I—" Her face fell when she saw the two women, the ashtray sitting between them. Liza turned on one heel and walked back into the house.

Cara followed her. "It's not what it looks like."

Liza was so furious she couldn't even bring herself to look at her friend, let alone give her the scolding she deserved. "You know she's not supposed to be smoking."

"She wasn't. I was. All right. I let her have one puff to see if she was over it. And she was! She said she didn't want any more."

Liza spun and shoved a finger toward Cara's face. "You're a nurse! How could you even let her—?"

"Honey. Really," Cara said. "Let her enjoy herself. What's it going to do to her now?"

A conscious choice to end Estelle's suffering was one thing. But Liza could not get behind doing it with the weapon that had given her cancer. It seemed too cruel to do that to Adam and Charlie. And her. Liza narrowed her eyes. "She could have another heart attack, that's what it could do."

Cara looked perplexed. "She had a heart attack?"

"That's how we found out it was spreading. The doctor said she had a cardiac episode, and while they were doing some tests, that's when they found out."

"Oh, shit. Liza, I'm sorry. I didn't know about her heart. Shit. I won't let her have any more. I promise."

"Adam can't know about the smoking." In her peripheral vision, Liza saw Estelle getting up and walking toward the sliding door. She lowered her voice. "They already have so many unresolved issues. All that anger. This could...he could turn his back on her for good. My mother's death was so sudden I didn't get a chance to forgive her. I don't want Adam to go through that...that *devastation* of realizing he could have done something before..."

Estelle was having trouble opening the door. Cara crossed the living room in three long-legged strides and helped her. "Sorry, Estelle," Cara said. "We're cutting you off. Nurse's orders."

Estelle shrugged. "No big deal. You know, I really think I could take it or leave it at this point." She worked herself into her recliner with a sigh. "Now, chocolate, that's a different story." She searched Liza's hands. "So? Where is it?"

Liza sighed. "I'll be back soon."

25

Liza was editing a paper for one of her summer classes—
Nutrition and Childhood Development—when Estelle
shuffled into the kitchen. Holding the filter pitcher with both
hands, she poured a glass of water and settled into the chair
next to Liza's. For a long time Estelle just stared at Liza's
moving pen. Finally, she spoke. "I've been looking things up
on Adam's computer whatchamacallit."

"You mean on the Internet?"

"Yeah. Seems like there's a lot of ways to kill a person
these days. Some of them have pictures."

Liza cut a glance toward her mother-in-law. She should
have never shown Estelle the Web. It was supposed to be a
fun distraction, not a way to research suicide techniques.

"Some ways you don't even need a doctor."

"Estelle."

"You get a tulip. You eat the bulb. They're poisonous."

"The Internet is full of lies," Liza said. "It'll probably just
make you good and sick."

"No. They say it will work. These are people who've had
experience. So, here's what we'll do. If I'm in the hospital and
it's bad, you'll bring me a tulip in a pot. I'll dig it out and eat it
when the nurses aren't looking. No one would blame you.
You just brought me a nice flower for my room. They'll say I
was out of my mind. Who would eat a tulip, for God's sake?"

"Estelle, I'm sorry, I want to talk about this, but now I
really have to finish this paper."

She peered over the tops of her reading glasses. "What's it
about?"

"Nutritional deficiencies in children."

"What, like rickets?"

"Among others."

"I thought Adam was going to have one of those
deficiencies. For a month straight, all he would eat was peanut
butter sandwiches."

"With the crusts cut off."

"He told you."

"He made you one."

Estelle blinked blankly.

"In your apartment."

"Oh. Right. See?" She threw up her hands. "I can't remember a thing."

"It's from the chemo. It'll come back."

"Some days not being able to remember is a blessing."

* * *

A few hours later, Cara dropped by. "How is she?"

Liza pressed a finger to her lips and gestured toward Estelle, asleep in her recliner in front of her soap operas. Nodding, Cara dropped her purse on the kitchen table. Her timing, as usual, was excellent; Liza needed a break. Estelle had been dozing on and off throughout the day, and Adam was out at a rare meeting where he actually saw clients face-to-face. She'd completed her paper, but the marathon study session she'd begun afterward was taking its toll. Molecules swam before her eyes; formulas danced and reformulated.

Cara poured them each a cup of coffee. "Get this. Millicent still reads to Randall Osten from the Bible."

"The daughter?"

"Swear to God. He's nearly immobile, a totally captive audience, and she sits there reading him chapter and verse, praying for some kind of deathbed conversion."

"A life-long Atheist." Liza thought about her father and his own disdain for organized religion and invisible deities. Someone like Millicent wouldn't stand a chance around him. "Talk about tilting at windmills. So why doesn't he tell her to leave?"

Cara shrugged. "She's still his daughter. He doesn't have anyone else." She dropped her voice. "Maybe taking Estelle in hasn't been a picnic for you and Adam, but I hope she's counting her blessings. I tell you, that Millicent gives me the creeps. I wouldn't want to be alone with her."

The phone rang. Liza started and grabbed for the receiver

before it could ring again and wake Estelle.

Charlie said, "Quick. Turn on the news."

Estelle was awake and blinking in her direction, as if to ask who had called. Liza put her hand over the receiver. "Charlie says turn on the news."

Her mother-in-law batted around the side table for the remote, disturbing Slipper, who jumped away. "What channel?"

"What channel?" Liza asked Charlie.

"Any of them."

Estelle flipped around until she found some sort of press conference. An attractive, dark-haired man in a suit read from a prepared text, cameras flashing all around him. His face looked somber, contrite. A tearful woman in a pink dress stood bravely beside him, clinging to his elbow. A very large rock glinted on her finger. "I will always love and respect my wife," he said. "She's been a wonderful mother to our children. I've asked for her forgiveness and I'm also asking for yours...I've dedicated my life to public service and hope that one day you'll put your trust in me again..."

"Who the hell's that?" Estelle said.

"Who the hell's that?" Liza asked Charlie.

"That," Charlie said, "is the man I'm going to marry. Don't tell Mom. Please. Don't tell *anyone*."

She excused herself from Cara's cocked eyebrow, walked into Adam's study, and shut the door. "That's the politician?"

"Yes, ma'am."

"Oh, my God." She could just see Charlie all over the news. The Other Man. Spun the wrong way, it could ruin his life, his career... "Charlie. If I were you..."

"I know. Deep cover. He already told me I shouldn't expect to hear from him for a while, until this blows over. Hell, I've waited this long, what's a few more weeks? Gotta fly. See you this weekend. We'll celebrate. With the appropriate somber tone, of course."

Liza hung up, and ducking under Cara's bemused gaze, returned to the living room to catch the rest of the story. "I don't even know who that *yutz* is," Estelle said. "What's the big deal?"

"He works for the mayor of New York," Liza said. "He's coming out of the closet. When someone prominent comes out, it's a big deal in the gay community."

Estelle's eyes widened. "The mayor is gay?"

"No," Cara said, pointing to the screen. "That guy. The *yutz.*"

"But he's married."

"Probably not for much longer," Cara said.

"Such a pretty girl," Estelle said. "What a shame. If he was gay, why did he marry her?"

Maybe he didn't want to disappoint his mother, Liza thought.

"Maybe he was in denial," Cara said.

"You are what you are."

Liza and Cara stared at Estelle. "I thought you believed it was a choice," Liza said.

"That was before. Some things, you don't get a choice about."

"He's happy," Liza said.

"Do you really think so?" Estelle asked.

"Yes."

"And there's no chance he likes women?"

Not anymore. "No."

Estelle sighed. "I always had a feeling about him. I was just hoping I was wrong."

"Sorry."

"I'm sorry. I'm sorry he'll never have children. I think he'd make a wonderful father."

"He can still have children," Liza said.

"I don't see how that's possible."

Turning away from Cara, Liza smiled to herself, thinking of the promise she and Charlie had made in college. "It's possible."

26

The kids were busy. Estelle tried not to be a bother and stayed out of their arguments. Liza had worked on a newspaper article until very late the night before. This morning she read over her nutrition homework during breakfast and went to class. Adam had already done three conference calls; now he futzed around with something on his computer. It was Cara's day off; she'd said Estelle could call any time, but Estelle didn't feel up to company. She was tired. Her back, hips, and knees throbbed with pain. Just thinking about putting on that *facacta* head wrap and drawing on her eyebrows felt like too much work. Instead, she dozed on and off in her chair for most of the day or did some knitting when her hands didn't weigh too heavily. Before she fell asleep this last time, she'd been watching Charlie's show. How he kept all those women from fighting was a mystery, because according to the tabloid newspapers, they all hated each other. Despite that, the show was pretty good. Charlie explained to her once what he actually did and how he kept it all running smooth, a harder job than the show he'd worked for initially because this one was live. They had to get it right the first time or make it seem cute and spontaneous when they got it wrong. Sometimes one of the women (mostly what's-her-name, the funny one with the big hair) talked about Charlie the Producer. The women seemed to adore him, not just on the show but off, too. They'd invited him to fancy parties—they gave him presents, tickets to their concerts, an expensive watch for his birthday. Sometimes, like today, the camera would cut over to him, near the edge of the stage, wearing an earpiece and holding a clipboard. He was such a handsome boy, a handsome man, and so good at what he did. Pride rose in her chest like warm bread on a windowsill. *I made him,* Estelle thought.

"Adam," she yelled from the chair. "They're showing Charlie."

He didn't answer.

"Adam!"

"I've seen Charlie, Ma," he said with a groan. "We see him in person every weekend."

I made him, *too.* No, she shouldn't be so harsh. She loved her boys equally. But Charlie made it so much easier. He was always so sunny and upbeat and much more patient than Adam.

But was her Charlie *really* happy? She again speculated what could have happened to a normal boy to make him turn queer (gay, she had to remind herself it was called gay now). Was it the flu she'd come down with while she'd been pregnant with him? Or that she hadn't taken care of herself well enough? Next, she tortured herself about the punishments she and Eddie had given him when he'd misbehaved, or had it been it the way the other boys, including Adam, had teased him? Finally she made it Eddie's fault. He'd been around for Adam, not Charlie. He'd been over the moon with Adam. He'd rush home from work, bring baseballs, a tiny mitt, maybe a toy truck. He'd sit up with her for the three a.m. feedings, touching Adam's tiny fingers and toes in disbelief, talking about their future. But when Charlie came around, Eddie apparently decided he'd done that already and could relax. He snored through the feedings. Adam's old toys were still good enough for Charlie's use. And he was working, always working. Yes, they needed the money, with two babies now, although he could have gotten a job that paid better. He had the skills but was too lazy to try. Maybe that made Charlie the way he turned out. He didn't have enough of a father at home to show him how to be a man.

She touched her abdomen, trying to remember the feel of Charlie growing inside her, but she was starting to lose that, too. She knew that on a bad day with her mother, Estelle would rub her hard, round belly and feel the sorrow drain away as if he had a magic power. It was one of those mysteries she could never share with Eddie. Even if she'd told him, he'd probably just shake his head and walk away.

Charlie had had another magic power. He'd kept Estelle's mother alive. Every day when Estelle came (having once again left Adam with Mrs. Steiner) she immediately went into the bedroom so her mother could say hello to both of them. She'd press an increasingly bony hand to the circumference of Charlie and whisper things in Yiddish. She claimed they were blessings for the baby, but Estelle remembered enough Yiddish from her childhood to know what her mother really said. She said she was waiting for him, God willing.

Miriam waited. She waited while the worst of the morning sickness abated; she waited while a dark line grew down the apex of Estelle's abdomen, which swelled so large that the neighborhood collective of old Jewish ladies speculated she might be having twins. Miriam waited, she was told, with the telephone by her side when Eddie took Estelle to the hospital (once again, leaving Adam with Mrs. Steiner). The birth couldn't have gone more smoothly; Charlie had crowned an hour after she and Eddie arrived at the hospital. For this Estelle thanked her mother's blessings and the magical powers of her second son.

Estelle turned her head to the living room window. The sun was sinking into the trees. Liza would be home soon, and they'd have dinner. Her daughter-in-law probably planned something healthy, with all those antioxidant-thingamajiggies to build Estelle's immunity. She'd eaten more greens than a flock of sheep, but more than anything, she wanted a thick, rare steak and a baked potato with butter and sour cream. Yet it would only cause an argument, as if there weren't enough arguments in this house, and Adam would give Estelle that warning look. She was getting tired of that look. She was getting tired of making conversation. Exhausted, even. Never would she have thought she'd be too exhausted to talk. Maybe if she had a pulsating bundle of magic to bless, a grandchild to look forward to, it would keep her going. Maybe. And maybe it would even keep Adam and Liza going, too.

* * *

"Ma."

She'd been sleeping. Dreaming about holding a grandchild. He had Liza's eyes.

"Ma."

"What?"

Estelle blinked. Adam. In one hand he held a manila folder, in the other, his keys. He looked angry. She tried to remember a time when he didn't look so angry. Maybe kindergarten. Or when he first met Liza. "My computer's on the fritz," he said, "so I'm running down the hill to finish something up on Dan's. You gonna be okay for maybe an hour or so?"

"Fine," she said. And as the door slammed, her eyelids drifted closed.

Then Estelle felt a terrible pressure in her lower abdomen. She grabbed both armrests of the chair and tried to hoist herself up, but it was so hard, especially on these horribly warm days, and it took her so long. Finally she moved toward the bathroom, feeling unsteady, weak, and light-headed, a hand braced on the wall. She got to the toilet, and while evacuating her bowels, dropped her head in her hands with the pain.

There's more blood, I know there's blood. I'm not going to make it. If I knew it was going to be this bad I wouldn't have even started. I would have killed myself right then and there.

She wondered how her mother made it through. How did she keep going all those days? Estelle touched her belly, trying again to remember how Adam and Charlie used to feel. The hard roundness. Before Adam, she never knew that pregnant abdomens were so hard. Her belly had gone soft now, road-mapped with stretch marks, but somehow just her hand upon it was enough, in that moment, for the clouds in her mind to clear.

That's when she saw the pink plastic case on the edge of the sink. She knew what it was; she'd used one herself, after Adam. Estelle's lip curled with revulsion; how could her daughter-in-law be so careless as to leave her diaphragm out, where people could see? Most likely she was in a hurry; Liza had been racing around like a confused chicken that morning, and she probably forgot, but still. Estelle decided to put it away for her. She flushed the toilet without looking (she'd stopped looking), washed her hands and picked up the pink case. She only meant to put it back in Liza's nightstand drawer, where she imagined it was kept. She only had the best of intentions. But then her heart sank. Adam wanted to start a family. Had he and Liza put it on hold, for her? To take care of her, for all these months? No. That wasn't right. They had to go on with their lives. They had to have this child. And she needed something to cling to—a touchstone, the curve of an abdomen swelling with magic. It gave her an idea. She fished a knitting needle from her basket. No one would ever know. After all, these things failed all the time. That's how she got Charlie.

* * *

Liza had been spending most of the evening at the kitchen table reading about carbohydrate metabolism. As she rinsed out her tea mug, Adam came into the kitchen. He started massaging her shoulders and pressed his body against her back.

The carbs could wait. Liza smiled at her husband's reflection in the kitchen window, letting herself melt beneath his hands. All evening he'd been in a state she could almost call a good mood. The air conditioning was working. The computer was working. The car was working. He and Dan had found the source of a leak in the laundry room and fixed it with only one trip to the hardware store. Estelle had passed a fairly trouble-free day and had been fast asleep for hours. His hands drifted to her breasts. She heard a cough from the guest room.

"Adam..."

He took her earlobe gently between his teeth.

"Adam. I think I just heard her cough."

"It's your imagination," he breathed into her ear. "She's out cold. I just checked."

"But..."

"Don't worry. Come on. We've got to take advantage of these windows." The hands slid south and worked their way into her panties. He groaned when he discovered how wet she'd become.

This was a window. Not the most romantic line she'd ever heard, but it was better than nothing. "I'll go get ready."

* * *

When a dejected Liza came back from the bathroom, Adam was already waiting for her in bed. She slipped underneath the covers and gave him the bad news about the hole in her diaphragm.

"So we'll go without it." He pulled her closer, his eyes soft as he met her gaze. "We wanted to get pregnant anyway."

She heard a scratching at the door and flinched before realizing it was Slipper, expressing disapproval at being ousted from her nighttime haunt. The noise focused her thoughts. "Adam, remember? We had this discussion...we'd agreed to wait..."

Adam drew a hand up her thigh, lightly brushing his fingers over her panties, which made Liza's breath catch. "How big is the hole, anyway?"

Big, she thought. *Big, hot, and hungry.* She swallowed as he stroked her in circles. *No. We can't risk it. Not now.* "It's big enough," she said, cursing her practical nature.

"You sure?" He teased down the waistband of her panties.

Part of her wanted him to rip them off with his teeth. But the sensible part of her prevailed and gently moved his hands away. "Adam...honey..."

"What?" The flesh that touched hers tensed.

"There are other things we can do besides inserting Tab A into Slot B."

He was still pouting.

"You'll like them. I promise."

After the other things—Adam quickly stopped pouting—

they pulled the covers around themselves. Liza rested her head against Adam's chest and stared at the badly painted ceiling. Slipper resumed scratching, stopped for a moment, meowed, and then, Liza assumed, huffed off to claim Estelle's recliner for the night.

"Maybe we shouldn't put the baby thing off too long," Adam said.

She squeezed her eyes shut. "You expect me to take care of your mother *and* a baby?"

"I work at home. I could help. I can change diapers and stuff."

"Whose?" Liza said. Cara had told her a thing or two about what happens toward the end.

"I just think it might give her something to look forward to. A reason to keep fighting."

"And I'm just supposed to bring a human life into this environment because—" No. The hole had looked suspiciously neat. Adam couldn't have possibly—

"What?"

"You could have just talked to me about this."

"I thought we were talking." He let out a harsh breath. "Liza. You don't think...why the hell would I do that?"

"You didn't?"

He turned away. "You know, it really hurts that you'd think I'd do something so underhanded."

Of course Adam hadn't done it. How could she have thought that about him? She'd just jumped to a conclusion. She'd been mentally stretched so thin she hadn't been thinking properly. "Adam. Adam, I'm sorry. I don't know what I was thinking, I don't know how I could have accused you..."

"Why would I force something on you that you don't want?"

She listened to him settling in, until his breathing became regular. "Honey. I'm sorry."

"Forget it," he said sleepily.

But the hole did seem awfully uniform.

* * *

The next morning Liza brought it to the expert.

"Hard to tell what did it in." Cara squinted as she held her neighbor's contraceptive device up to her overhead kitchen light. "Could be a puncture. Could be latex fatigue. How old is it?"

Liza shrugged. "Couple years."

"Heavy use?"

Liza smiled, but then her expression faded. "Well. We stopped using it for a while, before and right after Estelle got sick; we wanted to get pregnant. But lately, we've been using it every time."

"There's your culprit. You should get a new one every year. Even so, the failure rate is eight-seven percent. I'd go on the pill if I were you."

"Easy for you to say." Cara had had her tubes tied after her last child was born.

"Why not? You're in great health, you're under thirty-five, you don't smoke, you know all the vitamins and shit you're supposed to take. You guys do it like rabbits. Why kill the spontaneity by running into the bathroom to stick half a grapefruit up your coochie? When you're ready to get knocked up, just stop using it."

"We don't…"

"Mommy…" One of the boys, home sick, shuffled into the kitchen, looking feverish. Cara felt his forehead, gave him a baby aspirin and sent him back to bed.

"Dry spell, huh?" Cara said, barely missing a beat. "Well, that's natural. With Estelle across the hall, in her condition."

"There's that." Liza felt blood course into her cheeks and swallowed. "But…"

"Coffee?" Without waiting for an answer, Cara poured each of them a cup. She fetched two forks and the remains of a crumb cake from the refrigerator.

"Okay." Cara jabbed her fork into the pastry. "Spill."

"The baby discussion. We'd agreed to table it while Estelle…but…"

"What? He wants a kid? Now? Jeez."

Liza poked a tine absent-mindedly through the shiny clumps of crumb topping. "Because we apparently don't have enough stress in our lives."

"Honey." Cara pressed a hand to Liza's arm. "You're amazing for even doing *this* well. Hell, I think I'd be going after Dan with his hunting knives."

Liza chuckled to herself at the image. Cara the Amazon, chasing Dan the Gentle Giant around the house.

"But maybe you should cut him some slack right now."

"What?" Liza said. "Do what he wants? Have a baby?"

"Fuck, no. Just…maybe it's not a great idea to make any big decisions now."

"The thing is…"

Cara waited.

Liza lowered her voice. "I haven't been this…even with our problems, even with his mother sick, even though half the time he doesn't want to…I just…*want* him… No, not even him. I just want sex. Like, animal sex. Is that…completely inappropriate?"

"Depends how you do it," Cara said, eyebrow raised. "Oh, come on. Don't look at me like that. It's perfectly natural. Ever come home from a funeral and totally maul each other? It's the life force. So when Estelle's asleep, go get you some, girlfriend. But buy a new diaphragm first."

"So it doesn't look like sabotage to you?"

"I can't really say for sure. You're not thinking Estelle would…?"

That hadn't even occurred to Liza. "You're kidding me. You think Estelle—?"

"The woman wants grandchildren, honey, and she's running out of time. One of her boys is off the shelf. You're her only hope."

* * *

She brought it up with Adam later that evening, slipping into his office after making sure Estelle was asleep. "My mother," he said with a smirk, nodding toward her room. "My mother who can barely get out of her chair. My mother would rummage around in the nightstand and poke holes in your diaphragm to make sure you get pregnant because she thinks the thousand times a day she nags us to produce a grandchild are going unheard."

"It was Cara's suggestion, not mine."

"Right. Your suggestion was to accuse me."

"I'm sorry!"

He leaned back in his chair and drummed his fingers on the armrest. "Whatever."

"Maybe I forgot to put it away. Maybe she found it."

"Liza, I saw you. You pulled it out of the nightstand."

"Maybe she put it back."

"Maybe she knows where Jimmy Hoffa is, too."

She glared at him, swiveling in his chair. He looked so defeated. Then she began to soften. Perhaps she was being selfish. "Maybe we should…reopen this discussion."

He stopped moving. Rested his hands in his lap and looked up at her. "The baby discussion."

Liza nodded and perched on the edge of his desk.

"We want one anyway," he said, speaking more rapidly with each word. "It's not like we'd be doing it just for her. And maybe like I said, it would give her something to fight for."

Liza nodded again. "That's what happened to Miriam."

"My grandmother?"

"When your mother was pregnant with Charlie. Every day, she dropped you off with a neighbor and took care of her parents. And Miriam would pat your mother's stomach and say she's waiting to meet him."

"Mrs. Steiner." Adam leaned back again, his eyes focusing off into the distance. "She scared the heck out of me. Huh. For the longest time I thought Ma took me over there because I'd been bad."

* * *

Liza didn't put enough salt in her soup, or maybe Estelle's taste buds were on the blink again. Some things she could taste. Cara had brought Chinese food the other night and that was like heaven. Liza was upset about the sodium and what that would do to Estelle's heart, and she got even more upset when Estelle had said it wouldn't be a bad way to go. On top of that, Estelle could barely remember the basic things like where she put her checkbook. Adam did her finances now; she'd signed a paper with the bank. Liza kept reminding her to eat and gave her vitamins, lined up on a cloth napkin like shining jewels. Estelle couldn't remember what they were supposed to do. Something about cell walls, and that they cost a fortune.

"Don't waste those on me," Estelle told her. "Save your money. Save it for the baby."

Liza dipped a spoon into her bowl, readying another mouthful of the tasteless soup. "There's no baby."

If Liza suspected Estelle had done something, she and Adam had never said. "There will be," Estelle said. "And I hope to God you have a boy."

"As long as it's healthy, we don't care," Liza said.

"A boy," Estelle said. "You should only have a boy."

27

It was one of her home visit days, and Cara had fallen behind schedule. A normally unresponsive patient had been in a chatty mood. She'd had a flat on the Jeep; Triple A seemed to have better things to do despite her joking promise of a blow job to the first guy who came to her aid. At least if she had to be stranded, she couldn't have picked a more beautiful day: sun shining, not too hot, low humidity, a gentle breeze. She tried Randall Osten's home number to let him know she was running late, but neither he nor Millicent picked up the phone. When the wrecker from Triple A finally showed, a kid popped out, no older than seventeen or eighteen, and he stared at her boobs nearly the whole time he changed her tire. She hoped he remembered to replace her lug nuts. As she drove off, she grabbed her cell to try Randall again, but there was still no answer.

Fearing the worst, she swore under her breath and leaned on the accelerator. Maybe he was just in the bathroom or outside on his terrace. No one should have to die on a day like this. She hated losing any of her patients, and Randall had become one of her favorites.

When she pulled into the parking lot, Millicent's minivan was still there, alongside Randall's top-of-the-line Volvo that he hadn't been able to drive for years. She knocked. No response. She knocked again. "Randall? Millicent? It's Cara!"

Nothing. Then she heard something faint. A soft voice. Millicent's voice. Even and eerily calm. It sounded like she was reciting a passage from the Bible.

Cara fumbled out her key.

She found Millicent standing over Randall's bed. His head appeared forced back, his eyes closed, his chest still.

Millicent was holding a pillow. She blinked slowly at Cara. "You're late."

Cara checked Randall's pulse and found none. "You...you did this?"

"God told me it was his time. Pray with me."

"I will not." She whipped out her cell phone. "I'm calling 911."

"I've already called them." She smiled. "They're going to pray with me, too."

Then Cara heard the sirens. The police came, followed closely by the EMTs. Two cops confirmed what Cara already knew. They took Cara's and Millicent's statements. Millicent continued to claim it was God's will, that He asked her to do His work through her healing hands. Then they took Millicent away.

When the police finally let Cara go, she left a message for Dan to pick up the kids. She called Liza's mainly to hear Estelle's voice. Then sat in the Jeep for a long time thinking about Randall. She'd liked him. He was smart but didn't have to constantly prove it to everyone, like some people she'd known. He was funny, too. Over the last few months they'd become friends. *He didn't deserve to go like that. Suffocated. Christ.* She turned the key in the ignition and started to drive home. Halfway there, she remembered the brass urn on Randall's bookcase. It was too late for Randall, but maybe she could still help Estelle.

* * *

As if a mechanical virus were sweeping the neighborhood, now Adam's lawnmower wasn't working right. Dan came over after work to help him attempt to fix it. The green beast, as Liza called it, was in the driveway with its front two tires raised on cinderblocks, looking like a rearing animal. The Beast was overkill for a half-acre plot; a push-mower would have been kinder to the environment and provided some exercise, but Liza thought Adam secretly liked feeling like a rancher riding around on the thing. *What is it,* she thought, *about suburban men and their lawns?*

Each man worked on a beer, clinking the bottle down on the edges of the blocks between gulps. Perhaps attracted by the smell of tools and testosterone, one by one other neighborhood men came by, took a beer, and watched for a while. From the conversation Liza heard drifting into the house as she put up a load of laundry, not much was getting done except the emptying of bottles and the relaying of neighborhood news. Satisfied that Estelle was peacefully napping, and her classes done for the day with no exams tomorrow, Liza treated herself to a sweaty longneck and joined them. She took a seat on one of the railroad ties lining the driveway. By then it was only Adam and Dan again.

Adam wiped his brow with a forearm and asked Liza, "She's okay?"

"Sleeping."

"Sleep's good," Dan said. "How are you guys?"

Adam and Liza looked at each other as if deciding how much to give away. If it were up to Liza, she'd say they were horrible. She'd say that she and Adam argued at least once a day. Adam alternated between irritable and glum. Liza's hair was falling out in clumps, and she was developing a pimple the size of Mount Rushmore on her chin. She'd even snapped at Charlie. Sex with Adam, now that they'd agreed to attempt pregnancy, had become as romantic as a nineteenth-century gynecological exam. After being four days late she woke up this morning with her period and cried in the bathroom for fifteen minutes, not sure if the tears were of disappointment or relief, which made her cry for fifteen minutes more. Ironically, Estelle was the only one who'd been sleeping.

"Hanging in," Adam said to Dan. "So whaddya think? Just a new blade?"

"Yup."

"Hardware run?"

Dan checked his watch. "Can't. Cara's running late and I gotta go pick up the kids. I hate Nurse-a-Go-Go days. Never know when she's coming home."

* * *

Red lights swirled in Cara's rear-view mirror.

Like I need this now, she thought, swerving the Jeep to the side of the Thruway. She fluffed her hair and tugged down her neckline a smidge, showing herself to her best advantage. But the state trooper who walked up to her window didn't seem impressed. She would have to go to Plan B. *I'm racing back to a dead patient's house to steal the urn where he keeps his wife's ashes so I can give his suicidal dose of morphine to my friend so she can kill her mother-in-law, before the whole place gets roped off as a crime scene.*

No. That wouldn't work either. She took a deep breath.

"Did you realize you were going eighty in a sixty-five zone?"

Cara smiled. "I'm sorry, Officer. I'm a visiting nurse. I'm on my way to see a critical patient. She just paged me. She fell out of her wheelchair and can't get up to take her insulin."

"She should call 911."

"She didn't want to scare her neighbors."

"Where's your emergency tags?"

"Paperwork's still going through."

He appeared to consider her answers. Then he said, "Go on, but be careful. You want an escort?"

"No, but thanks anyway. I'm almost there."

When she finally arrived at Randall's townhouse, the unmarked squad car was still parked outside.

Yippee, must be my day for cops, Cara groaned, as she pulled up beside it. *Okay. Plan C. Pull something out of my ass.* It wasn't just the newest contents of the urn she wanted. She couldn't leave Mrs. Osten in the townhouse alone. If there were no other family members, and Millicent went to jail, Betty Osten could sit on the bookcase through probate and possibly even be auctioned off or disposed of in a way that would be more sinful than mere cremation. No. Betty and Randall needed to stay together.

Cara snuck in the open door. Two detectives were dusting the bedroom. She quickly slipped the ring off her left hand and stowed it in her pocket.

"Hey," one of them said, "this is a crime scene, what are you...oh. It's the nurse. What, you lose something?"

"Actually, yes. I was halfway home and realized I wasn't wearing my wedding ring. This was the last place I'd been."

"Knock yourself out," the younger one said to her breasts. "Just try not to disturb anything."

She pretended to look around the bedroom but didn't find the band.

"Anything turns up in here we'll call you," the detective said.

"Oh." Cara smiled and casually arched her back. "It would be so wonderful if you could do that. I'd be so grateful."

"No problem," he said, returning her smile. "So this means you're not really married now, doesn't it?"

"Gee. Guess not." *All right,* she thought, *time to make an exit before this one becomes a problem.* "You know, I remember washing my hands," she said. "I'll check the kitchen."

But she stopped in the living room first. There was Betty Osten, on the bookcase. Heart pounding, Cara reached for the urn. It was heavier than she remembered, and she adjusted her grip for the weight, curling her fingers around the cool brass. Also, she nabbed a book from the shelf that Cara thought Estelle might enjoy. Perhaps she and Liza could take turns reading it to her. Then she walked into the kitchen, paused in front of the sink, took a deep breath and yelled, "Found it! Thanks, guys!"

Next, she hauled her ass out of there before the younger guy could come out to see if being newly possessed of her wedding band meant she was truly married again.

* * *

Liza's Bug wasn't in their carport, and she didn't want to disturb Adam or Estelle, so Cara turned around and headed home. She sat in her driveway pondering her next move. Tomorrow. She'd drop by Liza's tomorrow on her way to the hospital. Adam had some kind of work thing on Friday mornings, if she recalled. But what to do until then? Randall Osten would hardly want Cara to leave his wife in the back of the Jeep.

"What's that?" Dan said, when she brought Betty inside.

Cara set the urn high enough on their bookcase so neither of her kids could reach it. "The less you know, the better."

"Crap." Hands on his hips, Dan stared at the urn. "Did another stray follow you home?"

"A patient's wife. And don't worry, she's not staying."

"Good," he said. "'Cause I don't like the way she's looking at me."

* * *

Charlie said he'd be up after the show, so of course, Estelle was perky and alert. Liza silently fumed. Weren't they good enough company anymore? Wasn't Adam, even though he was being an asshole lately, still her son, too? This made her feel guilty. She should just be happy Estelle was feeling well, whatever the cause. She should be happy that Estelle was doing well enough to troll after Liza asking a million annoying questions. *When's Charlie's train? What can we make for lunch? Are you pregnant yet?*

"I'm working on it," Liza said to the last one.

"Work, what work?" Estelle said. "*He* does the work. You lay back and think about what to make for dinner the next day."

This conversation was just too creepy to perpetuate. Lately, though, sex with Adam *had* felt like work. Her third job. *Manager, Reproductive Vessel.* The benefits sucked and the pay was lousy, but fortunately, the hours weren't long. She was reminded of a quote she heard somewhere, that insanity was doing the same thing over and over again, expecting different results.

"What, he's having problems?" Estelle said.

"Estelle—"

She waved a hand. "So you get one of those little nighties from a catalog. Eddie liked those. That's how we got Adam. You turn down the lights, you put on a little Frank Sinatra..."

Liza glanced at the clock. It was almost time for Cara to leave for work. *Save me,* she thought, willing her neighbor to get in her Jeep and drive up the hill. To make certain of it, Liza put more coffee on. Minutes later, Cara was at the door. For a second, something about her expression seemed odd. Like she was holding back a tidal wave.

"Estelle!" Cara forced that odd expression into a fake-happy-nurse smile. "You're looking so much better!"

Estelle had put on makeup. Liza had held her mother-in-law's hand steady while she drew on eyebrows.

"My Charlie's coming," she said.

Cara winked at Liza. "One big happy family."

Liza shot her a warning look.

Cara poured herself a cup of coffee. She was still grinning. But her eyes looked tired. Old.

"What happened?" Liza said under her breath.

"Tell you in a minute." She took a sip and set the mug on the countertop, and then raised her voice to chirpy tones. "Hey. You know? There's a sale on pillows at the mall and I almost got you one for that chair in your bedroom, but I couldn't remember the exact shade." She linked her arm through Liza's. "Let's go look."

"Yellow!" Estelle called toward them. "Yellow to match the afghan."

"Estelle, that's beautiful!" Cara said. Then lowered her voice. "I got it."

"I'll make you one," Estelle yelled back. "I'll make yours in green."

"Got what?" Liza asked.

"You're a doll!" Cara turned back to Liza. "What she wanted."

Liza steered them into the bedroom she shared with Adam and eased the door closed. "Cara. Please. No more pot."

"No. I got what she asked for in the hospital."

Liza's stomach dropped, imagining overdoses of pills, or maybe one of those tulip bulbs Estelle kept nagging her about. Or something else, like that freakish suicide machine Dr. Kevorkian designed. Maybe he used tulips. She reminded herself to get on the Web to find out. "Do I want to know how you got this?"

"Probably not."

"Did it involve breaking any laws?"

Cara's face changed again, her eyes and mouth softening as if she were about to cry. "Liza. The bitch killed him."

* * *

Liza listened, her hand on Cara's arm, as her neighbor explained how Randall's daughter smothered him with a pillow and confessed all to the police, saying she was only acting as God's instrument. As Cara mopped up a few overflowing tears, Liza felt hollow inside for Randall, whom she'd grown to know and respect through Cara's stories. And for Cara, because she'd bent one of her cardinal rules of nursing and became attached to him. And for herself. Essentially, this was what Estelle had asked Liza to do. When the time came, even if it truly was what Estelle wanted, would she have the nerve to kill her own mother-in-law? Based on Cara's reaction, would it be as horrible as she imagined?

"I'm sorry," Liza said, the only words she could get out.

"I just hate that his last thought might have been, 'Why is my bitch-face daughter smothering me?'" Then Cara shrugged, as if she were attempting to shake off the pain. "This crappy cloud sort of has a silver lining, though. For you guys." She explained that Randall Osten had not only left behind a beautiful townhouse and a homicidal daughter, but a dead wife who was currently on Cara's bookcase in a brass urn, guarding the vial of morphine Randall probably received from some sympathetic doctor yet never got the chance to use.

"She's in your house?" Liza said.

"It's on a really high shelf. And it's only temporary. I'll bring the goods by and then arrange a proper send-off for Randall and Betty."

Yikes. Talking about the means to Estelle's end was one thing, but actually having it in the house? Mixed in with a dead person's ashes? "No. Please. Don't bring it here. I'll come down."

* * *

It's creepy, Liza thought, staring at Cara's bookshelf, *having someone's remains in your house.* Liza and her father had spread her mother's ashes in a favorite meadow. She couldn't imagine keeping her outdoorsy mother inside, in an urn, on a shelf, like a forgotten, dusty book.

At least this was a very high shelf. Even Cara needed a stepladder. She plucked it off and handed it down to Liza.

Liza turned it this way and that. It was surprisingly heavy. "The top comes off?"

"You need a screwdriver," Cara said. "I'll get one from Dan's tool kit."

She left Liza holding the urn. "Don't keep me in a box," her own father had said, after they'd scattered her mother. "Just throw me in the ocean."

The idea of cremation made Adam cringe. His family was more traditional. His father had been buried, her mother-in-law had been proud to report, in a "proper" Jewish cemetery. Some day Estelle planned to join him. *By my hand.*

Cara came up the stairs, looking baffled. "Can't find the screwdriver," she said. "It's either in Dan's truck or still at your house."

"I know Adam has one." Liza checked her watch. "But he'll be home soon. Then he's got a conference call and I'm supposed to get Charlie. If we make it fast..."

Cara already had her keys.

* * *

"What's that?" Estelle's eyes roamed the urn containing Betty Osten's remains.

Cara was a much better liar, so Liza let her take the lead. "Oh. It's an old knickknack, used to belong to Dan's mother. Liza saw it and said she had something up here to polish it like new."

Estelle frowned. "A little toothpaste will do the trick. Why schlep it all the way up here?"

"We thought it would take a while," Liza said. "We didn't want to leave you alone."

"You can leave me alone. I'd have been fine."

"But isn't this nicer, all being here?" Cara said. "I missed you, Estelle, and I'm so glad you're having a good day. Hey, if you ever want to get out, come down to my house. We'll make dinner and sit out on the deck."

"You have the nicest neighbors," Estelle told Liza.

"Yes. You do," Cara said, and followed Liza down to the basement.

Cara set the former Betty Osten on Adam's workbench. Liza found a screwdriver. Loosened one screw, another, a third, then lifted the lid. But all she saw was a pile of gritty human remains. Ash, chunks of teeth and bone. A wave of nausea rippled across her stomach.

"Don't...tell me it's buried in here."

"Whaddya mean? I put it right on top."

Liza dared herself another glance into the urn. "There's nothing on top but..." She swallowed, willing the queasiness away, and in a small voice said, "Just more Betty."

"Give me that." Cara grabbed it away. "Goddamn it. I put it there myself. Damn it! Millicent, you bitch! Fuck. I can't believe this. She took it! The bitch took it!"

* * *

Charlie tossed his overnighter in the back of the Bug and settled into the front, adjusting the seat to accommodate the length of his legs and the insulated bag he'd brought from the city. It contained potato knishes for Estelle and two street-vendor souvlaki sandwiches for Liza and Adam. They were one of the few things Liza missed about living in Manhattan. Famished to the point of weakened knees by a tough morning with the divas, Charlie admitted to eating his on the train.

"How's she doing?" he asked.

"Great. Today. She always does better when she knows you're coming."

He sighed. "I just have that effect on women, I guess."

You don't know the half of it, Liza thought. She pulled out of the station's parking lot and headed up the service road leading to the Mid-Hudson Bridge. "Adam's pissed off about it. Stirs up all that childhood stuff. He's been in a mood since he woke up. Consider yourself warned."

"Done."

"And make sure you tell her she looks nice."

"Don't I always?"

"I did her makeup."

Charlie grinned. "The blind leading the blind."

"Fuck you," Liza said pleasantly.

"Don't tempt me," Charlie said. "It's been so long I don't think the equipment works anymore."

She mentally glossed over any references to Charlie's equipment. "Still in deep cover?"

"Honey, I'm so deep I might as well be straight. It's exhausting. A few words with him on the phone, it's—in some ways that's worse. Just magnifies the distance between us." He sighed theatrically. "What's that they say? Absence makes the heart grow fonder? Or does it just make the eyes wander?"

"Well, you could be in my shoes. Conscribed conception. At this point I'd prefer a turkey baster."

"Nothing yet?"

Liza slid a glare his way. "Check my purse; I have enough Maxi Pads for the Dallas Cowboy Cheerleaders. This is no way to bring a child into the world. You know what?" She smacked a hand against the steering wheel. "I can't do this. I won't. I know she wants a grandchild. But not like this. In a climate of sadness and desperation? It would be irresponsible of me. Adam and I are so stressed out that I don't know if I *want* to bring a child into this marriage right now. I swear when Estelle looks at me she's taking a mental sonogram of my uterus. Adam can barely keep it up long enough to..."

"Didn't exactly need to know that..." Charlie said.

"Sorry. But I've just had it! Cara's chasing some Bible-thumper around for her father's morphine, Adam and I can't go a day without snapping at each other, our sex life has devolved into discussions about basal body temperature and cervical mucus, my mother-in-law is giving me tips about how to get my husband hot in bed. Plus I'm getting a zit on my chin as big as Mickey Rooney..."

He raised a hand. "Hold on. Back the *tsuris* truck up. Cara's doing what?"

Liza sighed as they waited out a red light. "You don't want to know."

"Oh. Yes I do."

And while they drove up the west side of the Hudson toward home, the car shaded by the overhanging branches of ancient trees that guarded the string of monasteries, Liza told him the story. At the end, Charlie stared at her, eyebrows raised. "So the Bible-thumper smothers her father with a pillow. Ironic."

"But true."

"We ought to have her on the show."

"Too bad, she's in jail."

"With the morphine?"

"Probably not. If she's in jail don't they usually search you for anything like that?"

"Like I've been in jail?"

She thought about what Cara had said. "I think she probably just threw it out. If you know you have a suicidal dose of morphine in the house, and the father got it just for that purpose, why wouldn't you use that instead of a pillow?"

Charlie shrugged. "Both leave evidence. Maybe God didn't tell her how to use the syringe."

"Huh. I always thought people used pillows so they would get away with it."

He shook his head. "Fiber particles could get picked up in the autopsy. Now, if you're seriously plotting an easy out, try potassium chloride and epinephrine. In the right proportions, of course."

She threw a glance at him. "You know an awful lot about this."

"Watch a few of your friends die and you learn things."

He'd been just Charlie to Liza for so long that sometimes she forgot he'd also been a gay man in New York at a time in history when older friends and lovers got thinner and sicker until nobody talked about them any more.

Liza sucked in a deep breath and pulled to the side of the road. She couldn't have this conversation and focus on driving at the same time. Cars whipped by them, shaking the little car. She swallowed. "Estelle asked me to...end it for her. When it gets bad."

The expression melted from his face. "Oh, honey."

"She didn't think you or Adam could do it. I didn't know whether to be flattered that she trusts me enough to ask me to do this or insulted because she thinks I'd be cold-hearted enough to end a person's life."

Charlie appeared to ponder this a moment.

"Did you ever have to..." Liza cleared her throat. "Kill anyone...with...anything?"

He shook his head. "I've only heard about other people doing that. Older men. For each other. There were agreements."

"I told her I wouldn't do it. But she keeps bringing it up. She's been searching the Web and reporting her findings. You'll love this. The latest is tulip bulbs."

"Tulip bulbs?"

"They're supposed to be poisonous."

"Huh. I hadn't heard that one."

"That's why when Randall died, Cara went back for the urn. She thought she'd be doing me a favor."

"And it was gone," Charlie said.

"And it was gone."

Charlie appeared to think a while longer. "Is it a safe assumption that Adam doesn't know Mom asked you this?"

Liza flashed Charlie a guilty look.

"Honey. Aren't we keeping enough secrets from Adam?"

You don't know the half of that, either. "I know." She sighed. "But I just... it's all so touchy right now."

"So when did this start?"

"She first asked me in the hospital, but I wrote it off to the medication, thinking she was just delirious. Then when she kept bringing it up, I thought if I simply refused enough, she'd stop. Or hopefully, change her mind."

"But she's his mother. He has a right to know her wishes. And so do I. I'm her son, too. You keep forgetting. And you didn't have to get Cara mixed up in this, either."

Liza's hands tightened into the wheel. "Hey. I'm doing the best I can."

But now she felt horrible that Cara might get herself in deeper. She'd call her the second they got home, tell her to forget it. She'd tell her that if for some reason Millicent did reveal the location, Cara should simply turn it in or destroy it or do whatever the protocol demanded. "And I never *asked* her to get mixed up in this. Estelle's doctor wouldn't write a prescription. Cara's patient had morphine. Millicent told her to throw it away, but Cara wanted to save it for Randall and put it in what she thought would be a safe place, and when...with the pillow—"

Charlie touched her arm. "Honey. I meant that I could have helped."

She stared at him, growing aware that her mouth was hanging open. *How can he be so calm about*—? "You could do this? You could actually...kill your own mother."

"I don't look at it like that. Liza. I've seen what it's like at the end. I've looked into the eyes of people who were practically begging to go. Mom's a tough cookie, but...I don't want her to suffer like that."

"I don't either."

"We have to bring Adam in on this. It would be unconscionable not to, honey. Other things might be on a need-to-know basis, but this particular secret is not negotiable."

She sighed. "I know."

"We'll talk about this. The three of us. And then we'll talk to Mom."

Liza stared into the gray sky ahead. Then slid her hands down the steering wheel and turned the ignition. "Make sure you mention the eyebrows."

"I'll tell her she looks like Elizabeth Taylor."

28

Lately when Estelle thought about her mother, she didn't see the hollowed-out sick woman with bony fingers, but a young and pretty Miriam who took Estelle, just a child, to the park near their old apartment in the Bronx. She pushed Estelle on the swings and laughed. Estelle remembered the laughter, the music of her voice, the whoosh of the air as the swing went higher and higher. Then the memory changed, and her mother was kneeling at Estelle's feet with pins in her mouth, humming to herself, always humming.

"You're gonna make a beautiful bride," Miriam said. But she wasn't smiling or even humming anymore.

Her mother didn't like the match. Estelle had overheard her talking with the neighborhood ladies. She said Eddie was lazy *putz*, and she didn't like his parents. There was a rumor that an uncle was in the Jewish mafia.

But Estelle Rosenblatt was eighteen years old and wanted to get married, and no one could have told her differently. All her girlfriends were starting to get married and she wanted to be married, too. They could have Tupperware parties together, then be expecting together and take their babies to the park. She wanted to get married because she'd never been away from home before, not without her family. And in ten days she was going to be Mrs. Edward Trager. After the wedding, they'd go to Niagara Falls on the train and then home, or what she had started thinking of as home, the tiny apartment a block from Eddie's parents. His parents had paid for the first six months' rent to get them started. Eddie had wanted to do it on their own, but Estelle convinced him they'd be fools to turn down the money. If they had to make do on the salary he currently earned making furniture deliveries, they'd be living in her bedroom in her parents' apartment, and she wouldn't put up with that.

"He'll be getting promoted soon," she'd told her mother. "He'll be moving into the front office, and he won't have to make deliveries anymore. He'll wear a nice suit and help people write up their furniture orders and not get dirty. We'll get one of those really nice apartments on Riverside Drive."

Her mother had stuck another pin into her hem, frowned, and said something in Yiddish.

"What does that mean?" Estelle had asked.

"It means don't expect silk if you only got burlap."

* * *

It was as if a new person inhabited Estelle Trager's body when her younger son came to visit. A sagging shoulder lifted. A dark face lit up. The terrarium of Adam and Liza's yellow ranch house on Sycamore Street was a closed system. A simple scientific formula, a transfer of energy. All physical reactions required a catalyst, and in this ecosystem, the lit match, the sunbeam shining through a magnifying glass, the one good hard push was the act of Charlie Trager walking through the door. Liza could practically see the thermal reaction that resulted when Charlie appeared: the energy left Adam's body and entered his mother's.

"Look at you, all beautiful." Charlie leaned down to kiss her cheek.

Estelle beamed. She didn't say, "Liza did my hair and makeup." She didn't say, "Adam fixed my room up so I can sleep better at night." She just smiled at her baby, the answer to her sorrows, her touchstone, and said, like she said every week at about this time, "The train ride was good?"

"Fine," he said, like he said every week at about this time. Charlie talked about the show, and Manhattan, and Liza ached for her poor husband as he grew smaller and smaller.

"Adam got a big client this week," Liza said.

With an expectant smile, Charlie turned to his brother. Estelle watched Charlie watching Adam.

"It's no big deal," Adam said.

"Sure it is," Liza said. "It's a guy who just won a million dollars on some game show. He wanted to invest it, and his agent told him to call Adam."

"Hey, that's great. I met him. We had him on last week.

Great guy. Isn't he a great guy?" Charlie asked Adam.

Estelle was still watching Charlie watch Adam but Adam was almost gone. "Yeah," he said, his voice so small they could barely hear. "Great."

Then, like any thermodynamic reaction, the transfer of energy became complete and the system returned to homeostasis. Charlie checked his voice mail, a meal was shared, Adam regained his lost height, Liza did the dishes, and Estelle fell asleep in the living room recliner while Charlie regaled them with stories about the divas' latest tantrums. Equilibrium was restored.

* * *

"He was burlap," Estelle said.

Charlie had been in mid-sentence, something about too much foam in someone's cappuccino. "What's that, Mom?"

"Should have listened to my mother," she said, then muttered more of her almost-Yiddish.

Charlie turned toward Adam and Liza with a "please translate" shrug.

"She's talking in her sleep," Liza told Charlie. "She's been doing that on and off lately."

"Yeah," Adam said to Liza. "She was doing that this morning after you left for the train station. She wanted to help you plant flowers in the garden, I think."

"Flowers."

"Yeah. She asked if you bought any tulips yet."

Liza and Charlie looked at each other.

"Tulips," Charlie said. "In August?"

"Are you sure she said tulips?" Liza's stomach sank.

"Yeah. I'm pretty sure it was tulips." Adam narrowed his eyes at two of them. "What. Is there something significant about tulips? Another private joke?"

"Adam," Liza set down her coffee, "the three of us need to talk."

They left Estelle sleeping in her chair. The two men walked in front of Liza: Charlie first, then Adam. She sensed

Adam's uncertainty in the set of his shoulders. He'd started showing a few gray hairs since the move, but there were so many more now. It was attractive on him, somehow.

"Which?" Charlie said, and Liza nodded toward Adam's office. It felt like the most neutral space. Liza shut the door.

"Is this an intervention?" Adam said with a wan smile. "You want me to go to anger management again?"

"Adam. It's not funny. We have to talk about your mother."

"She wants to kill herself," Charlie said.

Adam's face sagged. "What?"

"When it gets bad." Liza twisted the hem of her T-shirt in her fingers. "She wants..."

"She wants Liza to do it," Charlie said.

Disbelief widened and then narrowed Adam's eyes. "No. You said no, right?"

"That's...that's what I told her...at first...but she kept bringing it up..."

"I'll tell her." Adam reached for the doorknob.

Charlie grabbed his arm. "Hold up. Let's just talk things out first before we go Neanderthal again—"

Yikes, Liza thought. "Charlie, is that really necessary—?"

But Adam was already shaking Charlie off. "No. Liza, she has no right asking that of you. Without even talking to me..."

"Adam," Charlie said, his voice calm but sounding rather condescending to Liza's ear. She cringed at the possible ramifications. This time, maybe Adam's punch wouldn't miss. He added, "Going ballistic won't make this go away—"

As Liza suspected, Charlie's tone only seemed to make Adam angrier. "I'm not supposed to get pissed off when my mother asks my wife to help her commit suicide? After everything I've done for her?"

"Remember? This isn't about you," Charlie said. "It's about what Mom wants and—"

"What Mom wants? What do *you* know about what Mom wants? I'm the one who takes care of her all week. Liza and me. All she does is whine and complain and ask when's Charlie coming, when's Charlie coming, and then you show up and it's like the heavens opened and God came down and made her well again. And then on Sunday afternoon, you get to leave. You go back to your quiet apartment and your job and your life. And we're here. With her. Hell, you think there haven't been times when I wanted to kill her myself?"

Liza reached toward him. "Adam..."

He put up his hands. "I don't want to hear it."

"I don't care," Liza said. "Charlie was right. It's not about you."

The glower slid from Liza to Charlie. "You may be on to something. Yeah, it's not about me. It's always been about him."

Charlie let out a loud groan and rolled his eyes. "Please," he said. "Can we put our Freudian whatevers behind us long enough to think about what's best for Mom right now?"

"It sounds like you two already know what's best." Adam darkened more.

"Yeah, I can see why you didn't want to tell him," Charlie said to Liza.

She snapped her head toward Charlie. "Oh, shut up, for God's sake. You're not helping."

"How long has she been talking about this?" Adam asked Liza.

She struggled for the right answer. Charlie stepped in and Liza's mouth went dry, fearing what he might say. "Look, that doesn't matter," he said. "What matters is Mom, that we honor whatever choice she makes—"

Adam ignored him and kept looking at Liza. "How long have you known about this?"

"Since the hospital."

"The second time?"

Liza looked at her shoes. "The first."

She expected him to rage, to put his fist through the wall. But instead, her husband simply crumbled. It started with a quake in his face, a tremble in his mouth. He sank into his desk chair and dropped his head in his hands. "Why did I bother?" He sounded like he was struggling to hold back tears. "Convincing her to get chemo? Taking care of her, taking her in?" His voice cracked as he softly said, "If all she ever wanted, all she ever planned on doing, was to die?"

Liza reached for him again. "Adam..."

He shook his head, waving her off. Then he took a deep breath, let it out, and looked up, his mouth tight, his expression resolute. "I'm done. I'm done with all of it. I just...I can't handle this anymore."

"Adam," Charlie began, his hands outstretched in a gesture of pleading. "Look, I get it. You're burned out. This isn't easy for anyone. So why don't you...well, take a break. Liza and I can handle this for a while..."

Color rose in Adam's cheeks. "Be my guest. She'd rather have you anyway."

Charlie opened his mouth to speak but Adam interrupted. "It's true. You're the only one who ever really mattered. I'm just some pathetic Charlie Trager substitute."

"That's not true," Liza forced out.

Adam looked up at her and said softly, "You told him first, didn't you?"

There was no good way to respond so Liza said nothing. But even in that, Adam found an answer. He made a slight nod of understanding and slid his glare to his brother, who seemed to be out of smart remarks. "Look," he said. "When you go back to your happy little life on Sunday? Take her with you."

"You know I don't have room for Mom," Charlie said.

"I wasn't talking about her."

"Adam..." Liza gasped.

He shook his head. "You need to choose. Him or me. 'Cause I'm tired of feeling like a schmuck, the straight version of the guy you wanted instead."

"Hey," Charlie said. "This isn't about—"

"I was talking to my wife," Adam said. "That is, if she still wants the job."

29

Little had changed in the six or so years since Cara last needed to visit the local jail. The visiting room still smelled like disinfectant and old coffee; the faces of the employees were still deathly pale. Soon after her arrival, a female guard shuffled Millicent Osten through the door and into a waiting chair. Millicent looked gaunt in the thin denim top and slacks.

"You're late," Millicent sighed.

Cara lit a cigarette.

"Can't smoke in here," the guard said.

Seriously? Cara turned around and glared. "You see me takin' out the pack, you can't warn me then? Or at least put up a sign? Jeez."

The guard pointed to the sign.

Cara rubbed her forehead with the heel of her hand. She knew that the hospital's rules had changed, but you couldn't even smoke in *prison*, anymore? *Seems like the one place you should be allowed to light up.* "Sorry. Nic fit. Bad day. Forgot to patch up."

The guard pulled one out of her pocket and sailed it onto the table. Cara blinked at it.

"New state law," the guard said. "Everyone 'round here's tryin' to quit."

"Filthy habit," Millicent said.

Bitch, you got balls lecturing me about filthy habits, Cara thought, smacking the patch on her arm. Finally, the guard left, and Cara turned back to Millicent. "I don't know why the hell I should, but I might be able to help you."

"I killed my father." She said this as matter-of-factly as one might report the weather. "Only God can help me."

"God's not gettin' you out of this, babycakes. But the state of your father's health might get the charges knocked down. And the state of your mind from watching him suffer for so long." She tilted her head sideways. "Gee, if you could only get someone in the medical profession to testify on your behalf."

"You...you would do that for me?"

She let her eyes settle into Millicent's as she thought about Estelle and her family, the help that Millicent could inadvertently offer them. "If you do something for me."

"What?"

Cara leaned closer. "The package you found in your father's refrigerator. What did you do with it?"

"I gave it to you."

"No. After that."

Millicent blinked in apparent confusion. "I don't understand. I gave it to you. I asked you to throw it out. You didn't?"

"Don't fuck around with me. I'm pretty much your only hope to save your ass, I've had a really shitty day, and I think this fucking patch is a bootleg."

"But I'm not... *messing* with you." Her gray eyes narrowed. "Maybe you're messing with me. Maybe you're just trying to make it look like I'm crazy. I'm not crazy!"

"I didn't say you were. Millicent. Please. Don't cry. I'm sorry. Jeez."

"I'm not crazy," she said, as soft as a whisper. "I just couldn't see him like that anymore. I couldn't."

"I know." Cara started to get up.

Millicent's eyes followed her all the way to standing. "You'll still help me?"

Cara felt for the bitch. The tough part, for her, the really tough part about being a nurse was that despite everyone telling her she shouldn't get attached to her patients, sometimes she did. There had been times when she'd sat with dying patients, when she just couldn't refer to them as patients anymore...they were people, friends, about to leave this world and their loved ones behind, about to leave Cara behind. Yet sometimes it didn't come fast enough. These people were in horrible pain, pain the morphine barely scratched, and they were scared. Not to die, but to keep living and suffering and helplessly watching the tormented looks on their families' faces. If not for a well-timed cigarette break or a few deep breaths, she might have done the deed herself.

Might have found herself in Millicent Osten's ugly shoes. Become one of those "Angels of Death" she'd heard about, going around nursing homes and taking people out. "I'll see what I can swing," she told Millicent.

"If you can't help me, please help my mother. I know that you…take care of things like that. Daddy told me about your work, the foundation you and the other nurses started. I think it's wonderful, really. Please get her a proper burial. It's what she would have wanted if he hadn't been so stubborn. I tried to convince him to let me take her but he wouldn't hear of it. If you can't help me, please. Help her."

"That," she said, "I can do."

And then Cara left. It made no sense to badger Millicent further. Clearly she didn't know what Cara was talking about. Maybe Cara had so much on her mind lately that she only *thought* she'd put the morphine in the urn. No. Impossible. She definitely remembered doing that. It had taken a screwdriver. It had taken effort. It wasn't as easily done as sticking something in a flower vase.

If Millicent didn't know anything, that left only one person who did. *Oh, my God. Randall.* Millicent just said she'd been talking to him about her mother. Maybe he'd had second thoughts about his notion that Millicent would never touch the urn and found a new hiding spot. Sure, he wouldn't have had the strength to do it himself, but with the various physical and respiratory therapists coming and going, perhaps he'd found someone to help. Maybe she should give the place one more look.

She drove from the county jail to Randall Osten's townhouse. There were no police cars in sight, but a sign was posted on the front door.

Crime scene. Do not enter.

Fuck it, Cara thought, fishing a pair of latex gloves out of her nursing bag. *In for a penny, in for a pound.*

The place looked good for having been tossed by the cops. But with the body, the alleged murderer, the weapon, and a full confession all in plain sight, not much tossing had been needed. The crime scene tape and signage were probably a technicality so the case couldn't be thrown out of court for improper procedure. Cara didn't think it was even under surveillance. She sighed. Her friend, Randall. The brilliant Professor Osten, now a forgotten bit of police procedure.

She didn't even know where to start looking. A desk drawer? A medicine cabinet? Randall was beyond something so obvious. *This is stupid,* Cara thought. Liza didn't even want the morphine any more. At least that's what she said. But after all, Millicent had once said only God could decide when her father's time was up. Cara turned to go. She'd violated enough regulations for one day; she didn't need to add a trespassing charge. But again, she thought of Estelle. Randall had been robbed of his choice; maybe Estelle could still have hers. Her eyes drifted from the blank spot where Betty Osten had been. Something didn't look right. A book on a low shelf looked slightly askew. It was Randall Osten's beloved copy of Karl Marx's *Communist Manifesto*. Cara pulled it out.

Behind it lay a plastic bag containing a vial and a disposable syringe.

30

Charlie put his arm around Liza's shoulders. "Honey. Give him some time, let him cool off."

This only made Liza cry more.

"Honey."

"No, and stop calling me that," Liza snuffled. She broke away and grabbed for a tissue from the box on Adam's desk. "He was right. I should have gone to him with this, and then to you. He deserves my first loyalty. I'm a horrible wife."

"Lizabelle."

Charlie made comforting noises and tried to reach for her, but she evaded him and flopped into Adam's empty office chair. She stared at the accounting program he'd left open and the headset he used for his conference calls. "No wonder he felt threatened," she said. "It's bad enough he resents the disparity in the way your mother treats the two of you."

"I'm afraid that particular Shakespearean tragedy predates you, my dear."

"Yes. But then I came along and underlined it for him. With a yellow highlighter and a lot of exclamation points."

"You're being too hard on yourself."

"Am I?" She glared up at him. "When you marry the congressman and something important happens in your life, how do you think he'd feel if you came to *me* with it first? Maybe a little betrayed? A little angry?"

He shrugged, the gesture so similar to Adam's that it hurt. "It depends."

"On...?"

"If he had my brother's temper and was stressed to the teeth," he cleared his throat and spoke a bit softer, "like we all are right now, I might want to bounce something dicey off someone else first."

Liza thought about this. "No. What gets to Adam is that the someone else is you."

Charlie recoiled as if he'd been slapped. "So what are you saying? That because you married him we can't be friends anymore?"

"I don't know what I'm saying." Liza glanced out the window. It was getting dark. She wondered where Adam had gone. Dan's? They were probably in the basement, downing a few beers. Maybe she should call, just to check. Make sure he was okay.

"I thought we'd gotten past this," Charlie said, running a hand through his hair.

"Apparently, some of us haven't." Maybe she hadn't. Maybe the idealist, love-struck eighteen-year-old girl inside her was still hoping that one day Charlie Trager would change his mind. *Stupid, stupid girl.*

"Adam, you mean."

Liza looked up at him.

Charlie's face melted. "Honey." She let him take her hand.

"I know." She sniffed. "We were a drunken aberration. An experiment. A mistake. Spare me the humiliating speech. This is just something I have to work through on my own."

Estelle's voice filtered through from the living room. "Hey, I can't get up. Adam? Liza?"

Charlie said, "We're coming, Mom."

Liza looked down at their entwined digits. He had nice hands. Pretty, graceful hands, like an artist's. But his fingers didn't fit in hers like Adam's. The thumb didn't reach around to stroke hers. She loved Charlie, but not like she loved her husband. Charlie was her friend but Adam was half her heart. It ached, that auricle and ventricle she'd promised him on their wedding day. *Will the pain ever stop? Can we get past this, the hurt, the anger?* She didn't know.

"Liza!"

"Be right there, Estelle." She reached for another tissue. As Liza walked into the living room, she made a mental note to tell Adam that tonight, when his mother needed help, she didn't ask for Charlie first.

"I thought I heard arguing." Estelle kept trying to propel herself out of the chair.

"It was nothing," Liza said, her mouth tight. "Here. Grab my arm."

"Where's Adam?" Estelle asked.

"He took a walk," Charlie said.

"It's bad luck to argue on Shabbat." She glared at Liza. "Especially with your husband."

"Adam's just a little stressed," Charlie said, mostly to Liza.

"Stressed?" Estelle winced, etching pain deeper into her face. "I'll show you stressed."

"Mom. Is it your back again?"

"Oh. Charlie. Worse than ever. I can barely breathe."

"You want a pill?"

"They don't do nothing anymore."

"Should we call the doctor?"

"Enough with the doctor. Just help me to the bathroom. Where's Adam? Liza. Where's Adam?"

"He'll be back soon, Mom." Charlie turned to Liza. "I'll handle things here. Why don't you try to find him?"

* * *

Liza called all the neighbors. She only got Cara's voice mail, at home and on her cell. Patty picked up on the second ring; she hadn't seen Adam, nor had Ted. Liza yelled to Charlie through the bathroom door that she was taking the car out to look for him, and that she'd have her phone. She started driving down the hill. How far could he have gotten on foot?

There was supposed to be a full moon tonight, but it hid behind a swirl of cloud cover. She scanned the sides of the road. No Adam. She didn't see him on the side streets, on the front porches of any of the other neighbors who were out enjoying the mild night, and who waved to her as she passed.

She turned around and started again. She passed Patty's house, the others, all the way down Sycamore hill until she reached the Miller's. Their collection of outdoor furniture was as empty as she thought it had been before except—in the chaise lounge next to the barbecue pit was a shape about the size of Adam.

Swallowing back the knot in her throat, she veered the Bug to the side of the road and walked across the lawn. The wet grass made her sandals slide around on her feet. The smell of earth rose to her nostrils. She called his name.

When he saw Liza, his face changed from surprise to anger to fear. "Is she—?"

"She's asking for you." Liza fought back tears. "I know, I should have told you, about her wanting to…. Frankly, I thought she was just being dramatic, that eventually she'd stop—"

"Look," he said. "Never mind about that now. Okay?"

* * *

Wincing, Estelle took Charlie's arm as he helped her into bed. "I used to change your diapers," she said. "Now you're helping me on the toilet."

"I guess we've come full circle, Mom," Charlie said.

She admired the quiet grace of him as he pressed a wet washcloth to her forehead. *He's a very gentle man, my Charlie.* Caring, considerate. In the bathroom he'd left Estelle her dignity, only coming in when she absolutely couldn't do for herself. *Someone this good, this kind, shouldn't have to be alone.* "Do you have somebody?" Estelle asked. "A…whaddya call it…a boyfriend?"

He looked into her eyes, as if deciding what to tell her, then glanced away. "I thought you didn't believe in that sort of thing."

"A person can be wrong." She lowered her voice. "So? A special someone?"

Charlie shrugged, a light flush rising into his cheeks.

"You do," she said. "I know that look on my sons. Adam looked like that when he brought Liza home. Tell me. This special someone. Is he a good person?"

"Yes," Charlie said. "An upstanding citizen. He's even Jewish."

That's good, at least. "And does this upstanding citizen have a name?"

Charlie smiled. "You're going to laugh. His name is Adam."

"Your brother knows this?"

"Not yet. I've only told Liza."

"Between brothers there should be no secrets," Estelle said. She gave Charlie a warning look. "Or husbands and wives for that matter."

He pressed the washcloth back to her forehead. "Mom. Liza and I were just friends."

"Please. You can't fool me. You looked at her the same way, once."

He gave her a flat smile. "So is the pain getting any better?" he asked.

Fine, she thought. *So don't tell me. I know what's what. I know my boys.* "Some."

"Maybe you'll sleep a little?"

"From your mouth to God's ear. If I do, wake me when Cara comes. We have to talk."

"Sure." He kissed her cheek and started to leave.

"Charlie?"

He turned toward her half-closed eyes. "Yes, Mom?"

"I don't care that all those therapists say it's the mother's fault. I did something right with you."

* * *

Adam practically leapt from the car while it was still rolling into the carport. Not waiting for Liza, he shoved the back door open and called out, "Ma? Ma!"

Liza closed the gap behind him in time to see an exhausted but stunned Charlie in the hallway, eyes wide, gesticulating wildly for his brother to shut up. "I just gave her a couple more pain pills and got her settled in for a nap."

"Then she's okay?" Liza peered into the guest room. Satisfied that Estelle seemed to be sleeping soundly, she eased the door closed.

"As okay as she can be," Charlie said. "Considering."

"What happened?" Adam asked.

"We were feeling a little woozy and needed some help on the toilet." He dropped his voice. "Did you know about the blood?"

Liza started feeling a little woozy. Adam paled a bit. "Blood," he murmured. "What blood?"

"She acted like it was nothing. A side effect from the chemo. I asked her how long it's been going on and she said a while."

"Let me guess," Adam said. "She didn't want to worry us."

"Bingo," Charlie replied. "Anyway, she's out. We're supposed to wake her when Cara gets here. Mom asked for her. She's coming up the minute her shift ends."

Adam groaned. "She needs a doctor. If she's bleeding like that, she needs to go to the hospital."

Charlie's eyebrows shot up. "You think I didn't try? Look. She likes Cara. She'll listen to her. Maybe she can convince her to go to the emergency room."

"Right. Because everybody else has all the answers. God forbid she listens to me."

"Yet funny how she was asking for you," Charlie said.

"Yeah? Since when?"

"I…think I left my headlights on," Liza mumbled, and drifted off to the kitchen door, mainly to disappear from the rapidly escalating conversation. Her hand was around the knob when she heard Charlie's voice, lowered a bit.

"After you stormed out of here like a little bitch diva, that's when. She was asking for you, and all over Liza for driving you away."

Liza froze, still gripping the knob. She turned it, opened the door an inch, and closed it again. Waiting for her husband's response.

After a few seconds of silence, Charlie said, "Liza's a good woman."

Adam snorted. "And you'd know about good women."

"Surprisingly, I would. Enough to know that you have one. She's got a big heart. She loves you. And she hasn't run out of here screaming yet. So don't fuck this up."

Liza turned the knob again and opened the door. This time, though, she stepped out of the house, so they wouldn't see her tears.

* * *

"I don't like her breathing." Cara moved her stethoscope over Estelle's chest. "Or her color. Liza. Get my phone out of my bag. Hit star-seven and ask for Joey. Tell him Cara wants an ambulance. Estelle? Liza's calling the paramedics, okay, hon?"

Estelle shook her head.

"They're on the way," Liza said.

"Ma," Adam said, louder. "They're on the way."

"No hospital," Estelle wheezed out.

"We can talk about that later," Cara said. "You might not even need to go to the hospital. Right now they're just going to help you breathe." She pressed a hand to Estelle's arm. "They're going to make you more comfortable. You want to be more comfortable?"

This got a nod.

"Okay." Cara smiled. "We're all here and we're going to take good care of you."

"Wanna go home," Estelle mumbled.

"You *are* home, Estelle. You're home with Adam and Liza and Charlie."

"No," Estelle said. "Home. Mother was right. I had burlap. Should have listened."

Adam cocked his head. "What the…?"

"What's she doing with burlap?" Charlie said.

Liza shrugged. "Estelle. What about burlap?"

"Shit. No heartbeat. Back up." And Cara was on the bed, pushing at Estelle's chest, counting to herself, as the sirens got louder.

* * *

Adam slumped into the hard plastic seat. Suddenly, Cara swung through the doors to the waiting room. Liza sat up taller and felt a knot tighten in her throat. "She's stable," Cara said. "You boys can go on back. I just gotta borrow Liza for a minute."

She stood. Both men turned to look at her. Liza's gaze drifted from one to the other. Then it settled onto her husband's face. He had that lost, little-boy look once more, as he had in the Middletown emergency room almost a year ago. Had it only been ten months? It felt like a decade. A lifetime. She tried to touch his arm, as if she could transmit strength, but he pulled away yet again.

"Come outside," Cara said, as Charlie and Adam disappeared behind the doors. "I'm dying for a smoke."

Liza followed Cara out. The clouds had cleared. The moon shone whole and proud, winking off the sea of windshields in the parking lot. It had gotten colder, or maybe Liza hadn't noticed before. Feeling the chill creep through her body, she wrapped her arms across her chest. Cara's lighter scratched into flame and she touched it to the end of a cigarette. After a couple of puffs, her neighbor's face began to relax. "Cripes," she breathed. "I've been trying to cut down, but I just couldn't take it anymore. And those patches are so fucking useless. Maybe I've built up a tolerance or something."

"So," Liza said, after a long silence. "How bad is it?"

Turning a clear-eyed gaze on Liza, Cara blew smoke out the side of her mouth. "It's bad, honey. And it's just gonna get worse."

Liza's heart sank. For herself, but mostly, for Adam and Charlie. "We're talking...what? Weeks? Months?"

"Hard to say. Could be more. Could be less. But there's fluid in her lungs. Her heart's weak. This was a close call. Next time we might not be able to save her."

Next time, Liza thought. "Save her for what? To prolong a painful death?"

"Preaching to the choir, sister. I'm just here to help my patients. Speaking of that, I left something for Estelle. In her room. Top left drawer of the bureau near the window. And if anyone asks," she dropped the cigarette on the ground and mashed it under the sole of her sensible nurse shoe, "you have no idea where it came from."

31

Estelle's doctor wanted to keep her in the hospital for a few days. It made no sense to Liza, but her name wasn't on the health proxy. Weak and overmedicated, Estelle didn't argue the decision. Beaten down by their mother's failing health, Adam and Charlie didn't argue the doctor's call, either. Each night, when the ICU nurse "suggested" they all go home, Liza wished she could go somewhere else. An empty hospital room. Cara's house. Back to California. How easily Adam could compartmentalize, Liza thought. Once they got home, he went to sleep, not a word whether he expected her to join him or stay out, other than to say, "I don't want to talk about it" to every syllable she tried to utter. For the first two nights, Liza solved her own dilemma by staying up late studying until she couldn't see anymore, then crawling into the bed in the guest room, too tired to care about Adam's silence, too tired to care about the woman who might have once died there, or the prognosis of its current occupant. She'd sit at the kitchen table for hours reading about the sodium-potassium pump. Yet she couldn't help but put herself in the role of the membrane, the pump, marshaling the passage of equal concentrations of Adam and Charlie. How dare he ask her to choose, when they were both such a large part of her life? Like asking her to choose between sodium and potassium. And what would Adam have said if she had told him she was done with both of them, that her choice was none of the above?

No. She'd been Charlie's friend for fifteen years. It wasn't fair to make him bear the brunt of Adam's unreasonable request. From the kitchen table, she could see Charlie's socked feet sticking out of the blanket, Slipper curled up between them with a protective paw over one of his ankles. He'd wanted to book a hotel room so he could be near Estelle, but Adam—Adam!—insisted he stay with them.

On the third night, as she was reading the same paragraph on carbohydrate metabolism for about the sixth time—and wondering if it wasn't too late to get a refund on her fall tuition—she heard footsteps. Adam, wearing sweatpants and a T-shirt, drifted into the kitchen and drew a glass of water from the faucet. Still, apparently, avoiding any extraneous conversation or eye contact with her.

Enough, she thought. "So this is how it's going to be?"

"I don't want to talk about it."

She gestured toward a sleeping Charlie in the living room. "You seriously expect me to choose." Liza knew her timing sucked, but she didn't care. She needed one thing in her life that wasn't eating away at her or else she felt she'd explode.

He huffed out a breath and sat across from her at the table, looking as if his bones were dissolving. "I didn't mean...look." He lowered his voice. "You guys have a history. Do I like that my wife slept with my brother first? Not really. But I can't change that."

"You..." she blinked at him, feeling her voice get small. "He told you?"

"Well, not in so many words." He rolled his water glass around in his hands. "But when he came home for Christmas break that one year it was pretty damned obvious. We had a couple beers after Mom went to bed and he started crying about this girl who broke his heart. He only had one female friend that I knew of. I could do the math."

She felt the flush burn all the way up into her scalp.

Adam let out a long breath and slumped deeper into the chair. "You were kids. He was confused. He hadn't been, uh, 'out' for all that long. And it's sort of...to your credit that he, uh, chose you."

Please, shut up, she thought. But he didn't. "He...uh...well, probably felt he could trust you on some level."

"Yet you don't trust me," Liza said. "Even though all that happened years before you and I met."

"It's complicated," he said.

A knot of anger punched into her chest. "What isn't? Relationships are messy, Adam. Love is messy. You choose someone and you can't pick one bit of baggage from column A and another from column B. You get the whole thing. You get the mother-in-law. You get the wife who is never going to be Martha Stewart. You get the guy who could never love you the same way you once thought you loved him, and you just have to fucking deal with that because you married his brother."

Adam stared at her.

"Yeah." Liza shoved some hair out of her eyes. "I said, 'the way I once thought I loved him.'" She almost wanted him to make something out of it, to yell and scream, so they could get it all out in the open. But he just shook his head.

"What?" she asked.

"'Practical Liza' with a spreadsheet for ovulation and a category for everything is talking about how messy life is."

"Did you ever think that's why I have all the spreadsheets? Because I don't deal very well with the mess?"

"I just wish you'd told me. About him."

She held up her left hand in a fist, knuckles facing him. "I made my choice. Does that mean nothing to you? 'With this ring, I thee wed, forsaking all others'? Remember that?"

"I was there," he said. "I have a vague recollection."

A loud groan came from the living room. "I was there, too," Charlie said. "Hello? Awkward house guest trying to get some sleep here."

"If I recall, Cara offered you *her* foldout," Adam said to his brother.

"Which comes with a kid who likes to bang people on the head with toy cars and a sixteen-year-old cat with razor-sharp claws and gas. But you guys are making me reconsider."

Liza said, "Adam, can we please talk about this…"

Charlie sprang out of bed, taking the blankets with him. "Not listening." He stormed through the kitchen, grabbed his cell phone from the counter, a fifth of something from a cupboard and disappeared out the sliding glass door to the deck.

"I just can't *deal* with this, Liza. With my mother…I don't have enough room in my head to do *kumbayah* and make a spreadsheet of our conflicts. Why are you making me do this now?"

She looked down at her hands.

Slipper leapt from the top of the washing machine and ran to the sliding glass door, batting her paw against it and mewling. A hand reached up from the lounge chair, opened the door to let her out, and closed it again.

"Even your cat likes him better."

"Adam…" she whined. "That's not funny. At this point, it's just mean."

He sat back in the chair, looking glum. She returned to her book, mainly so she wouldn't have to look at him. After a few moments of silence, he said, "What are you studying?"

Her gaze didn't budge. "Nutritional Chemistry."

"Didn't you take that last fall?"

"That was Organic Chemistry."

"I don't know how you can focus on that now."

Instead of thinking about my dying mother-in-law and the humiliation of finding out you knew about Charlie and me? Had always known? "Self-defense."

He yawned. She glanced up at his face. In the almost-year since Estelle's tumors came into their lives, he appeared to have aged two decades. Why was she hectoring him like this? With Estelle— "Why don't you go back to bed?" Liza said softly. "It's going to be a long day tomorrow."

"Can't sleep." He hesitated, and said in an oddly hostile tone, "Are you coming in?"

"I don't know. Is that an invitation or a warning?"

"Which one will make you stop talking?"

She'd been just about to apologize for not telling him about Charlie. And for all the times she went to Charlie first. Screw that. And screw Charlie. So much for his promise that they would take the secret to their graves. Maybe her answer to Adam's ultimatum *should* have been "none of the above." With one last glare, she gathered her books, snatched her pocketbook off the counter and left.

Cara's foldout might come with a bratty kid and a farting cat, but at least it was in a house with no one named Trager in it.

* * *

Liza must have overslept. Because it was quiet in Cara's house when she woke. Too quiet. A note taped to the empty coffeemaker read that Cara had gone to work and would meet her later at the hospital. She made herself a pot and crawled back under the covers, curled into a ball, and listened to the groan, wheeze, and drip of the ancient device. Her head was pounding, her heart ached, a shiver went through her body. Everything around her was crumbling to bits. She wanted to call her father. Even though he wasn't especially good at sugar-coating and they hadn't talked in a while, at least hearing his voice might make this day bearable. As she was hunting around for Cara's phone, the doorbell rang.

She ignored it.

It rang again. She peered through the side pane. *Charlie.* Dammit.

"I know you're in there, Elizabeth Barrett Browning Stanhope," he said. "Don't make me use this key."

"She gave you a key?"

"What can I say? I'm charming. Now will you open the damned door?"

She clicked open the lock and stormed back to the couch. He stepped in but she refused to look behind her. "I don't want to talk to you," she said.

"Tough. You have to. My mother is dying and you have to be nice to me. Haven't you been paying attention to any of those Bette Davis movies we watched?"

"I don't know how you can joke about this."

"Why stop now?"

She huddled under the covers. A kitchen cupboard creaked open, dishes clinked, and she heard the sound of pouring. Footsteps grew louder and stopped. The thin mattress dipped. He actually got onto the bed and—. She peered out. Charlie sat next to her with his back against the couch cushions, his legs straight out in front of him, neatly crossed at the ankle. He held a mug of coffee and offered it to her. She declined. He shrugged and took a long sip. Feeling humiliated all over again, and irked at his cucumber-cool demeanor, she burrowed back under the blanket.

"You told my husband," she said. "I can't believe you told my husband about us."

"I didn't tell your husband. I told my brother. How was I supposed to know that one day you'd marry the guy?"

"You promised me. The night Adam and I announced our engagement…"

"The horse was already out of the barn, I'm afraid."

She could have kicked him. But he was holding a cup of coffee—in Dan's favorite mug—and she didn't want it to go flying all over Cara's living room. "Let me get this straight. You lied to me about making a promise you'd already broken."

"Semantics," he said.

"You're not helping your cause."

"It was an untenable situation. You were marrying my brother. It was already weird, with Mom yelling about your hippie upbringing; I didn't want it to get weirder. For any of us. Remember when Adam told Mom you were pregnant? It was sort of the same thing. I punted. Yes. It was a mistake to lie to you like that. And I'm sorry. But…"

"You weren't supposed to have told Adam at all. Even when he was just your brother."

He sighed theatrically. "Liza. When I went home for Christmas break, I was a broken man reaching out for solace from my experienced older sibling. My heart was in a million little pieces after you had your way with me."

"Had my—you are so full of shit. I might have been a virgin, and definitely had too much to drink, but what we did felt awfully mutual." She peeked out of a corner of the blanket to glare at him. "So don't blame this on me."

He raised his eyebrows. "Mutual? Do tell, Lizabelle. Huh. Not bad for my first and only experience with the, um, other side of the aisle."

"Beginner's luck and a lot of tequila," she said with a sniff, and relieved him of his java. Which should have been hers. But it smelled funny. Probably that cheap store-brand Cara bought. No wonder she always came up to Liza's house for coffee. "Does the congressman know?"

"You mean the congressman who has two children with his soon-to-be-former wife? Yes. He knows about..." She was waiting for him to make some joke of it, but he simply said, "you."

"Good," she said. "Because secrets suck."

"Tell me about it."

"We should go to the hospital. Adam's there?"

"Yes. He's with Mom." He looked at his watch. "The ventilator tube should be out by now. They're probably yelling at each other as we speak."

"And where does he think *you* are?"

"Getting coffee." He took the mug back and sipped from it. "And it's a good thing I did. That swill at the hospital is dreadful. Come." He gave her shoulder two firm pats over the blanket as he got to his feet. "Get dressed. "We'll bring the rest back for your husband."

32

Estelle looked so tiny in the bed. So tiny that at first, when Liza and Charlie rounded the corner to her room, Liza thought they'd taken her away for testing. But there she was, half-dozing, little more than a head and a torso on a pillow. Her color was bad; her cheeks had a yellowish-gray cast. There were reddish-brown circles under her eyes. And she wasn't wearing her wig. According to Estelle, it had been too much trouble in the hospital, and after the first day, she'd asked Liza to take the thing home. Her hair, which had never completely fallen out from the chemo, was beginning to grow back: downy white patches amid the still-long clumps. Liza promised herself that when her mother-in-law's new hair grew a little longer, she'd cut it even all around, and when a few months passed and more chemicals leached out of her system, Liza would help her dye it back to her original shade, whatever that was. She'd learn to make the eyebrows more even. Maybe she'd even ask Estelle how to use a little blush and mascara on herself. Estelle always said it would bring out the depth of her brown eyes.

"Hi, there." Charlie bent to kiss Estelle's cheek. "I'm back. And I brought you a friend."

"My Charlie," Estelle said in a sigh, as if he were a long-lost lover.

"Adam and Liza are here, too," he said.

Estelle turned her head toward Liza and stared, her eyes widening. "*Shvanger?*" she said.

Adam, Charlie, and Liza all looked at each other. Liza could read nothing on Adam's face, so she turned to Charlie. "Is that one of her doctors? Is a Doctor Shvanger supposed to see her? Estelle, have any doctors seen you today?"

Estelle blinked a few times, as if she were waking up from a dream. Her words came out thick and slow. "Doctors. The only doctors I see are on this thing." She nodded toward the television, where a soap opera was playing, a very large caption crawling across the bottom of the screen. "I see nurses.

They've been very nice. But so many."

"Ma. That's not right," Adam said. "The doctor should be checking on you."

"What's to check? They can't do anything for me."

"They can make you comfortable," Liza said.

"Comfortable." Estelle sniffed. "That's what they say when you're gonna die."

Liza's gaze dropped to her hands. Without even looking at her husband, she could feel an aura of fear, enveloped quickly by anger, radiating from him.

"Don't talk like that," Adam said.

"It's okay, *tateleh*. I haven't had such a bad life."

"Ma."

"I raised two good men. And when I see your father, I'll tell him we did all right."

"Ma. Stop."

"You'll take me home," Estelle said.

"If they say you're ready—"

"Adam. Charlie, Liza, tell Adam to take me home, for Christ's sake. If I have to die here I'll kill myself."

* * *

While Estelle was in the hospital, Adam, Dan, and Dave had painted the guest room, laying down a new and even coat of white on the ceiling, all special paint that had no chemical smell. On the walls, they applied a shade of yellow Liza and Adam could live with. Patty and Cara had washed the curtains, steam-cleaned the carpet, and filled the vases with fresh flowers. They worked quietly, companionably. Beers were opened, sipped, clicked down on furniture. There was no mention of decapitation by the window, which still would not stay open, despite Adam and Dan's earlier efforts. And there was absolutely no mention of anyone who ever might or might not have died here.

* * *

She was released after what seemed like forever. The nurse who brought the forms talked, and talked, and talked, giving the kids so many instructions that it made Estelle's head swim. Fortunately, Liza wrote them down, nodding and asking a lot of questions. Estelle couldn't stop staring at her daughter-in-law's face. Something was different. But she couldn't wrap her muzzy brain around it and simply closed her eyes, following the rhythm of the nurse's voice.

Another nurse came to the house a few days later, early in the morning, a young man with nice eyes but no sense of humor. Liza said where he was from, but Estelle couldn't grasp the word; it kept sounding like "hospital." Maybe the hospital did that, like they had done for her mother: sent a nurse around to check. *Although this one, such a sourpuss.* But she was always glad to see Cara, who stopped by every day before work, usually with chocolate.

"Teach me how to knit," she'd said, nodding at Estelle's untouched knitting basket next to her recliner. "Maybe if I had something to do with my hands, it'd be easier to stop smoking."

"Teach, what?" Estelle said. "I can barely think."

Cara smiled warmly. "Then maybe a little piece at a time. Whatever you feel up to. It'll be really fun to learn. Maybe I can make something for the kids."

And every day before work, Cara sat with Estelle. She practiced her stitches and told dirty jokes that made Estelle laugh so much she sometimes forgot the pain.

One morning Estelle had an awful craving for strawberry jam. Funny, she never really cared much for jam before. Liza went out to buy some and Adam had a telephone meeting, leaving her alone in the living room with Cara. They chatted about nothing: the weather, a woman who'd been on Charlie's show. And then for a few seconds, silence fell between them.

"So what's it like?" Estelle asked her.

Cara looked up from her knitting. The girl learned quickly. Already a few inches of mostly even stitches trailed from her needle. "What's what like, Estelle?"

"You know." She dropped her voice so Adam wouldn't

hear and get upset. "Dying. If I do…the injection. What's it like to die?"

"Don't know, hon. Never have."

"But surely you've had other patients…does it hurt?"

Cara shook her head. "Not if you're tanked up on morphine, it won't. Everything just kind of…shuts down. But a doctor once told me fear can intensify how bad you feel pain. Estelle? Are you afraid?"

It doesn't really feel like fear. "Not as much as I thought. It'll be nice to see my mother and father again. Eddie the schmuck, may he rest in peace, not so much." She aimed a quick glance toward the back hallway to make sure Adam was still in his office with the door closed; still, she kept her voice low. "But the kids…oh, Cara, I'm sick to my stomach about leaving the kids. Adam and Liza, they barely speak. Liza, my beautiful daughter-in-law, she looks so tired. Even Charlie's not my Charlie. And I'm doing this to them. And the worst part is if I had it to do over again…"

Cara tossed her knitting aside. "No, no, no, no, no," she cooed, crossing the room to kneel next to Estelle's chair and grasp her hands. "It doesn't do any good to blame yourself now. That just eats away at what you have left."

"But…"

"Shhh. Honey. It's okay. And remember. Just because you have the morphine, you don't have to inject yourself if you're not ready. Think of it as an option. It's completely up to you."

Estelle felt the wave of fatigue roll up her body, and her eyelids were too heavy to keep open. "No. Was gonna say…if I had it to do over again…I might have done the same thing."

* * *

One day, a couple of weeks later, Cara's kids were sick and she couldn't make it over. The dour hospice nurse came and went. Adam attempted once again to fix the window. Estelle slept most of the afternoon in the living room recliner, and Liza checked on her between chapters. She had an exam tomorrow on nutrition and cell regeneration.

"Can I get you anything, Estelle?" Liza asked, finding her awake and pawing around for something on the side table.

"Lip balm," she croaked out.

Liza started to pass her the tube, but seeing Estelle's shaking hands, gently applied the balm to her mother-in-law's chapped lips.

Estelle pressed her lips together and swallowed. She turned dull eyes on Liza and mumbled a few unintelligible words.

"It's okay," Liza said. "You just get some rest."

Adam came out from the guest room. From his face, Liza could tell he'd made progress against the evil window, if not vanquished it altogether. She forced a smile at her husband and, knowing how important it was for him to feel like he could fix *something*, she hoped to transmit a mental embrace of comfort. After all, she could compartmentalize, too, until he was ready to deal with her spreadsheet.

Estelle mumbled something. She kept looking at Liza's face as if she'd never seen it before.

"What's wrong?" Liza said, pressing a hand over hers. "Are you hungry? Do you want another jam sandwich? Do you need to get up?"

Liza felt her hand being lifted by the force of Estelle's. Still looking at Liza's face, Estelle raised her arm, her fingers shaking somewhat, and pressed the flat of her palm against Liza's abdomen. Surprised and not really knowing what to do, not knowing if Estelle was having some kind of hallucination from the pain pills, a bad dream, or from the cancer, Liza just watched as their combined hands rested on her belly.

She felt Adam next to her. "Ma, what are you—"

"*Shvanger*," Estelle said again, her hand withdrawing, her face settling into a smile.

"Ma? What's that? Is that Yiddish? It's the same word she used in the hospital," he told Liza. "Is that someone we're supposed to call? Crap." He stalked off to his office. "I'm gonna look that up on the Internet."

"Estelle?" Liza said. "Would you like me to call Cara? Do you want Charlie to come up? His…friend…has a driver. He said it's no problem; he'll be here any time you want."

"Pregnant?" Adam yelled. He darted back out. "Liza? *Shvanger* means pregnant. Ma, I told you, Liza's not…"

Liza froze where she stood, her hand drifting to her belly. As Adam stared at her, the hardness in his face began to melt into the faintest of smiles.

Estelle's eyes fluttered open, taking in the still life of the living room. The last image before her lids fell again was her Adam, looking befuddled but almost happy, and his Liza, who was lost in contemplation.

You'll see, she thought. *He'll be a comfort.* Then both of them dissolved into a dream. And what a nice dream. Estelle was with her mother. The young, pretty mother who pushed her on the swing. The wind blew at Estelle's skirt, and her pigtails flew out behind her as her mother pushed her higher, and higher, and higher.

A Note on the Yiddish

For the uninitiated, Yiddish is a language derived in part from German, and in my family, often used by the older generation to say things they didn't want the kids to understand. Yiddish is undergoing a revival of sorts lately, spurred on by a younger generation exploring their Jewish roots and by the Yiddish Theater. I, for one, am very glad for this. Doing my little bit to keep Yiddish alive is one way I connect with my ancestors. Plus, they have some creative curses, and it's always fun to learn how to curse in another language. I do not know why. Also, spelling varies, depending on your source. So don't blame me if your *bubbe* spells it differently.

Bupkes (sometimes spelled bopkis): Nothing. Literally, "beans."
Bubeleh: Darling, honey, sweetie. Regardless of age.
Dreck: Crap.
Facacta (sometimes spelled *farkatke*): Lousy, ridiculous.
Farshtinkener: Rotten, as in a rotten thing or person.
Feh: An exclamation of consternation or annoyance. As in, "Feh, the farshtinkener dishwasher is on the blink again."
Libling: Darling.
Macher: Big shot.
Meshugge (sometimes spelled "meshuge"): Crazy.
Meshuggeneh (sometimes spelled "meshugeneh"): The feminine form of "meshugge."
Noodle kugel: A kind of pudding made from egg noodles, fruit cocktail and some other dense foodstuffs designed to give it the weight and consistency of a concrete block.
Putz: A nicer way to say "schmuck." This is more "Yinglish" than Yiddish.
Shvanger: Pregnant.
Tateleh: An affectionate name for a child. Grown men do not like being called this by their mothers.
Tsuris: Troubles, worries, stress.
Yutz: Hapless, clueless guy.

Acknowledgments

I love this part of crafting a book. Well, I love most parts of writing. Not the part where your eyelids are sticking together and for the life of you, the perfect word dances just out of reach. But the part where I get to thank people. Without their help, this novel would have remained a skeletal NaNoWriMo project withering away under an iffy title in a forgotten folder.

Thank you to Bette Moskowitz, Anne McGrath, Ann Capozzoli, Isabelle Burkhart, Heather Cassano-McIntosh, and Mary Leonard, for their fabulous constructive feedback over many cups of tea in many different places.

As always, a key to the executive washroom goes to Tom De Poto, my first and favorite reader. For their technical expertise, thank you to Stephen Hise, Carolyn Steele, KS Brooks and Ed Drury. Big smooches to Donna Dillon, Yvonne Hertzberger, Al Kunz, and Stephanie Brooks for helping me with the fine-tuning when I could no longer see the words. And to my virtual family on Facebook and Indies Unlimited for the laughter and support. You know who you are. And the PNN ladies and the DBs for always having my back.

Thank you to Paul, my supportive husband, who still has not run away screaming. And to my wonderful blended, extended real-life family for forgiving the occasional unreturned phone call or e-mail. Okay, a whole lot of them.

About The Author

Laurie Boris is a freelance writer, editor, proofreader, and former graphic designer. In addition to *Don't Tell Anyone*, she is the author of two more works of contemporary fiction: *The Joke's on Me*, published through 4RV Publishing, LLC in 2011; and *Drawing Breath*, self-published in 2012. She has contributed to two anthologies and is a contributing author and associate editor for Indies Unlimited. When not playing with the universe of imaginary people in her head, she enjoys baseball, cooking, reading, and helping aspiring novelists. She lives in New York's lovely Hudson Valley with her husband, Paul Blumstein, a commercial illustrator and web designer.

Connect with Laurie online:
Website: http://laurieboris.com
Facebook: http://www.facebook.com/laurie.boris.author
Twitter: http://www.twitter.com/LaurieBoris
Goodreads:
http://www.goodreads.com/author/show/4824645.Laurie_Boris

Other books by Laurie Boris
The Joke's on Me
Drawing Breath
Indies Unlimited: Author's Snarkopoedia Volume 1 (Contributing Author)
Indies Unlimited: Tutorials and Tools for Prospering in a Digital World (Contributing Author)

5·13

Made in the USA
Charleston, SC
02 May 2013